Shakespeare's Blood

Peg Herring

Gwendolyn Books

ISBN: 9781944502195

It will have blood, they say.

Blood will have blood.

Stones have been known to move, and trees to speak.

Augurs and understood relations have,

By magot-pies and choughs and rooks, brought forth

The secret'st man of blood.

Macbeth, Act III, sc. Ii

PROLOGUE

1596 A.D.

Kirkfort Willie Reid followed his henchman down the stone stairs, watching his step carefully lest he slip on the slimy surface or tread on something disgusting. Circling the moss-encrusted well, they turned down a passage barely high enough to navigate at a crouch, where he took care to watch his head as well as his step.

Finally they came to a rough wall constructed across the passage end, forming a tiny cell. A horizontal slit somewhere above let in a narrow ray of light, and in it sat a man, hunched and still. As footsteps sounded outside his prison he looked up briefly, his ruined face catching the light. Willie's man took a key from a hook ten feet back, tantalizingly visible but out of the prisoner's reach. He moved to unlock the door, but Reid gestured a curt negative. The stench was bad enough from outside the cell.

The prisoner had a high forehead and a pale face that formed a perfect oval. A nose once long and slender was misshapen now, and breath wheezed through it laboriously. His bones stood out sharply, the cheeks hollow, the formerly muscular frame shrunken. Eyes that had once sparked with fire and good humor now were dim, like lamps about to sputter and go dark. He did not rise to meet his visitors, having no hope of mercy.

"Have ye considered, Johnny?" Reid called through the grated door. "Ye dinna look well. A bit o' venison or an apple'd serve better than bread and water, would it nae?"

There was no answer from the prisoner, who lowered his gaze to something apparently more important to him than the outlaw Scot who held his life in his hands. Willie knew what it was, had in fact inspected it carefully. It was a small wooden box, about six by eight by three inches, containing a sheaf of papers that John studied intently whenever light in his prison permitted it. After he'd examined them himself, Willie had ordered a minute examination by his clark. Neither he nor the learned fool could explain why the papers were so important to the prisoner.

Though dressed warmly in breeks and wrapped in a heavy woolen cloak, the outlaw shivered in the dank the prisoner seemed no longer to notice. "Come nae, Johnny. A bit o' help from ye and I am a happy man. I will set ye free and gie ye food. Cook's roastin' one o' th' new turkeybirds for dinner. T'would be easy t' hae yer freedom." The mere mention of the meal made Willie's mouth water, and he rubbed his ample stomach.

The prisoner spoke with some effort, loosened and missing teeth making it difficult to enunciate clearly. "You do not intend me to leave this place, Reid, as we both know well. It makes not a whit of difference whether I tell what you want to know or do not."

It was true. They had beaten and starved him. He was skeletally gaunt. His left shoulder was broken, and he held the arm against his side to keep the pain to a minimum. They had met with no success. Reid noted the captive no longer denied that he knew what they wanted him to tell. He had simply decided to die rather than do it.

"Ye spoke wi' Robert Maxwell and th' auld rogue went missing right after. Ye got what ye wanted fro' him, and I'll get it fro' you as well!"

"I doubt that." There was no fire in John's denial, merely weary certainty.

The burly outlaw's jaw clenched, and for a moment he considered ordering another beating to force what he sought from the prisoner. Further torture was not wise, however, due to John's fragility. When he died, his secret would die with him.

Reid turned to go, throwing casually over his shoulder, "Well, then, best to let you think on it a day more Johnny." To his henchman he said, "No bread. We'll see how he fares on water alone."

"Might I have pen and ink?" The prisoner's tone held no dismay at the further reduction.

Glaring through the narrow opening, Reid gave the door an angry thump with his beefy fist. "Have it and be damned," he replied. "Mayhap with your last words, ye'll write the location I seek." The stomp of his frustrated departure echoed off the stone walls and died away.

The prisoner looked at the papers in his lap, considering. He smiled despite his weariness. "Mayhap," he whispered through broken teeth. "Mayhap I will."

CHAPTER ONE

"Take my picture in front of the sign, so I remember where this roll came from," Mrs. Flowers called in a voice that carried to everyone within a quarter mile. She mugged for the camera, pulling herself as erect as possible though *erect* was hardly the term due to the woman's arthritic spine. Mercedes dutifully snapped the picture, and immediately the camera's automatic rewind began a businesslike whirr. That made it photo number one hundred forty-four, no doubt to be titled: *Leaving Castle Canready*.

It was the sixth roll in six days. Helen Flowers eschewed digital photographs, so Mercedes had in her suitcase a bag of undeveloped rolls of film, neatly marked in order of use. There wasn't a moment of her tour of Britain for which Helen would not have visual evidence to show family and friends, people unknown to Mercedes but to be pitied all the same.

At times she pitied herself. Her long-time neighbor and current traveling companion was condescending in most instances, nasty on occasion, and giddily fatuous in the infrequent moments when she tried to be pleasant. Still, her son had offered to pay Mercedes' way if she accompanied his elderly mother on her Bucket List tour of the British Isles. A month ago, it had seemed like the opportunity of a lifetime. Now Mercedes wondered why she hadn't figured out that Mr. Flowers considered it well worth a few thousand dollars to not be the one who traveled with his mother.

"Oh, darn!" Mrs. Flowers tottered unsteadily along the stone walkway. "I've set my bag down somewhere." She said this as if it was the first time such a thing had happened, but by now Mercedes was used to it. Since she traveled at the lady's expense, she was expected to smooth the way and keep track of an extensive array of equipage. "I suppose it's in the powder room." Her petulant tone, irritated with the bag for being left behind, made the nasal whine in Helen's voice more strident than usual.

"No problem. The bus is over there, see?" Helen frowned myopically in the direction indicated, where six motor coaches lined up like racing ponies at a starting gate. It was a little like that, too. Each tour guide strove to be a few minutes ahead of rival tours to cut down the wait time at points of interest they would all be stopping to see.

The Americans had been sternly cautioned not to call their conveyances *buses,* but old habits die hard, and in the states a bus was a bus. Mercedes counted. "It's the fourth one down. You'll see the Lion on the side when you get closer." Helen had boarded the wrong coach once already, and rather than admitting she was wrong, insisted she'd been misinformed. "Get on board, rest your feet, and I'll be right back with your bag."

"Hurry, dear. I need my sunglasses. I have a rotten headache from diesel fumes!"

"I will." Women labeled *companions* in an earlier era would have empathized with Mercedes' position. In return for the chance to see England, Scotland, and Wales, she was expected to respond cheerfully to anything from retrieving lost items to impossible yens for curly fries in Windemere at ten p.m. There was no respite except when Helen was asleep, and even then the younger woman often lay awake listening to high-pitched snores and mumbled, unconscious moans of complaint.

Re-entering the castle with a brief explanation to the woman at the door, she checked the floor-plan layout on her guide pamphlet and found her way to the rest room they'd visited earlier. The W.C. was on the lower level, which wasn't called a basement but should have been. Rest rooms in centuries-old buildings are often eccentric, since the plumbing was added at a much later date. Closets become miniature bathrooms and pipes run along the walls like odd adornments, making shuddery clanks and other tortured sounds as they operate. Water pressure may be anywhere from normal to nil. This "loo" had its toilet tanks attached to the wall at the ceiling height, for gravity-assisted flushing, she assumed.

Scanning the room, she located the familiar canvas tote of extra-large proportions on the floor under the ancient sink. Pulling the bag out, she slung it over her shoulder, noting that it weighed a ton. No wonder the old woman kept setting it down. She vowed to reorganize at this evening's inn. For a second she imagined her friends' teasing: "A place for everything and everything in its place, right, Mercedes?" She raised her shoulders slightly in self-defense. She couldn't help it if she liked things tidy.

As she exited, Mercedes became confused in the warren of passages. What she'd thought was the way to the stairs was instead a blind hallway, ending abruptly in a tiny circular room that smelled of orange cleaning agent and something else, odd and objectionable. Twin pillars halfway down on either side framed what might once have been the entry to a larger room, but now the space was blocked off, empty except for a door marked *Staff Only, Please*. Smiling at the polite addition of please to the order, she turned to retrace her steps.

Something on the left caught her attention, and Mercedes leaned in to peer into the shadows behind the pillar. Her eyes widened in surprise and horror, and a small sound of distress escaped her. Stepping forward, she gripped the cool stone of the pillar and bent close to be certain her eyes were not deceiving her.

A woman sprawled, half-lying, half-leaning between the wall and the pillar. Her head was tilted so that her dead eyes stared coldly at Mercedes as if displeased with her. The woman wore the uniform of the castle's female employees, plaid skirts and sashes over crisp white blouses. This woman's costume was missing its sash, but a more jarring departure was the jeweled dagger that protruded from her chest, just below the laminated card that proclaimed, *Welcome to Canready Castle* and her name, *Sylvia*.

***

The policeman was plainly embarrassed that visitors from America had been troubled with what he called a "bad bit of business." A well-built, auburn-haired man of about thirty, he introduced himself as Jared Graham and shook Mercedes' hand formally, his calloused palm feeling rough in hers. She was sure he must have mentioned his title as well, but she couldn't remember it. The whole of law enforcement officialdom was foreign to her, and this was foreign officialdom to boot. Contenting herself with calling him "sir," she reported the little she knew.

"I'm sorry that you were caught up in this, Miss Maxwell," he said when she'd finished. "There's likely an angry boyfriend behind it, no danger to you or the others." His gaze met hers a little longer than necessary, and she noticed he had very nice eyes.

"Where did an enraged lover get his hands on an antique dagger?"

Graham frowned, his handsome face creasing where the sun had begun tiny wrinkles. "It's a replica, Miss Maxwell. You didn't see them in the shop?"

"I avoid the gift shops in these places." She made a rueful grimace. "It's not snobbery, just lack of cash to spend on trinkets. Penniless college student, finished now but with lots of loans to pay off."

When he smiled in understanding, even more lines appeared. She decided they were an asset, giving the otherwise babyish face a more grown-up look. "Many of your countrymen—and women—find gift shops the most interesting Scottish landmarks." His tone was gentle, as if he didn't want to offend her with his humor. "All sorts of weapons are available in the castle shop, among them a copy of an 11th-century dagger. Not meant for murder, of course, but adequate enough in determined hands."

With some reluctance, Graham made interview-ending movements, closing his notebook and recessing his pen point with a decisive click. Taking her arm, he guided her out of the small room where he'd interviewed her and back into the main hall. Direct eye contact signaled his underlying meaning as he said, "I'm sorry we could not have met under other circumstances."

"Yes," she replied, "It was awful. That poor woman!"

"An innocent woman like yourself is perfectly safe. I shouldn't repeat this, but from what the manager here reported to me, this Sylvia was a bit of a scamp."

CHAPTER TWO

"'Is this a dagger which I see before me, the handle toward my hand?'" The dark-eyed man muttered Macbeth's words as he watched the antic scramble at the castle. Two policemen entered, then more official-looking folk, and finally, stretcher-bearers departed with a bagged corpse.

After two full hours, the watcher wandered to the castle for the second time that day. With a camera dangling from his neck, he looked like any tourist. Entering from the left this time, he approached a different clerk, who would not remember him from the morning crowd. She was assertively decorated, nails a hard blue, eyes edged with black, and lips stained a flamboyant red. Strong scent emanated from her tiny kiosk. None of it made up for her sullen expression.

"I'm sorry, we've closed for the day. There's been a bit of an accident."

"Not serious, I hope?"

She thought about lying but finally admitted, "Quite serious, sir."

"I see." As he stood wondering how to proceed, Fortune smiled on him. A man escorted an attractive brunette to the door, assuring her it was quite unusual for visitors to find corpses in Scottish castles. The man seemed vaguely familiar. The brunette he'd seen a few hours ago. Pretending to consult a pamphlet on Ben Nevis from a rack near the entry, the watcher eavesdropped unobtrusively.

"Here's my card in case you think of anything more you can tell us." The police sergeant was young and solicitous, and it was easy to see why. The woman was naturally attractive, dressed simply in clothing that flattered her slim figure. Dark brown hair fell to her shoulders in waves that curled toward her face. Luminous green eyes lit a pale complexion, and her features were made unique by an expression both intelligent and warm. This woman would see through flattery, but she wouldn't blame a man for trying.

"You'll be glad to be on to Dumfries," the sergeant was saying. "We're sorry to have kept you."

"Not at all. It's the others waiting in the coach who've been inconvenienced."

"Yes, your Mrs. Flowers came to inform us of that, and to retrieve the bag she sent you back for, fearing we might misplace it." His expression remained bland, but he rolled his shoulders in an unconscious gesture that signaled either impatience or humor.

The watcher moved off before they noticed him, heading to the parking lot and his car. Ignoring the work of assiduous castle gardeners who'd planted hundreds of tulips and sweet-scented hyacinth for the enjoyment of visitors, he went over the morning's events in his mind.

They had agreed to meet early in the day, and he'd found Sylvia setting out napkins and sugars in the characterless, stuffy tearoom. Things had not gone well from there onward. Sylvia indeed possessed the book, which she'd fetched from the staff room to show to him. Her demand had been greedier than he could have imagined.

"You've got the money, Vincent, I know it. I saw your picture in that magazine."

He'd been prepared to get the book from her with sweet words and a small gift, but she'd held out for cold, hard cash. When she realized how angry she had made him, Sylvia had taken up the book and hurried away. When he followed, she retreated into the ladies' room with some of the visitors, confident he wouldn't dare to follow.

Demonstrating the great patience of which he was capable, Vincent had backed off, letting Sylvia think he was gone. Down the hall was the gift shop, and there he'd found the weapon with which he could punish Sylvia. "O happy dagger!" Juliet exults upon finding a weapon at her moment of need. The Bard's words fit perfectly, as always, leading him toward his destiny. Vincent slipped behind the counter, slid the glass aside, and hid the dagger in his jacket while the school-girl clerk rang up postcards for a woman in a fleece suit and trainers.

Twenty minutes after she'd gone into hiding, Sylvia ventured out of the ladies' loo, certain her pursuer had given up and left the castle. Instead, Vincent was waiting for her in the passage. As she passed he simply stepped out, caught her from behind, and stabbed false-hearted bitch in the chest. Sylvia had died almost immediately, like Juliet. As he pulled her behind a pillar, Vincent felt a wave of exultation as she took her last breath.

The feeling was short-lived, for Sylvia no longer had what she'd offered to sell him. Remembering it now, anger rose again, and he felt the blood pound inside his head. He'd spent precious moments searching the corpse and the area around it. He found nothing.

The book had to be in the ladies' room. He stepped toward the door, but as he approached, three women came along, a pair of old ladies and the attractive brunette. The older women chatted animatedly about fortifications, and he could hear them through a louvered vent even after the door closed. The brunette came back out and went on her way, but the elderly women remained, still talking.

Panic almost overtook him. How much time before someone discovered Sylvia's body? Forcing himself to remain calm, he pictured the corpse in his mind, searching for details he hadn't consciously observed in the heat of the moment. There was something. What was it?

Of course. Sylvia had worn a plaid sash when he first saw her but it had been missing when she left the lavatory. Waiting impatiently, he heard the rush of water and the scrape of paper towel torn off the roller. The women finally left, still discussing motte and bailey and crenellated stone. As soon as they rounded the corner, Vincent rushed inside the room. A quick search revealed nothing. Again he forced himself to imagine the women who had come and gone.

The two old ladies were of little interest, but he recalled the brunette had gone in and come out almost immediately, too quickly to have used the facilities. Squinting his eyes in order to picture her, Vincent realized she'd carried something upon leaving that she hadn't had before, the sort of canvas bag all American tourists seemed to require. The book had been in the lavatory, but it was there no longer.

As he watched the same brunette board the motor coach, he repeated the names he'd heard. "Dumfries. Mrs. Flowers."

***

With apologies from the department, the castle staff, and their tour guide, the group was soon on its way again, only a few hours behind the all-important schedule. Things returned to normal fairly quickly once they were away. The incident, though tragic and shocking, affected none of the group personally.

Their cheerful coach driver sped them expertly along through rhododendrons in full bloom and past sheep that dozed along the verge of the roadway, not even looking up as the huge, noisy interruption passed them by. Paul, the tour guide, proposed skipping a side trip planned for that day, and as a result they reached the hotel in Dumfries in time for dinner, despite the delay at the castle. This pleased Helen Flowers, who, though excited to be part of a police investigation, was put out that the sergeant had spent little time questioning her. "After all, if I hadn't left my bag behind," she told Mercedes, "you would never have discovered that poor woman's murdered body."

CHAPTER THREE

After dinner Helen watched the news, which she did each night, dreading that something horrible might happen somewhere in the world without her knowing about it. Mercedes repacked their bags, as she'd promised herself. She'd worked out an orderly rotation, keeping small suitcases stocked with clean clothing so that only every fourth night did they have to open the larger bags. Recalling the heaviness of Mrs. Flowers' carryall, she emptied it onto the bed. An unfamiliar object wrapped in a plaid strip of thin, cheap wool bounced onto the bed. "What's this?"

"I have no idea," Helen answered, taking yet another double-dipped chocolate peanut from the bag beside her. "It isn't mine."

"It was at the very bottom." She removed the plaid, which had been rolled around the object several times, and gave a gasp of surprise. The small book inside the wrapping was obviously old, its dull brown cover soft, velvety, and smudged with finger marks. It smelled of old paper, destroyed by the very ink it held.

"Let me see that," the old lady demanded, and Mercedes reluctantly passed the book to her. Having recently earned a degree in history, she was aware of basic protocol in preserving artifacts and documents. Instinct said to examine it with caution, but it wasn't her call.

The cover was simply a strip of leather, perhaps five inches by ten, folded in half over the inner pages, making a volume about as wide as it was high. The whole was held together by a leather thong threaded several times along the left edge through both cover and pages. The book was handmade, and judging from its battered condition, someone had carried it around in a pack or a pocket.

The old lady opened the cover which, dried to a state of fragility, crackled ominously. Inside were a dozen handwritten pages, the style neat but cramped, as old writing tends to be. There was no title page, only a notation on the inside cover, at once intriguing and disappointing: *An assimilation of information concerning the death of William Shakespeare's brother John Shaksper in Scotland, circa 1608.*

Mercedes rolled her eyes in disbelief. Any bright high school student knew that John Shaksper was Shakespeare's father, not his brother. The brothers were Gilbert, Richard, and Edward—no, Edmund. The Shakespeares were hardly adventurous types, so it was unlikely that one of them had died four hundred miles north of home on the wrong side of the Scottish border.

"What's Shaksper?" Helen asked.

"When William went to London, he changed the family name, pronounced Shax-pair. Nobody knows why. He spelled it differently at different times, too, but that wasn't unusual in that age. Spelling was phonetic, not standardized, and it varied from person to person, or in his case from day to day for the same person."

Helen Flowers evinced no interest, though she might repeat the information later as if it were something she'd always known. She squinted at the difficult handwriting. Mercedes waited silently and a little impatiently. The booklet was intriguing, even if it was incorrect. If the account concerned a John Shaksper who died in Scotland, he might at least have been a cousin to the most famous Shakespeare of all.

Making no attempt to apply logic to what she saw, Mrs. Flowers jumped to the least logical but most interesting conclusion. Laying a heavy hand on Mercedes' arm, she exclaimed, "I've found a book from the 1600s, and it's about William

Shakespeare!"

"I don't think it's that old." Mercedes examined the homemade volume. Although yellowed, the pages were intact, the words and letter formations modern if flowery. "If I had to guess, I'd say 1800s.

"Listen to the opening paragraph." Helen read slowly, as she deciphered the crabbed handwriting. "It begins, 'On the death of Angus Reid in 1867, his home was bequeathed to the kirk at Kirkfort.' *Kirk* is church to the Scots," she informed Mercedes pedantically, forgetting they'd been told that by Tour Guide Paul only that morning. She touched the paper lovingly. "I need more light. My eyes aren't what they used to be."

Moving to a small table, she dragged a heavy brass lamp across its wooden top with a scraping sound that boded ill for the table's antique varnish. Switching the light on she muttered, "That's better. Let's see, where was I? 'At first a church, the place was converted to a fortress, hence the name of the surrounding village. The structure was left to deteriorate for decades and was determined to be beyond saving. As vicar, it fell to me to prepare the property for demolition, removing items that might be of value for eventual sale.'"

Mercedes formed silent conclusions as she listened. As she'd guessed, the book was from the late 1800s, not the 1600s. A nineteenth century minister had apparently written it to chart his progress on what he considered a historically important task.

Mrs. Flowers read on. "'In the oldest section of the house, which dates from the 1300s, workmen found a hidden alcove, undisturbed for centuries. In this cache they found nothing that appeared valuable to them, but two items that interested me. One was a box, beautifully made and wrapped in waxed cloth to preserve it. Not so well protected was a journal stored in a leather pouch that had disintegrated over time. The outer pages, both front and back, were damaged as water seeped slowly through the stone wall of its hiding place."

"That's too bad. If there was a box, why not put the journal in it for safekeeping?" Helen frowned at whoever had made such a careless decision before reading on. "'Inside the box was a loose sheaf of papers. They had been wrapped yet again to protect from damage but had been folded and unfolded many times, showing signs of much perusal. It was a very old, handwritten script of *Macbeth*, a rough copy such as actors might use for rehearsal. Lines had been marked and notes written in the margins to cue entrances, exits, and so forth. I took the script to a learned man who disabused me of the notion that it might be an original in Shakespeare's own hand. It had been, he said, copied by a semi-literate clerk. Still it was of interest, and I gave it to the local museum for display.'"

Helen stopped, running her fingers idly over the rough paper as she pictured the vicar's find. "I wonder which museum that would be? I'd like to see it." Mr. Flowers had been a professor of English at a small college, and his wife had absorbed some of his interest in literary history, though it was a superficial and generally snobbish interest.

In the hallway a woman murmured something and a man laughed as a door slammed, cutting off the sound. Adjusting her glasses, Helen returned to the text. "'The journal was very difficult to read and in a most decrepit state. Despite my careful treatment, the pages often disintegrated when touched.' Oh, that's too bad."

An amateur in the 1800s would have known little about methods of document preservation. If the journal had been historically important, this well-intentioned vicar had probably damaged it with handling, as Helen did now to his work, her careless fingers touching the friable paper and bending the desiccated leather cover.

Still she read on. "'It became a hobby of mine to attempt to transcribe the journal, page by page. It was the diary of William—known as Willie—Reid, a notorious outlaw. I knew of Reid from local legend, but it was difficult to glean his story from the decaying pages. I applied myself to research in an attempt to learn more about the events described in the journal, and the story that emerged is quite amazing. Beginning in the Year of Our Lord 1868, within these pages I will put forth what I can compile of the matter, along with my comments and conclusions.'"

Mercedes' approval rose somewhat. The vicar had not saved the journal, but he had preserved the information it provided in his own notebook.

"There! It's not original, but it's still a piece of history." Helen's watery blue eyes dared her companion to argue. "I wish he hadn't given up the script. That would surely be valuable."

"It's in a museum, where it should be." Mercedes' fingers itched to hold the book, which was interesting, even if the vicar was wrong about there being a Shakespeare involved. "I wonder how it got into your bag."

Her companion's enthusiasm was not to be slowed by practicalities. "I don't know, but we must get it to someone in authority at once. It's a very important find." When on her high horse, Helen Flowers was as imperious as Queen Victoria at her queenliest.

"Who would we tell at this hour of the night?"

"Paul, of course." She closed the book with a clap, sending up a musty smell and causing her roommate to wince at mistreatment of an antique. "He's very knowledgeable."

Mercedes tried not to smile. Their smooth-talking tour guide had great patter and a way with fussy old ladies, but she doubted Paul was an expert on historical finds. Still, he might know how they could contact someone who was, since he spent a lot of time in museums.

"You should take this to him immediately."

"We can do that in the morning. I'd like to—"

"He won't have any free time during the day. He'll want to make some calls tonight."

Mercedes would have liked some time to examine the booklet herself, but Mrs. Flowers insisted. She obviously imagined Paul phoning up the PM to let him know there was news on the historical front thanks to Helen Flowers, visiting American.

Realizing it was useless to argue, Mercedes pulled on a soft pair of black, plastic-soled slippers. She'd already changed into the sweatpants and a baggy T-shirt brought along for comfort on idle evenings, but she saw no reason to change to visit Paul. He was used to informal Americans, and the advantage to her present outfit was that the book fit into the roomy pocket of the pants. Picking up two drinking glasses from a tray on the dresser, she said, "I'll look for ice on the way back. Maybe we'll have a slightly cold soda before bed."

Paul was not in his room. She checked the lobby, which was empty. Probably in a local pub. The guy deserved a pint after catering to his charges' demands, large and small, all day and managing to appear pleased about it.

The old hotel was charming, and she spent a few minutes wandering the lobby, admiring the ancient wood beams overhead. They hung low enough that the college basketball player she'd dated until recently would have had to duck to pass through. She read the inevitable plaques listing important events associated with the place, a chronology of additions to the original structure, and several people, famous and infamous, who'd visited there.

There was a fire on the hearth, apparently for the enjoyment of guests, since the night was not cold. As it crackled, she savored the woodsy aroma and waited for Paul's return.

They had stayed the night before north of Carlisle and crossed into Scotland that morning. In addition to the unplanned discovery of a murder, today had been full of marcher barons, family feuds, and outlaws both English and Scottish. Tomorrow was Robert Burns, if she remembered correctly. It was hard to keep track on a three-weeks-of-Britain tour. One saw so much in a day that it became a jumble sometimes, each stop impossible to appreciate separately from the next. Of course the dead body she'd found would make a permanent memory of Canready Castle.

"It's lovely, isn't it?"

Mercedes turned to see a man beside her, staring into the fire. He was an inch or two taller than she, compactly built and sturdy as an oil derrick. His face was more whimsical than most Scots she'd met. Sandy blond hair, a little long for fashion, fell over his right eye, and he pushed it back now with a gesture that was half-impatient, half-unaware. Her first thought was of a Celtic chieftain, one who needed both strength and charm to survive. The man had an allure that was not explained by his looks, a masculine aspect that drew her to him.

He spoke again, and she realized she'd been staring. "The fire. It's nice."

"Oh. Yes. Very nice."

"I saw you reading the placards. Are you interested in Scottish history?"

"Yes." She felt like an idiot, unable to form a sentence in this man's presence.

"I'm interested as well. My uncle is a professor at the university in Glasgow, and that's his specialty. Have you heard of

Allan Rankin, perhaps?"

"No."

He nodded. "Well, he made certain I heard my share of history, and it stuck."

She wondered if he knew of an outlaw named Willie Reid but decided against asking. "I love Scotland," she said, and then regretted it. It sounded so fatuous, an American tourist one day into her visit making such a sweeping statement. "I mean, what I know of it."

"Is this your first trip over the pond, then?"

"Yes. A neighbor in Detroit wanted to come. Her son didn't want her to travel alone, so she asked me along."

"And is she a pleasant traveling companion?"

"Not bad," she hedged. "I'm very lucky to have the opportunity."

Actually, a repertoire of Helen stories was growing that, while aggravating at present, would be funny when shared with friends at home. The old lady styled herself an expert on everything, so any comment made in her hearing might initiate a lecture on the subject. Mercedes had been criticized for shaving her legs, since the hair would grow back twice as thick; reading too much lest she ruin her eyes; and wearing trousers too often, which might someday inhibit her ability to bear children. Grinning at the memory, she reflected that Helen was living proof of the origin of the term "old wives' tale."

The man watched her, and she guessed he sensed the truth of her situation.

"Perhaps you'd like a drink? I've an hour or so before work, and I know a place that's an excellent example of Edwardian décor."

She was tempted. He was charming, and she was a sucker for a Scottish accent. But Helen awaited her return, and she hadn't yet found Paul or ice. "I'm sorry. I can't." She moved away before she changed her mind. Two attractive men in one day, but neither acquaintance was likely to go anywhere. She'd never see the nice police sergeant again, and she knew better than to get picked up in a hotel by a strange man, not matter how intriguing he might appear.

There was no ice machine on the premises, which was not a surprise. She rapped at Paul's door again after twenty minutes or so, but there was still no answer. Finally she took the creaky but ambiance-inducing elevator once more, returning to the room with neither of her errands complete.

The lights and the television were off, which was unusual. Most nights she took care of that after Helen fell asleep, often sitting upright with the remote in hand. Closing the door softly and slipping the security chain into place, Mercedes pulled off her shoes. As she did so, an odd sound came from the other bed. It was neither the snore of an elderly sleeper nor the sigh of a person settling into rest.

After Mercedes waited motionless for a few seconds, there was a rush of breath that ended in decidedly abnormal rattle. Switching on the light, she froze as she took in the sight before her. Helen Flowers lay on the bed, her head bleeding from what had eventually been her death blow. Worse, her eyes had been gouged out, leaving two bloody holes where they'd once been.

CHAPTER FOUR

When the police came into Mercedes' life for the second time that day, it was in the form of one Inspector Callard, Crimes Management Division, who was not nearly as pleasant as Sergeant Jared Graham had been. Though not an old man, Callard appeared to be the sort of person who decides early on that life is a disappointment. The hotel manager who trailed behind him with questions about procedure and a return to normal operations paused in the doorway under Callard's baleful glare. The inspector kicked the door shut in his face.

As he turned his gaze on her, Mercedes read an opinion in the piercing, dark eyes. The only person on this trip who'd known Helen, she was the likeliest suspect. "Miss Maxwell?"

"Yes."

"Did I hear someone call you Sadie?"

"Not Sadie. Mercedes."

"Ah." His grunt dismissed Americans and their eccentric names. "We must talk, Miss Maxwell, about this evening."

She didn't remember much of the first few minutes after her gruesome discovery. She must have gone for help, vaguely remembered a nervous clerk who followed her to the room and then hurried to phone the police. The night manager had opened his office to them, and she had been seated inside and given that British panacea, a cup of tea. The drink sat before her now, cooled to tepid. No one had thought to offer a warm-up, though she shivered from shock.

Paul had tried to speak to his charge while the inspector saw to the crime scene, but a sober young police woman informed him Miss Maxwell could see no one until she'd been interviewed by Inspector Callard. That was how Mercedes learned his name, since the man himself offered no pleasantries. He simply braced an ample buttock atop the borrowed desk and began a barrage of questions.

Callard had a little mustache faintly reminiscent of Hercule Poirot, but he had neither Poirot's urbanity nor his trimness. The polyester suit strained at the job of holding him in, and he made no attempt when he sat to adjust his clothing to a more presentable state. The coat hung unbuttoned, pilled at the lapels and bulging at the pockets. The shirt gaped at regular intervals, its buttons strained against the buttonholes. The pants stretched up and across his belly so that the top section of zipper was visible, exposing a gap where it hadn't been pulled fully into place. She looked away.

"Mrs. Flowers was dead when you entered the room?"

"No, I don't think so. What alerted me to her, um, condition was a sound." Mercedes shuddered at the memory of the death rattle, the first she'd encountered and hopefully the last.

Callard rose and looked out the room's one small window, hiding his face from her and snapping a finger against the slat of a blind for a moment. Suddenly he turned back accusingly. "Mrs. Flowers had money?" His face, heavily-jowled and splotched with red patches, conveyed intelligence, but Mercedes had already guessed it was the kind that's seldom moved once a conclusion is reached. A woman was dead. Her roommate had killed her for financial gain. A logical and oh-so-simple conclusion.

"She was comfortable, I guess." Absently she moved a bobble-headed Scotsman doll on the manager's desk into better

30

alignment. Becoming aware of the gesture, she stopped herself. Fidgeting made a person look guilty. She should suppress her need to put things in order.

"And will you get this money now that she's dead?"

"Of course not. I'm her neighbor, not her heir. She offered me the chance to go to Britain at her expense, and I agreed."

"Why did she do that?"

"Because there was no one else, and she wanted to see Britain before —" she stumbled on the last words as the reality of the very dead Helen Flowers formed a horrifying picture in her mind. She hugged herself, rubbing her arms as if to keep the blood circulating.

Callard digested this, adjusting the facts to fit his theory rather than vice versa. "So she paid your way. Was Mrs. Flowers...difficult? Hard to please?"

"Truthfully, yes, but I expected that. I knew her well enough to see ahead of time that she'd be demanding. I thought it was worth it for the chance to come here."

"But after several days of waiting on this disagreeable old woman you were not so sure?"

He'd been talking to the others. Helen had made no friends on the tour, carping about everything from the very first day. England didn't have enough rest rooms. The food over here was not like at home. A person couldn't get a cold drink to save her soul. And so on. She'd made no effort to be quiet about it, either. The fact that she was slightly deaf caused her to speak loudly, as if everyone else was too.

"Mrs. Flowers was quite sharp with you at times, I

31

understand." Callard had apparently switched motives but not suspects. No profit, so the roommate had killed the old woman in a fit of rage.

"Look, I can't say I enjoyed her company, but I had no reason to kill her. It would take a crazy person to do that to a helpless old woman."

"There was another murder today as well." The small eyes lay flat in his fleshy face, like reptiles she'd seen at the Detroit Zoo.

"Well, yes, but what has that to do with this?"

"You were present at both."

Mercedes felt her jaw tighten in anger. Who did this guy think he was? "As were forty other people who had nothing to do with either crime!" She struggled to calm herself. "I left the room. I came back. She was dying, and I called for help. She was alone when I left. In perfect health. That's all I can tell you."

"Why did you leave?"

"To find ice." For some reason she didn't mention the notebook. Maybe it was this slovenly man's instant assumption that she was capable of killing and mutilating a seventy-two-year-old woman. Since he suspected her already, what would he think if she confessed that only two hours ago the victim had found a mysterious, possibly valuable book? She might be more suspect, accused of both murders, since it was at the moment still in her pocket.

The book couldn't be connected to either death, so mentioning it would serve no purpose. There was no telling how long since Helen had looked in the bottom of her bag —two days ago, maybe, when she'd needed her heavy sweater. Mercedes didn't believe the book had any great value, but Helen had. It was hard to know the right thing to do.

Tears formed and threatened to spill down her cheeks. The poor old thing had lay dying even as she'd returned, her skull crushed by a blow from some heavy object. How had someone gotten her to let him in? And why had he done that to her eyes? Mercedes' chest felt like it might fly apart as she tried to calm her raging fears. How had this happened to an innocent tourist?

An odd jangle interrupted the mental questions, and Callard dug in his pocket for his cell phone. He had put in a call to Helen's son, Lloyd Flowers, who now called back. Once Lloyd was aware of the situation, he asked to speak to Mercedes. Callard passed the phone to her without comment. Shocked but supportive, Lloyd sensed her fear after a few moments. Offering reassurance that things would be all right, he asked to speak to the inspector again. She put Callard back on and heard Lloyd, somewhat like his mother in temperament, stating that the inspector was an ass if he suspected Mercedes of anything remotely illegal or immoral. As far as she could discern, Callard didn't take the message to heart but only glowered at Mercedes as if she'd caused yet more trouble.

After more than an hour the inspector called an end to the interview, unable to expose the American tourist as a heartless murderer. Paul waited outside the door, his professional politeness replaced by real concern. "I've arranged a different room for you tonight. We can decide in the morning what you want to do, but whatever you need, I'll try to arrange it."

"Thanks, Paul. Right now I'd like to try to sleep."

Try was the word. Since the hotel was full, they put her in a maid's room in an old section where guests were not usually housed. It was tiny, smelled of cigarettes, and the bath was down the hall, but it was quiet and she felt safe in the quaint, 1950s atmosphere, removed from corpses and policemen's questions.

Mercedes pulled off her sweatpants and stretched out in the narrow bed. The book laid in the pocket, softly curved as if it had spent years that way. Should she give it to Callard? Leave it in the room for someone else to find? Destroy it? It probably wasn't genuine history. The time was wrong, the contention that it concerned an unknown Shakespeare brother ridiculous. Most likely it was someone's attempt at fiction. Tomorrow she'd look it over and decide what to do with it. She already knew she would not leave with the tour. It didn't feel right to go blithely on after Helen's death.

Glancing at the clock, Mercedes considered and rejected the idea of calling Lloyd Flowers. It was still not late in the States, but she'd be intruding on his grief, and honestly, she didn't know him well. She would have liked to talk things over with someone, but she could think of no one who could help her sort through the things she had to decide. In the end she tossed in the single bed for another half hour before she gave up, turned on the light, and pulled the book from the pocket of the pants left folded over a ladder-backed chair.

***

The hotel clerk thought the man approaching her was nice-looking, though she wasn't fond of chin beards. "Sorry to be a bother, but there's a woman in the second-floor hallway who can't get into her room. She's in a rather angry state, and I thought I'd stop on my way out and tell you."

The girl, *Glynis*, according to her badge, grimaced around an impressive wad of gum. "I'll go up and let her in. What's the room number?"

He slapped the counter gently in self-recrimination. "I should have thought to look."

Right, her eyes said, but she kept her professional smile. "I'll

34

see to it."

The man moved off and Glynis headed for the stairs, which was much faster than waiting for the decrepit old elevator. As soon as she was out of sight the dark man reappeared, slipped behind the counter, and bent over the computer. "Should be easy enough if that lack-wit can do it," he muttered, moving the mouse into position and clicking on *Guests, Current*.

A list appeared of those presently registered and their room numbers. Flowers, Helen was still listed in room 24A. That was no longer true. Vincent had watched until they took her away. The brunette wouldn't be left there, so where had they put her? He'd learned her name, but there was no Mercedes on the list.

There, Maxwell was listed at the bottom, but no room number was given. "Where are you?" he whispered, but the computer gave no further hint. Hitting *Back*, he returned to the original screen and moved off, mission incomplete. Glynis returned moments later, convinced that the lady the dark man had reported must have made her key work after all.

CHAPTER FIVE

Mercedes beat the skimpy pillow into the shape she wanted, pulled the paper-thin sheet up around her waist, and took up the notebook again. It was hard to read the vicar's writing, and he was no Shakespeare. To give the man credit, dealing with bits of disintegrating paper might make assembling a complete story difficult. Worse, Willie Reid had written in a sort of half-literate shorthand, leaving some passages open to interpretation.

The journal begins in the spring of 1609. Reid makes no explanation as to why he started it, but I deduce that he recorded everything about a certain captive, hoping to glean clues to his secret.

The prisoner was delivered into Reid's hands by chance. A ship's captain who plied the lucrative salmon trade between Scotland and England was invited to sup with Reid on business. In the course of the conversation, he mentioned he'd seen a fellow Londoner in the village below the castle. Since Reid was unaware of the man, and since he made it his business to find out about such things, he casually asked how the captain knew this Englishman. "He is a player," the man replied. "I have seen him on the stage and know his face well."

Having heard of no troupe in the area, Reid became interested. Why was an English actor wandering Scotland alone? Spies later reported that the man walked along the coast each day, climbing among the rough formations and occasionally wandering off along a river, often wading in the fast-rushing water as far as a mile upstream. Willie decided the man was looking for something. He became determined to discover what it was.

Men were sent to ask questions about the Englishman. He claimed to be a playwright, come to the area to learn the tale of Black Douglas' fall at Threave Castle. He spent little time writing, which gave the lie to his story. The man was careful, and it took two weeks of watching before he was seen passing a letter to a sailor on the dock. The sailor was waylaid and the message seized. It was in code, but the very existence of a coded letter told Reid enough. The poor wretch who'd been charged with delivering the letter was forced to reveal its destination, which was even more telling. It was meant for Robert Cecil, Spymaster for Elizabeth Tudor.

Mercedes stopped reading and absent-mindedly arranged some cracker crumbs on the nightstand into a neat pile. She summoned what she knew of Cecil, but that was very little. It was said that Elizabeth I had been fortunate in her ministers, but Mercedes had always believed it was more her canny choices than luck. On impulse she hauled her tablet out of its case, booted it up, and consulted the worldwide web. Cecil was listed as a successor to Francis Walsingham as Spymaster. Both had been exceptionally good at their admittedly creepy job.

There were only a few paragraphs on Tudor spies, but she noted that among the spies recruited in Elizabethan times was Christopher Marlowe, the playwright. She supposed those associated with the theatre made good spies, being required to wander the countryside in their profession as well as being skilled at playing roles. Spymasters of the day, like Walsingham and Cecil, trained their agents in the use of ciphers, which the prisoner had apparently employed in his letter. A player and a spy? It was possible. She returned to the vicar's account.

Once Reid learned that the Englishman was a spy, his long walks along the coast took on greater meaning. If the Crown had sent him here to find something, it could mean wealth. Kings and queens of the day generally operated with an eye to profit.

Being fairly new to the area, Reid needed an informed source. He invited the sea captain to dine a second time and brought up the subject of treasure. The sailor, a scoffer at such things, assured him that any tales of treasure ships lost in the area were blather. Willie asked innocently what tales there might be.

Reluctantly, since he believed not a word of it, the sailor recounted the tale that Sir Francis Drake had died with a great prize unaccounted for. "The story goes," the captain told Willie, "that Drake took a rich vessel in mid-ocean only a few days out from Plymouth on his last journey. The ship, a galleon named the *Madre de Dios*, was heavily laden with gold from Mexico City, where the Spaniards minted coins from the mines of the colonies and sent them home to fatten King Philip's coffers."

Drake's men had spotted the galleon by pure luck, the story went, but surprise at the meeting was overcome more quickly by the English than the Spanish. She was overtaken in a short time with no loss of life on the English side. The heavy, full-rigged galleon was a problem as well as a prize, being much larger than the English vessels.

On board the ship was a chest of gold coins along with other prizes. Rather than load his vessels with heavy items to carry both out and back, Drake chose a skeleton crew for the galleon and ordered them to return it to England with its treasure. In command he put a man well known to him, one John Falstaff. Drake went on his way to the

Caribbean, trusting Falstaff to take the ship into port. Drake never returned from that voyage, nor did the *Madre de Dios* ever reach England. According to the old sailor, the crew was not as true to England as their officer was. They overtook Falstaff and threw him overboard, taking the ship and the treasure for themselves.

Mercedes stared into the shadowy corners of the room, silent except for the soft click of a battery-operated clock. It was common knowledge that Spain had garnered great wealth from the New World in the 1500s. Drake, one of Elizabeth's most skillful and lucky captains, had taken his share of it, making his Queen proud and himself famous. What had that to do with Shakespeare? She read on.

Not daring to return to England, the men supposedly sailed north to Scotland and found a deserted section of coast where they unloaded the chest of gold coins and hid it, intending to return for it in the future. Their plan was to sail southward and sell the galleon and the rest of its contents to French privateers who would not question its origin. Once the ship was disposed of, they could reappear, claiming they'd been shipwrecked and survived only by chance.

The mutineers were unlucky, or perhaps Divine Providence saw fit to treat them as they'd treated John Falstaff. A storm wracked the vessel off the Isle of Man, and the mutinous thieves perished in the sea but for one found floating on a piece of ship's timber. He supposedly told the truth as he lay dying of his injuries.

Here was the weakness in the story, the old captain said, for was it not high drama for the man to die halfway through the telling, before he could reveal the hiding place of the treasure? With as much coastline as Scotland possessed, it was impossible to tell where to begin a search. It was a sailor's tale, spun to

39

entertain other sailors, and nothing more. Drake himself died in the Indies on that last voyage, and though his men confirmed that a Spanish vessel was taken, it was likely the ship was lost at sea and never reached Scotland or anywhere else.

That was the sea captain's story. Despite his dinner guest's dismissal of the account as "spun yarn," Reid concluded there might be something to the story if one of Cecil's spies was searching the local coast. New evidence of the treasure's whereabouts must have surfaced, and Cecil had sent a man to find the location and report to him. Already Reid had stopped John's letter from getting to England. All he had to do now was stop the man himself.

In those days in these parts, Willie Reid was a law unto himself, and if he wanted a man to disappear, he did. Kirkfort Willie arranged for the Englishman to be waylaid the next time he left his inn. John was brought to Kirkfort castle, and from there he would not depart alive.

The old-fashioned dial telephone rang sharply at her side, and Mercedes glanced at the clock to see it was seven a.m. The day was lightening outside, and she saw peeks of sunlight through dispersing clouds. She'd spent hours deciphering the pages of the vicar's work, and it was hard to shake off the story and return to the here and now.

As she picked up the phone, Mercedes realized what she wanted to do. The vicar's story had captured her interest, and she wanted to know more. In the two weeks remaining of her stay, she would visit the place where Willie Reid had lived and look at the *Macbeth* script the vicar had turned over to his local museum. Along the way she'd finish reading the vicar's account and decide if the notebook was worthwhile or not. If it was, she'd turn it over to the authorities before she returned home.

The caller was Paul. Assuring him she was coping, she added, "I'm going to stay in Scotland. Once Inspector Callard is satisfied I'm no psychotic killer, I think I'll wander around on my own."

"I'd be happy to download some information on local attractions," he offered. "I was raised not far from here, so I know the area well."

"Thanks. I'll miss your sparkling repertoire, though." It felt odd to strike out on her own. After only a week, Paul's face and mannerisms were as familiar as people she'd known for years. Still, she thought she'd chosen a good path. She couldn't travel on as if nothing had happened, but at the same time, going home with the corpse didn't feel right either. She was free to explore Britain at her leisure. She might as well seize the chance.

***

Vincent watched carefully as each tourist stepped onto the growling coach. The trim brunette didn't join them. There would no doubt be things to do concerning the woman's death. Mercedes might even be a suspect.

The old one had been so easy to fool! He'd knocked on the door, apparently very agitated. "Someone has fallen on the stairs, a young woman. I'm afraid she's badly hurt!"

"Is she dark-haired, very pretty?"

"Yes. Please, may I use your telephone to call for help?"

That was all it took. The silly old hag had unhooked the chain and directed him to the phone. After that, making her tell what she knew of the book took only seconds. He'd smashed her skull and left her posed as Gloucester. The old man in King Lear who trusts wrongly and loses his eyes as a result was perfect for an old woman so quickly duped into offering her life to him.

41

But again the book was not where he expected it to be. With hands clawing at him for mercy, the woman sobbed that the girl had gone to give it to Paul. At first he resolved to wait for the brunette's return, but he found it hard to stay with the old woman once he'd finished her. Like a cat when the mouse has gone limp, he wanted to be away.

And Paul, how had he not recognized Paul? Did he have the book now? Did the police know about it? There'd been no search of Paul's room, no evidence they were suspicious of the glib tour guide. Vincent had to act quickly to arrange a surprise for his old friend.

***

Lloyd Flowers called at eight to report that arrangements had been made concerning his mother's body. When he asked about her situation, Mercedes assured him her arrest was not imminent. "Use whatever money Mother had left in her purse for your needs," Lloyd urged. "You deserve it. When I talked to her last she said you'd been the perfect choice." His voice trailed away as he added, "I can't believe it."

Nor could she on this bright morning. It was hard to accept the grisly scenes of yesterday, hard even to recall her sleepless state of a few hours before. She was sorry for poor Helen, but those matters were out of her hands. Energized by the desire to know more about the vicar and his theories, she'd already begun to look forward to solving the puzzle of Willie Reid's prisoner.

CHAPTER SIX

The motor coach stopped mid-morning at a pub in the Moffat Hills, its occupants unaware that death followed them. It was a breathtaking spot, with green hills stretching in all directions and the cozy pub nestled in a copse of trees under the crest of the highest one. As he assisted each person off the coach with a steadying hand, Paul cheerfully gave directions to the loo and cautioned the passengers to return in exactly twenty minutes. As soon as his flock of forty dispersed, he stepped aside and took out his phone, his expression altered from the friendly mask of seconds ago.

In seconds a bored voice asked if he could be of assistance. "I'd like to leave a message."

"Do you know your party's extension?"

"No."

"What name, sir?"

He gave his name and was connected, but he got his party's voice mail. Leaving only three words, "Mother of God," he hung up and paced until the call was returned.

As he waited, Paul recalled his youth, spent just south of where they were. A long-ago rainy day had started things, when four friends found an intriguing item in the attic of his home. Only twelve or so, they'd loved spending time in the dark and dusty room at the top of the house, where grownups seldom went. They could smoke next to the tiny circular window and the olfactory evidence floated away in the breeze. That summer's day, Paul's pudgy best friend Bubble had brought along a cousin who was visiting from England. Younger and therefore anxious to be included in their adventures, the newcomer had tolerated a lot of abuse, most of it from him, he had to admit.

Sprawled on the wooden plank floor with the rain beating on the roof above, they'd been surrounded by items stored over time farther and farther away from the active part of the house. Boxes and trunks that had once been useful migrated up one staircase and then another as they became full of miscellanea, broke a handle, or simply went out of fashion. Now they rested here under thick layers of dead flies, dust, and the spoor of mice and invading squirrels. A haven for youthful discussion and experimentation.

Vincent had begun it, opening this box and that and sifting desultorily through the contents. At some point the book caught his attention, and he went silent for some moments. Finally Paul said, "What have you got, Vincent? I don't see a centerfold."

He read aloud, and soon they were all interested. As the afternoon wore on, they took turns, reading with difficulty but enthusiasm the account of the prisoner being starved to death in an old castle they knew was nearby. At the end they sat wide-eyed at what they'd learned. There was treasure nearby, and only they knew about it.

Vincent had become manic about the gold, insisting they hunt for it that whole summer. The others, fearful of the brooding, volatile Vincent, had done as he demanded. Nothing came of it. Vincent often cursed the vicar for giving away the script, which he was sure held the key to the treasure's hiding place.

He'd also insisted that he keep the vicar's journal. Paul protested it belonged in his house, but Vincent had looked at him in that way he had and said, "Your family's let it rot up here for years. I'll keep it safe."

There'd been no more discussion. Weeks later, when they exhausted their ideas about where to look, all except Vincent lost interest in the search. Paul had mentioned the matter to his father and learned to his disappointment that lots of people knew about Drake's treasure. "A fool's chase, a myth hunted for centuries," Father scoffed. Paul, Bubble, and Squeak accepted that their dream was just that, a dream. Vincent never did, as far as Paul knew.

When he was fifteen, Vincent had a terrible row with his father, a brooding, hard-drinking hulk of a man. The boy was thrown into the streets and told to make his own way in the world. A day later he was gone from their lives, and for a long time no one knew where. Years later, Paul had been surprised to see Vincent's face in a national magazine. He looked much the same, except he wore a goatee and dressed rather better. He was, the magazine said, a respected writer and reviewer specializing in Elizabethan drama. Who could have predicted that? Paul wondered briefly at the time what had become of the vicar's homemade book, but there was no way to find out.

Within ten minutes the phone rang. Paul had by then fended off several offers to buy him a pint from nattering tourists who thought he should be honored to drink with them. Smiling with his lips, he said he had to wait for a return call from the tour offices. Going around a corner to prevent anyone hearing, he said, "It's Paul."

"What's going on? Why the message in code?"

"Do you know there's been a second murder?"

"Do you think I'm an idiot? Of course I know."

"The woman who died at Canready Castle was Sylvia Brickett."

There was a pause as the caller placed the name. "Vincent's old girlfriend?"

"I know. She used to be pretty, but she'd let herself go. And she was married once, so the name was different."

45

"Do you think Sylvia had taken up with Vincent again?"

"I don't think so. I saw her quite often, since I make this trip several times a year. Whenever we'd stop at Canready, I'd look her up, you know."

"For a good time call Sylvia?"

"Something like that. Anyway, yesterday she was bursting with excitement, and I asked her what was up. She wasn't going to tell me, but then she couldn't hold back."

"Sounds like Sylvia in more ways than one," the other put in dryly.

"Right. She had a book that Vincent was going to pay her a great deal of money for."

"Sylvia never seemed to me the type for books."

Paul chuckled. "I didn't say she'd read it. It's the attic book, the vicar's story."

The man once known to his friends as Bubble thought about that. "The summer we spent looking for treasure."

"Yes. Vincent left it behind when he ran away, but Sylvia kept in touch with his mother. When the old lady died, she helped to clear the house. There was a box of things she kept for herself, but she hadn't gotten to the bottom of it until recently. There she found the book, wedged under the cardboard liner."

"It wasn't very thick. I remember that."

"Sylvia remembered Vincent telling her about our search and insisting there were great riches to be found."

"Something about Shakespeare, wasn't it?"

"Yes. She skimmed through and saw the name and a mention of coded letters. It happened she'd seen Vincent's picture in the papers a few months back. You know, he's made a name for himself in certain circles."

"As what, a circus freak?"

"Shakespearean drama critic. Anyway, Sylvia located him, and he said he would like to have the book back."

Bubble said in a rueful tone, "I've wondered what he did with it. We should have gone after it once he'd left home."

"We were all afraid of his old man. Anyway, Sylvia said Vincent couldn't hide his eagerness to get his hands on that journal."

"What do you think he knows that we don't?"

"I made some phone calls this morning, checking who's visited certain sites and looked at certain documents. Vincent's been studying records on the *Madre de Dios*."

"So he's figured it out?"

"Some of it, maybe, but he'd need the journal for specifics."

There was a pause. "If the book is what we hoped it was, a guide to the treasure, I'd like a look at it myself. I assume Vincent took it from Sylvia and killed her?"

"He might have killed her, but I think he lost the journal somehow. I think the old woman who was killed last night found it."

"The tourist?"

"I don't know where it is now. Either Vincent took it from the old woman, or the girl who was traveling with her has it."

"She said nothing about finding a book." Bubble paused. "Why would Vincent have killed Sylvia?"

"She must have asked for too much money and made him

angry. You know he never was completely sane, Bubble."

"No one calls me that anymore." He paused, but Paul made no correction, so he returned to the subject at hand. "Vincent will get the book, if he hasn't already. When he does, I'll get it from him."

"And how will you do that?"

"I have a few ideas. Vincent doesn't know about us, that we're aware the book's been located. He'll think Sylvia kept its existence to herself out of greed."

"It was luck, really, that she couldn't resist telling me about it."

"Yes. She must have been one of those who doesn't believe in Drake's treasure."

Paul stared at the wall. "I've thought about it over the years. Have you?"

There was a pause, as if the other was gauging his answer. "I thought Vincent took the book when he ran away. That must have been some row if he went off without it."

"Knowing Vincent's old man, it was."

"So our old friend is after the treasure, and he intends to leave us out of it."

"Vincent's not stupid." Paul straightened a bit. "If he's around, he's seen me, and that's unnerving. Strange as he was as a kid, who knows what he is now?"

He left off, and the man at the other end spoke reassuringly. "Vincent knows nothing. Just relax and let me see what I can find out on this end." With no further comment the call was disconnected. Paul was more than relaxed. Someone had come from behind and rendered him unconscious.

CHAPTER SEVEN

With the morning on hold until Callard was finished with her, Mercedes returned to reading the vicar's account. She took her breakfast up to the room: an apple, a cheese Danish, and a glass of orange juice. The old servant's quarters were like a rabbit warren, with hallways that twisted this way and that and short stairways leading up or down to single rooms. She got lost twice on the way, balancing her pastry atop the juice glass and retracing her steps in frustration. Finally she found the correct door and opened it with the old-fashioned metal key.

On the floor were several sheets of paper, information on a variety of sites within a fifty-mile radius, maps of the area, and some handwritten notes tailored to what Paul had noticed were her interests. Since her current focus was the vicar's journal, she set the downloaded pages on the nightstand, lining up the corners with her usual precision, and returned to the small leather-bound book.

Reid writes of visiting "Johnny" almost every day. The prisoner's condition is of concern. His strength fades rapidly from the conditions he endures, and Reid frets over how to make him reveal his secret before he dies. John's attempt to send the coded message and his intent to leave Scotland indicate he had located the treasure, and Willie wants badly to make him tell what he knows. When they first questioned him, however, John almost died under the beatings. Reid hurriedly called in a physician, who concluded the man's heart was weak and could give out at any time.

This ended the torture, but Reid believes that withholding food will bring results. The man's ration is halved, then halved again. For a while John receives only bread and water. When he still refuses to speak, he is allowed only water and finally nothing in his last days of life. When Johnny finally dies, Reid's entry shows no regret for his barbarous actions, only for the fact he never learned the man's secret. May God have mercy on both their souls!

Mercedes stopped to consider Willie Reid's inhumanity. Why would John die rather than tell what he knew? Probably he'd sensed he would die either way. As she munched on the apple, she tried to imagine him sitting in a tiny cell, cold, hungry, and wracked with pain from injuries left untreated. Her imagination conjured images she'd rather have avoided: the skittering of rats, the reek of the cell's filth, and John's probable disorientation, even madness. He'd endured weeks, maybe months of slow death as his captor watched and gloated. The harshness of life can be terrible, and man's cruelty to his fellows is the worst, being consciously done.

Once the facts of the prisoner's last days were told, the vicar took pains to establish the historical truth of his major characters. Willie Reid, he reported, was a figure documented in history, having been once arrested by the Scottish wardens for his crimes and subsequently freed by his relatives in a well-publicized gallows rescue. The vicar admitted he could find no record of a prisoner who died in Willie's clutches, but that was not surprising. Records from the time were often missing important pieces of information, and to whom would the outlaw report that he'd starved a man to death in hopes of getting him to tell the location of Drake's treasure?

As far as Mercedes was concerned, the question was what in

the journal led the vicar to conclude that "Johnny" was William Shakespeare's brother. Pulling her feet up yoga style to ease the cramp in her thighs, she read on, intrigued by the story her practical side whispered was probably pure fiction.

The true identity of the prisoner is never known to Reid. He identifies himself only as John Romeo. It is possible John finally lost his wits due to the ill treatment he had received. He asked for pen and ink, and thereafter labored day after day, making holes with the pen nib in a working script of Shakespeare's *Macbeth* which he'd had with him at his capture. At the last he wrote a letter to Reid, asking that the script be returned to William Shakespeare of London, whom he calls "his beloved friend." He recounts their long association and says he many times viewed William's plays from backstage where he watched, assisted the players, and even took part himself. Along the margin of the first page of the script he wrote a line from the play: "By the pricking of my thumbs, something wicked this way comes."

Was it some odd joke? Mercedes asked herself. A man in a fetid, clammy cell, starving by inches, takes the time to beg for the return of Globe Theater property? If John's request had a purpose, what was it?

I considered that these pinpricks might form a message for Shakespeare or someone to whom he might relay the script. This is not true as far as I can determine. The holes seem random. At the back of this book I have listed the letters indicated by the pinpricks, but in the end I gave up the attempt and turned the script over to a museum recently established in Kirkfort.

Turning to the end to see what he meant, Mercedes found that the last sheet of the vicar's book was separated from the rest of the pages. The paper had split where the leather thong wore against the holes it passed through. There was a long list of letters, faithfully copied from the script by the vicar. Scanning them briefly, she saw no pattern to the letters, no discernible words.

acsbtiusoaltoubartspehgenpepfianrpapomentmalint
weoinhbnioeweoilekneatiaquisznetquuomememfoeindpo
muneniocaaineneieistvcbhlklaenenieieaxasenwpinititche
cnenhointenehoinrwewexuxbeembpomattwetytlpoemen
pomdeneibrnoingereqrutagihctmxbienmrpcrmrweniailm
svjrcrbhoxcrnsfhkeeyuwfhkaeybutsjhrheilbfefohkoegbljo
edtysgkpfwlbnawjhytjafgvhprnkawgmoiecnyjtiedmdegde
gjvyjxiwchlegtebhuhrbesmoeeunilcepsrrltrkewemdntepi
nskenttwlethmrbiarvnumwcoynfjobeclrgoujooid

After some minutes' scrutiny, she gave up trying to decipher it. Outside the room, movement had picked up. The hotel was in full operation, with staff beginning the ritual of cleaning out the signs of departed guests and setting up amenities for those of the future. What about the room she'd occupied until last night's horror? One guest stayed on unexpectedly, and poor Mrs. Flowers, she thought sadly, had departed in a much more serious sense. Did the notebook hold the reason for an otherwise senseless death?

Setting the loose page on the bed table beside her, Mercedes returned to where she'd left off earlier. Here the vicar had turned to attempts to identify the prisoner.

Being in my youth enamored of the stage and the works of Shakespeare, I knew that Romeo was a name the playwright invented. Apparently to amuse himself, he frequently used names that end in the "ee-o" sound: Gromio, Mercutio, Antonio, and so on, but there is no record before then of a real person named Romeo, first or last. If the prisoner had been Italian, the spelling would no doubt have been the traditional "i-o", since the "e" would make the name Ro-MAY-o in Italian. So this was, I decided, an assumed name, a logical conclusion assuming John was indeed a spy.

She shook her head. The vicar was too easily convinced that Reid's information was correct. What if the outlaw had it all wrong and poor John Romeo told nothing because he had nothing to tell? Even if he withheld his true name, he might have had other reasons for it, not the least of which was a refusal to let his captors have something he could deny them.

She paged through the book quickly, noting the vicar seemed to tire of his project as time passed. Entries became shorter and shorter, some mere notations: *No success* on one day, and an angry *What does he mean?* on another. Finally the entries stopped altogether. All that remained was the list of letters on the last page, which he'd obviously once had high hopes for.

Glancing at the jumble of letters again, Mercedes squinted at it, turned the page sideways and upside down, and held it to the light, hoping to find something that stuck out, a grouping or repetition. Nothing appeared. Finally she set it aside again, leaving the vicar's story to percolate through her brain for a while.

Taking up Paul's list of places of interest, she found a map and located Kirkfort. It was a coastal village to the southwest of Dumfries. What drama had played out there, unseen, unknown, and unresolved?

There was a light knock on the door, and a strawberry-haired young man informed Mercedes that Inspector Callard requested her presence downstairs. She was pretty sure the word *requested* was the messenger's idea, not the sender's. Promising to be right down, she ran a brush through her tousled hair then straightened the room, more from habit than anything else. Not wanting to leave the book lying out, she pulled her tablet out, slipped the slim volume into the zippered pocket on the outside of the case, and slid it under the bed. The loose papers Paul had copied for her she slid into her purse to look at later. Glancing approvingly at her tidy little space, she left the room.

CHAPTER EIGHT

Callard was somewhat less convinced today that Mercedes had killed her employer, since there was no evidence to support his theory. She hadn't touched the iron that was the murder weapon. There was no blood on her anywhere, and she was left-handed, while the blow that killed Helen Flowers had come from the right. "I told you, no sane person could have done that to her and then calmly answered your questions."

"You'd be surprised at how much a clever madman, or madwoman, can hide," he replied stiffly. "However, the medical examiner informs me the killer would have had signs of what was done on his clothing." He didn't elaborate on spatter patterns, for which Mercedes was grateful. Still, the inspector wasn't happy about giving up the easy answer, and he took it out on her, insisting she keep him informed of her whereabouts for the next few days.

"I'm going to see the countryside," she told him, "but I'll call each evening and let you know where I am."

"And report anything you think of that may pertain to this matter."

She swallowed a pang of guilt. "Of course."

The suit the inspector wore today was newer, though no sartorial prize, and he smelled faintly of cooking grease, probably sausage. "The body will be returned to Detroit as soon as we've finished with it." She tried not to let her mind focus on what that entailed. Rising to indicate the end of the interview, Callard held out a plain white envelope. Inside was a surprising amount of cash. "The money from Mrs. Flowers' purse."

"She was carrying all this cash around with her?"

For the first time, a hint of humanity crept into his expression. "Some roommates might kill for six thousand dollars in cash," he replied, "but I think you'd be smart enough not to let me see it if you had."

Mercedes made her way back to the old section of the hotel, this time managing to find her way with no false turns. The place was deserted at this time of day, the cramped, musty hallways silent. Callard was convinced of her innocence, much as he hadn't wanted to be, so maybe it was time to tell him about the book. She could say she'd just found it and relieve her niggling sense of guilt. If the book did have something to do with the two murders, or even one of them, the police would discover it, and if it didn't, they'd return the book to its rightful owner. Rounding the last corner, she made up her mind. Callard might still be around if she hurried. She'd take it to him right away.

Her tablet was missing, case and all. She peered under the bed in disbelief. A glance around the room showed that nothing else was gone, but the laptop was the only thing of value. Thirty seconds in the room had gotten the thief what he wanted.

Hurrying down the stairs, she found Callard finishing up with the manager. "Could I speak to you?" He agreed tacitly, indicating the manager's office. That long-suffering gentleman once again put his work on hold and moved away with a sigh.

Briefly she told him about finding the book, being unable to give it to Paul the night before, and returning to her room to find it gone. "I didn't think it was important, but the fact it's been stolen means it might be what the killer was after in the first place."

Callard moved to the farthest point of the small office, as if separating himself from her lest he lose self-control. "Two women dead and you didn't think you had to tell me everything?"

Mercedes looked down at her hands. "I didn't know about the book at the castle, and when we found it later, I didn't believe it was genuine. But now that it's been stolen —"

"It's more likely your computer is the thief was after." His tone implied that no old book would be worth the effort of breaking into her room.

"The book concerns lost treasure." As soon as she spoke, she regretted it, for an expression of disbelief formed on the inspector's unattractive face.

"Miss Maxwell, at times tourists are offered things by unscrupulous people. Due to their inexperience, their unfamiliarity with history or with local legends, they are...duped." He scratched at a stain on his lapel, egg, it appeared. "Mrs. Flowers might have believed she'd bought something of value, but—"

"She didn't buy it. It was put into her bag, possibly by the young woman who died at Canready Castle yesterday."

"Possibly." He was humoring her. "But you've dealt with a lot in the last day, and you mustn't overreact. I've spoken with Sergeant Graham, and he says this Sylvia Tate was involved with a disturbed young man. They probably argued and he lost control, with tragic result.

"Now Mrs. Flowers' murder is the act of a depraved individual, and we can find no connection between the two. The first was a crime of passion, a single stab wound to the heart, while Mrs. Flowers' death was—" He searched for an acceptable term— "the result of frenzy: the choosing of an unknown victim, the mutilation—" He stopped as Mercedes winced. "A book is unlikely as the cause of such a crime."

"I thought it was a hoax," she had to admit, "but if Helen

thought it was valuable maybe someone else did, too. What if she called someone after I left the room and told them she'd found a book worth thousands of dollars? People have been killed before in the mistaken notion there was money to be gained."

Callard grunted assent, and she went on. "Last night I read parts of the book. I don't believe the man held prisoner was a Shakespeare, and I don't understand why the writer thought he was, but the account is interesting. I think someone wants that journal."

"But you no longer have the book."

"No."

"I don't doubt your good intentions, Miss Maxwell, but a modern madman is a more likely answer than a long-dead vicar."

She gave up. The man didn't want to hear her theories, had already settled on his own. She should be grateful he'd opened his mind enough to clear her of suspicion of murder.

After Callard left, Mercedes sought out lunch in the hotel dining room, frustrated at his disregard of the missing book. Over a tasty salad and a crusty, still-warm croissant, she argued with Callard in absentia. The man seemed just shy of incompetence, though personal antipathy might color her judgment. Still, two murders and a theft within twenty-four hours, wasn't there a chance they were related?

The rental car she had arranged that morning was delivered a few minutes after three, a tiny Chevy model not even offered in the U.S., as far as she knew. The friendly tick of the motor promised reliability and good gas mileage. She planned to store the bulk of her luggage and take only a small bag, so the tiny trunk was no problem. After signing the proper forms, she accepted the keys, retreated to her third room in the same hotel, this one much like the second but down a different hallway, and took a very long nap.

There was no schedule now, which was restful after the hop-on, hop-off pace of the bus tour. Shock and the lack of sleep over twenty-four hours finally caught up with her as well. Before drifting off, Mercedes shed a few tears for Helen Flowers, who had done nothing to deserve her terrible death. Her last conscious thought was relief. If the killer had been after the vicar's journal, he had it now. She need no longer be concerned. It was a matter for the police.

When she awoke, it was after two in the morning. Once again wide awake in the middle of the night, Mercedes didn't even have the vicar's book for entertainment. She still intended to go off on her own, but without her tablet, it would be harder to plot her route. With its roundabouts and traffic lanes opposite what she was used to, driving in Britain would be a challenge. Recalling there were several maps in the information Paul had provided, she took the folded sheets out of her purse. Shuffling through for the clearest map of the area, she stopped cold when she found a smaller sheet sandwiched between the others.

Immediately she realized what had happened. While hastily tidying the room earlier, she had swept up the loose page from the back of the vicar's book with the sheets Paul had provided. Now she laid the single sheet directly under the light and studied once again the letters the vicar had copied from John Romeo's script.

Even after trying every trick she could devise, she could make nothing of them. In all likelihood, Callard was right, and the "vicar" who'd written the book was a scam artist who, for fun or profit or both, had mocked up some old paper and rehashed the legend with some creative touches of his own. Even if parts of it were true, she had no resource for researching the story with her laptop missing. Even her cell phone was gone, since she'd left it on the bedside table. Reluctantly she put the sheet aside, wishing she knew who could tell her if there really had been an outlaw named Willie Reid.

Glancing back over Paul's information, she brightened, reading aloud: "Dumfries has a large library with an impressive collection of local information."

***

It was mid-afternoon when the death of Paul Prescott was discovered. He wasn't at the coach at departure time, and after ten more minutes, the driver got out and looked for him with no success. That started a nervous stir among passengers who'd been close to two murders in two days. They were herded inside the pub again and provided with free drinks while the police were called and a search mounted.

Paul was found hanging upside down in a corner of the pub's wine cellar. A large tub had been set under him to catch the blood that slowly obeyed the pull of gravity. Though the cellar had been checked earlier, the body was positioned behind the wine racks in such a way that it could not easily be seen in the darkness of the back corner. The guide's feet had been tied together and the rope thrown over a rafter, then he'd been hauled up and his throat slit. Investigators later found that his luggage was missing, probably taken when the driver went inside to use the facilities. The constable who'd found the body was half sick, and the American guests were near to panic.

Someone was en route from the company office to make arrangements for the group. Many would go home, a few would join another tour, and one couple planned to ignore the triple disaster, rent a car, and strike out on their own.

A conference call between the involved council areas pooled information on the three murders. Inspector Callard held that one of the Americans was the killer, and investigations had been launched into each person's background. There was no apparent deviant among them. The group was mostly married couples and elderly ladies in groups of two or three, none likely to begin a killing spree.

Sergeant Graham, Inspector Callard, and the Moffat village constable discussed Mercedes Maxwell by telephone. She had been in the hotel at Dumfries at the time of Paul's murder. Callard had interviewed her, had gone to her room to look for the stolen laptop and book. Since it wasn't possible to be in two places at once, Miss Maxwell could not be Paul's killer.

"She might be involved," Callard insisted. "With no motive, it's hard to say who is part of it."

"She seems harmless to me," Jared Graham said diffidently, and Callard rolled his eyes in disgust. The young man was obviously taken with the girl and couldn't see past her attractive exterior.

Callard chewed a fingernail absently and spit the shard off to one side. "What about this missing book?"

"It seems an unlikely trigger for murder," Graham replied, and the constable agreed. They rang off, and Callard glared at the window without seeing what was outside. "She read the thing," he said to himself. "If she learned something important, Mercedes Maxwell must be required to tell what she knows. Even if she doesn't understand it herself."

CHAPTER NINE

Mercedes didn't like to waste morning hours. She had breakfasted, packed her smaller bag and stored the rest in the hotel manager's closet, and practiced driving British style before most businesses opened. Around nine, she left the car in a public lot and walked a short way up the inevitable Queen Street toward the library.

The area bustled with morning traffic: a bus with squealing brakes, bicyclists with tinkling bells that warned pedestrians of their approach, and a crush of people making their way on foot with the efficiency typical of mornings in the city. Halfway down a sloping street, she found the library pictured in the pamphlet. The Provincial Historical Society of Dumfries and Galloway was just opening its doors for the day.

Inside, she met a pleasant woman who looked pretty much like a librarian of antiquity should, light brown hair sprinkled with unashamed gray, half glasses on a cord around her neck, and a tweed skirt paired with a high-necked blouse. The sweater thrown over her shoulders and the sensible, crepe-soled shoes completed the picture. Did the job description read, "Must look like a Maeve Binchy creation"? As she explained what she wanted, the woman watched her face carefully, apparently having trouble understanding her Midwest American accent.

"I'm on vaca—on holiday, and I'm interested in some of the clans from this area."

"Any name in particular?"

"Reid?"

The woman was well-versed in the historical material she

tended. "The Reids are an interesting family, noted for their military temperament, but they are mostly associated with other areas. Falkirk and Loch Leven, I think, perhaps Perth." Mercedes looked disappointed, but the woman gave a mischievous grin. "However, this area was home to a Reid less military and more arbitrary, shall we say?"

"Willie?"

"You've heard of our outlaw?"

"Yes, but only enough to make me curious."

"I can give you some books to look through, but I know the basic facts. Willie was a distant relative of the fourth Earl of Montrose. No one is sure how he came by his holding on the coast, at Kirkfort. Some say the land was a grant from the family to keep Willie away from them. Others say he simply found a ruined kirk, converted it to a fortress, and set himself up as a laird. Whichever, he held sway over this area for twenty years, gaining a reputation for ruthlessness and greed. For example, the Reids of the time were feuding with the Douglases, a powerful clan. Willie sided with Douglas against his own kin and managed to double his holding."

The librarian ended with the vague memory. "I believe Willie met with a bad end." Striding purposefully through the aisles, she collected several pertinent volumes. The place was quiet, the atmosphere restful, and the memories it evoked pleasant. Mercedes found a secluded table and lost herself in the intrigues and eccentricities of the Reid clan.

Willie was a footnote to Clan Reid (Red) history, but in a book that dealt more with Kirkfort itself, she found a short passage outlining his life. It confirmed his double-dealing, his greed, and his neighbors' dread of him. In 1629, the wardens of Scotland finally put an end to Willie's wickedness. He was hanged from his own castle gate, and his body left for the ravens. There was no mention of anyone finding the man's personal journal.

Returning to her own world two hours later was like awaking from sleep, a slow return to awareness of things around her. Mercedes blinked, conscious now of the soft clunk of books shoved into place, the scent of wood polished to a lemony shine, and the hardness of the chair seat under her. Approaching the library desk, she set the books on the counter. "Thank you," she said. "Willie wasn't a nice man, but he got what he deserved at the last." As the librarian nodded agreement she asked, "Is his castle still standing?"

"It's long gone, pulled down in the eighteen hundreds sometime. The stone was used for other building projects. I believe the Presbyterian Church took over the property, and there's a hospital on the site now."

That fit with the vicar's claim he was assigned to evaluate the place when it was bequeathed to the church. So they had decided against selling and instead used the land for a hospital.

"There's a library in Kirkfort itself, small but very well stocked with materials on both history and local lore. I understand they receive some sort of endowment." She sounded a bit jealous. Libraries aren't often gifted with extra funds.

Was it worth a trip to Kirkfort? The place was definitely out of the way, and what would she find that the vicar hadn't in all his time there? "I don't suppose there's any record of a Shakespeare visiting this area."

"No." The librarian never stopped working at her current task, stamping the date on a stack of magazines before her with efficient movements, ink pad to paper, over and over. "The English lay claim to all of them, especially the famous one. But there are those up here who have an alternate author theory."

"They claim a Scotsman wrote Shakespeare?"

"Ben Jonson." She smiled at the look on Mercedes' face. "His parents were Scots, though he's often thought of as English. He spent long periods up here, getting his muse back, I like to think. He could very well have done the plays and handed them to his friend William."

Mercedes wanted to ask why someone would do that when he, too, earned his living as an author, but she kept to her purpose. "I've heard Scotland is connected with a legend concerning Francis Drake and a lost treasure ship. I'd thought of writing a story about that for a magazine back in the States."

"Well, then, we'll have to see what we can find, won't we?" The woman started purposefully down the rows of books. "That story's been around for centuries, mostly discounted by experts. If Drake's treasure hasn't been found by now, it's probably scattered and buried under silt at the bottom of the sea. Every coastal town has its shipwreck legends, you know."

"But the publicity could bring tourists to the area."

"I suppose that's good." She stopped before a shelf of history books and chose one. "I only have one account here that mentions the legend. If you're heading north, they have an extensive library of Scottish history at the University of Glasgow."

Mention of the university struck a chord of memory. The man at the inn had mentioned an uncle who was a history professor there. Such an expert might be able to shed light on the vicar's claims, might be able to tell if the single page she still had from the journal was authentic or not.

"Yes, Glasgow is a possibility. Can you give me an address for a Professor Rankin in the history department there?"

65

"Certainly." Heading back to the desk, the woman consulted the Internet briefly then took up a quarter sheet of scrap paper thriftily cut and saved for such purposes. She copied the professor's office address and phone number down.

While she did that, Mercedes read the short passage that confirmed events mentioned in the vicar's account. Sir Francis Drake took a rich Spanish vessel, the *Madre de Dios*, on his last voyage, but it never reached England. A sailor rescued by fishermen claimed he and his mates had hidden the treasure ashore, but no one knew for certain if he'd been one of Drake's men or not. Most believed that either the sailor was delirious in his last moments or the fishermen had lied.

The tale of the lost treasure ship was appealing, however. In the 1500s, it was estimated that over 170 tons of gold and 8200 tons of silver were shipped to Europe from the New World. At least ten percent of it had been lost between continents. *Madre de Dios* was a problem for treasure seekers due to varying accounts of where she might have gone down. Eager hunters had searched the south and western coasts of Scotland, attempting to figure geometrically where the ship might have been coming from when it crashed against the rocks off the Isle of Man. Luce Bay was the focal point of most searches, but a few easterly sites were tried when nothing was found to the west. There was too much coastline, however, and too few clues to whether the treasure was in a cave, underground, or somewhere no one had thought of.

"It's as I said," the librarian said pedantically. "If there were treasure, it would have been found by now."

"Still, it could make a good story."

"If your readers know who Drake was." A slightly superior tone crept in, a hint that Americans were not known for their interest in history. It was, after all, true that most of them couldn't name ten of their own past Presidents.

"Sir Francis is in all our books," Mercedes assured her.

"Well, you seem to know a bit of history."

"It was my major. I've just finished my degree, and I'll be teaching history and English."

The librarian took up the stack of magazines she'd finished stamping. "You mean you will teach American," she said with a droll smile.

Mercedes left the library and walked uphill to her car, pulling on the sweater that it's always a good idea to have in Scotland. Programming the car's GPS for the Glasgow address, she headed for the E05. Despite the lack of detail, she'd confirmed to her own satisfaction that the vicar's conclusions were at least possible. The puzzle wasn't solved, but she'd taken a step forward, and she was anxious to know more.

What if Kirkfort Willie had silenced the one man who knew where the treasure was? She hoped the charming Celt's uncle at Glasgow University did indeed know his history. Maybe once she presented her evidence, he'd send someone to Kirkfort to re-examine the original *Macbeth* script. If the prisoner of Kirkfort wrote in code what he knew, she had the message in her possession. The thought was both exhilarating and frightening, for she suspected that two people had died so someone could get the vicar's notes on the subject.

Suddenly it was three people. Mercedes stopped at a small inn outside Glasgow, planning to drive into the city early in the morning. The lobby was characterless, like many motels in the States, and the traffic rumbling by would probably go all on night, but it was convenient. As she filled out the check-in card, a newscast on the lobby television caught her attention. "—Paul Prescott was guide for a motor coach tour of Britain. The grisly crime was discovered when he did not rejoin his group at a small pub outside Moffat. Police know of no motive, but since it is the third death associated with this particular tour, they will look carefully at those on the Village Tour Coach."

Mercedes froze. Paul was dead? A "grisly" murder? An image of Paul with no eyes flashed before her, but she pushed it away. What did it mean? If the murders were about the journal, the killer had it now. Why would he kill Paul?

On an impulse she tore up the registration card. "I'm sorry. I've written the information in the wrong places. May I have a new one?" The bored clerk handed her a second card with no comment, and she started again. Name: Mary Martin. That was generic enough. She filled in the rest, letting her creativity form the answers. When she handed the card to the clerk, she said, "I'll be paying in cash. You do take American, don't you?"

CHAPTER TEN

The book was missing the essential page, the one that listed the letters from the *Macbeth* script. In a rage, Vincent shattered all four of the cups left on the little setup tray in his hotel room, throwing them against the wall and listening to the satisfying crash as they disintegrated into pieces. The resulting noise helped him force his mind to a state where he could think.

Had Sylvia removed it, or had the Americans? Instinct told him the brunette had it. The tablet he'd stolen from her was password protected and therefore useless, and he'd tossed it into a rubbish bin. The cell phone, too, defied his efforts to open its files. Disgusted, he stomped the thing until the screen went blank. Pacing for a while to calm himself, Vincent had a sudden inspiration. Picking up the hotel phone, he got a number from information and reached the hotel in Dumfries. "This is Sergeant Tate with the Dumfries police. The inspector would like a word with Miss Maxwell."

He sat staring at the wall for a few moments as he waited for someone to ask someone. *Where will you go, Mercedes Maxwell? If you are innocent, you could be anywhere, but then you don't matter.* He pulled a map of Scotland out of his suitcase, still waiting for the clerk's return. *If you have stolen my property, then where will you go? Wherever it is, I'll be right behind you.*

The clerk returned and Vincent listened for a moment. "Oh, yes, of course. I'm sure the inspector had forgotten. Did she say where she was going? And you gave her directions for that?" Another pause. "Perhaps she has, but we haven't heard of it. I'll check with my sergeant, she may have spoken with him. Thank you."

***

Concerned at the news of Paul Prescott's death, Mercedes called the Dumfries police as soon as she reached the tiny room she'd been assigned. Surprisingly, Callard himself came on the line within seconds after she'd identified herself. Surely his shift should be over by seven in the evening. "Everything possible is being done to find the killer, Miss Maxwell." The inspector's voice took on a new tone, a diffidence he hadn't shown before. "Now, this book. I wonder if you can tell me more about it."

Yesterday he'd dismissed the book as phony. She straightened a stack of pamphlets on the nightstand, meant to acquaint her with Glasgow's points of interest. One of them had a coffee ring that went all the way through to the back. "As I said, it was an account written by a nineteenth-century vicar who said he'd found an old journal. With it were some papers supposedly taken from a dying prisoner, papers that might have a coded message about Sir Francis Drake's treasure. The vicar transcribed the journal, since the original was decayed beyond saving. I think he also did some research on the matter, but he never finished it."

"Did this vicar write the prisoner's message out word-for-word?"

"As far as he could decipher it." Should she mention the page she possessed?

"I wonder if you can remember any of it." Something in his voice made her pause.

"I don't think so. It was only random letters."

"I see." He sounded disappointed. "If you remember any of the letters, even bits of them, I want you to write them down and send them to me at the first opportunity."

"Why?"

"I've asked around, and there is some interest in this journal. No one believes in treasure, of course." He gave a small laugh, and her belief that Callard wasn't the type to laugh often made Mercedes doubt his sincerity. "Still, we'd like to investigate further, if you recall anything."

"All right." Her mind worked on the inspector's shift from curt dismissal of her story to "some interest." Callard had learned something that made him want to know more about the notebook. Concern for her safety seemed to be secondary, even though three people who'd had contact with her in the last few days had been brutally murdered. Had the inspector been bitten by the treasure bug?

Mercedes found herself unwilling to share anything more. She glanced through the ancient, wavy window glass and scanned the street as if expecting to see Callard peering up at her. The street was empty except for two women, one pushing a baby in a carriage. She was smoking, and Mercedes frowned in unconscious disapproval. "I'll call if I remember any of it."

"Where are you now, in case I need to reach you?" His voice was casual, but the tone relayed anticipation of her response.

She paused only a moment before replying, "Edinburgh."

With the phone still in hand, she pondered the situation. On impulse she rummaged through her purse and pulled out the card given her by the police sergeant at Castle Kinready, Jared Graham. She dialed his number and got a recording asking that she leave a brief message.

"Sergeant Graham, it's Mercedes Maxwell, the one who found the body yesterday? I wanted to speak with you about something."

71

She paused. Her questions weren't easily explained in a voice mail. "I have an appointment with Professor Rankin at Glasgow University tomorrow morning. I intend to ask him about things that possibly concern these murders." She couldn't go into the whole Willie Reid story now. "I'll call you and explain after I've seen him. Goodbye." She hung up feeling a bit more secure. Graham had obviously liked her. She was pretty sure he'd be willing to help.

By the time she went to sleep that night, Mercedes had explained away most of her fears. It was paranoid to think this all revolved around her. She'd told Sergeant Graham where she was, so no one could claim she was hiding. It wasn't the police who made her uneasy, it was Callard himself. Tomorrow she'd explain that to Graham.

***

The next morning Mercedes had the worst continental breakfast of her life: stale pastry, terrible coffee, and juice so watery it hardly merited the term. When she phoned the university, she was told Professor Rankin was indeed a person likely to be able to help with her quest. He had no summer classes scheduled, but luckily he came in several days a week to work on a text he was preparing for publication. She could see him at eleven. With her usual precision, Mercedes marked a route from her inn to the university, not willing to trust the GPS one hundred percent. She informed the clerk at the cramped front desk she'd be staying a second night. Her plan was to visit the professor and then make use of the university's library. Perhaps tomorrow she'd head to Kirkfort and see the script for herself.

She had three hours to find the place and do some research. Although she'd confirmed Willie Reid's identity and at least the rumor of Drake's hidden treasure, she hadn't connected Shakespeare to the story in any real way. Maybe that was the fictional part, but she wanted to know more about the man. Without her tablet and phone, she hadn't even been able to confirm basic information.

There was no problem finding the university. The well-known tower stood over the city like a beacon, and one had only to head toward it. She wished she could linger among the city's highlights: the Victorian architecture; the amazing cathedral, built in the 13th century and somehow spared destruction in the Reformation; the impressive red sandstone art museum; and the distinctive Glasgow taxis. She'd looked forward to visiting the quaint, bustling city that stood with one foot in Dickensian squalor and the other in twenty-first century Renaissance, but for now she simply followed the polite orders of the GPS voice. Once in the visitors' parking lot, she sat before the magnificent glass-front library and waited for it to open for the day.

The nice thing about libraries is that they're very much alike. A feeling of camaraderie accompanies each visit. All who enter are in search of knowledge, and those who persevere are likely to find what they seek. It was no problem for Mercedes to check the online catalog to find where books on Shakespeare were, then follow the plan of the library's layout to make her way there. In only a few minutes, she had surrounded herself with several satisfyingly heavy volumes and started on Honan's *Shakespeare-A Life*.

***

The officer on duty at Dumfries station wasn't sure he'd heard correctly when the caller told him what the matter was. The man spoke as if he'd run a long way, but his breathing problem was incipient panic, not distance.

"Would you repeat that last part, sir? You say a woman is dead at the library?"

"Yes, dead!" the man all but shouted, but then his voice became a whimper. "She has no hands, and her tongue is cut out! Come quickly, please!"

***

William Shakespeare, born Shaksper in Stratford in 1564, had no brother John. There were precious few facts known about his life, and most of them were disputed by scholars and pseudo-scholars alike. Had he left Stratford because of trouble with the law? Had he grown to dislike his wife Anne after their three children were born and in effect ignored her for twenty years? Had his acting ability been so lacking that he only got small parts such as the ghost or the dying king? And most important of all: had he really written the works attributed to him, perhaps the best use of language known to man?

There was wide disagreement there, with weighty minds from Mark Twain to Isaac Asimov holding forth. Mercedes was aware of the arguments but had never thought about it much, since they were opinions and opinions vary. It was one of those interesting historical questions that made for long discussions and gave historians the chance to show off their expertise. One book purported to prove that Shakespeare was two men, William Shaksper from Stratford and the 17th Earl of Oxford, Edward deVere. It was convincing unless you read other arguments: for Ben Johnson, for Francis Bacon, for Christopher Marlowe, and even for a collaborative group of London playwrights concerned about censorship.

She settled in and skimmed several sources, making notes on a small legal pad and adding comments as scholars disagreed with each other. There was a lot to read. Had any other author been so studied, so minutely examined, and yet remained so mysterious? The man did not emerge from historical record. Only in his work did one glimpse his substantiality, and even there were contradictions. Did he see women traditionally, as chattel to be tamed as Petruchio tamed Kate? Or did he see them as viragos goading men to ruin, like Lady Macbeth? Or, as Mercedes liked to think, were they simply individuals to be drawn, lifelike and human, from their own utterances?

Her watch beeped a warning. Her time in the library had flown by, but she was used to that. During research she entered the past wholeheartedly, immersing herself in its ambiance. Pulling the yellow pad to the center as she set a book off to one side, she scanned her notes and made a mental summary. William Shakespeare, a young man with what today would be an eighth-grade education, had dared to take on subjects like royal power, quarrels among the nobility, and historical murder. He had addressed themes of love, hatred, racial bigotry, ambition, even incest and homosexuality. Was it possible that a "country bumpkin," as some described him, could have depth of knowledge about all these things?

Mark Twain thought not. Assuming Stratford was a backwater town and the education to be obtained there would have been third-rate, he contended no one could prove Shakespeare ever wrote anything. Mercedes would have argued with Mr. Twain that someone from Hannibal, Missouri, with no college education and an apparently shiftless disposition might be rejected by many as classic author material.

But it was time to meet Professor Rankin.

CHAPTER ELEVEN

A helpful young woman at the library desk gave directions to University Gardens, where Rankin's office was located. Mercedes had specified the era and location of her study when speaking to the professor's secretary, and she'd made notes of what to ask in case he was short of time. She needn't have worried. Professor Rankin was either at his leisure or gracious enough to make it appear so.

The office she was ushered into could not be called messy, but neither would Mercedes connect the term *neat* to it. The office was organized, but there was a definite quality of surfeit to the place, as if it held everything it possibly could. Folders covered every conceivable surface, and extra books were shelved horizontally along the tops of the upright volumes. Several sources lay open on the desktop as if ready for reference at a moment's notice, and sticky notes littered magazine covers, stacks of printed sheets, and even the computer screen.

Not at all what one imagined a leading scholar of Scottish history to look like, Allan Rankin instead brought to mind one of Dickens' Cheeryble brothers. Mercedes fought the urge to look around for the other one. His face was moon-shaped, with shiny cheeks and a rounded nose, all tinted bright pink against the paleness of his complexion. His forehead shone, too, and the very little hair remaining on top of his head was cotton-ball white, curled into fine wisps. An ancient tweed suit-coat hung over the back of his chair, and despite the warm day he wore a sweater vest over a long-sleeved white shirt, probably as substitute for a necktie. About her height and not overly large elsewhere, Rankin's stomach rounded before him like a concealed basketball. The hand he presented to her was dry, cool, and soft.

Unaccustomed to lying, Mercedes had given her real name when she made the appointment. She consoled herself that no one in this ivory tower would connect such a common Scottish name to the recent murders.

"Miss Maxwell, is it?" Rankin made a courtly gesture toward a chair and waited until she was comfortable before resuming his seat. Perceptive gray eyes took in her mannerisms, her posture, and her unwillingness to look him in the face. "What may an ancient historian do to help you?" He smiled to acknowledge his own pun.

Now that it came to lying to this kindly, genteel man, she felt nervous. "A librarian at Dumfries said you might help me find information about an outlaw from Kirkfort named Willie, probably William, Reid."

Rankin's pointy white brows descended briefly as he searched his memory. "I recall bits and pieces," he said after a moment, "but let's see what Merlin has to say." Turning to a computer on his left, he tapped the keys for a few moments. "Merlin is our search assistant, but I've added a device that refines my questions and eliminates less helpful matches."

Despite her nervousness, Mercedes smiled. Who hadn't had the daunting task of sorting through page after page of websites that might relate to a subject but probably don't?

"All right," he continued, "I've typed in Willie/William Reid/Scottish outlaw/Kirkfort. Is that correct?"

"Yes."

"Very well, then." In two minutes they had everything known about "Kirkfort Willie" Reid, which was exactly what she already knew and no more. Taking in her expression, Rankin apparently sensed more than intellectual curiosity. Leaning back in his chair, he suggested, "Why don't you tell me the whole story, Miss Maxwell?"

She had arrived planning to tell the professor a few facts in a tapestry of lies. Within fifteen minutes, she'd told Allan Rankin almost everything, from her serendipitous chance to visit Britain to the body in the castle to the subsequent murders of Mrs. Flowers and Paul Prescott. Without knowing why, she felt he could be trusted and would help if he could.

When she was finished, Rankin sat quietly for a moment, digesting the information. "No name mentioned for the vicar," he finally muttered, running a stubby finger across his bottom lip. "Did you know the Maxwells in that area had a long-standing feud with the Johnstone clan?"

She acknowledged his reference to her own family with a grin. "But they all joined together when it was time to fight the English, right?"

"Of course. Have you heard how Scotland was created?" She answered with a shake of her head. "It seems God said to Gabriel, 'I'm going to create a land of great beauty for the Scots. They'll have wonderful hills, crystal lakes teeming with fish, beautiful landscapes, and fantastic views of the sea. I'm going to give them sheep and cattle and flax, and I will show them how to make whiskey as well.'

"Gabriel says to God, 'You're blessing the Scots above any other people on the face of the earth. Why do they get such wonders?'

"'Ah,' God replies, 'I haven't told you who their neighbors are going to be!'"

For the first time since hearing of Paul's death, Mercedes relaxed a tiny bit. She chuckled along with Rankin, who smiled to see that his intention had borne fruit.

Returning to the subject of the book in a roundabout way, he summarized the climate of the time. "There were Reids who held lands near the marches, and I'd guess this Willie was a relative. England and Scotland had no formal border for a very long time, and various means were tried to keep peace between people on the two sides. Wardens from each nation were commissioned in attempts to punish raiders. Laws were enacted such as the Hot Trod, which said that a victim of a raid could pursue the offenders over the border if he notified the warden of his intention and carried it out within six days of the raid."

"Like modern-day hot pursuit."

"Exactly. Nothing worked, however. The wardens were often as crooked as the outlaws, and both sides seized any excuse to attack the opposition. The feud I mentioned between the Maxwells and the Johnstones was not the only one. Scot fought Scot, but on the other side, the English Reeds were feuding with the equally English Halls, so one couldn't even tell at times whether he'd been attacked by friend or foe, so to speak."

"Tough people for tough times."

"I would guess that the wardens, or maybe a powerful clansman, went after Willie Reid, and he ran or was sent to the west to find his own way in the world. He sets up in an old church, makes it into a fortress, forces the locals to submit to him, and lives like a king on two hundred acres. It's not so unusual for the time."

"Until he was arrested and hanged."

"Yes. That's why I have doubts about this vicar's claims. If a

79

man like Willie wrote his crimes down, he most likely would have destroyed the evidence."

"Or hide the pages where no one would find them." Mercedes turned pensive. "I suppose some of my ancestors were as bad as Willie, but I'd rather not know for certain."

"Yes," Rankin agreed. "History is much easier to take in the objective."

She leaned her elbows on Rankin's desk. "But if it is true, it's a fascinating story. It's amazing that the prisoner never gave in, never told his secret."

"Indeed. What could be so important he would die rather than tell it?"

She saw Rankin's statement as a gentle hint she'd hit upon another reason to disbelieve the vicar's account. "Maybe John did lose his wits."

"Not inconceivable in such a case."

"Senselessly poking holes in the manuscript does suggest madness, but I've taken a liking to John. I don't want to believe he became a babbling idiot at the last."

"There may be other explanations." Rankin was being tactful now. "But if the script has been available all this time and no one has made sense of it..." He let the sentence hang.

There were pieces missing, things that would add up if she had more information. "The vicar thought the prisoner was John Shakespeare, William's brother."

"Does he say that Reid believed John to be Shakespeare's brother, or that he himself believed him to be?"

"The outlaw called him Johnny, but the name they knew him

by was John Romeo." She shook her head. "But there is no such name as Romeo. Shakespeare made it up."

"So I've heard."

"Maybe there was such a name once. Suppose John Romeo and Will Shaksper met at some point. Later Shakespeare might have used the name when he retold the old Pyramus and Thisbe legend." A line from the play popped into her head. "O happy dagger!" A replica of an Italian dagger had been used on the woman at the castle. Did that mean something, or was it coincidence?

"I agree, Romeo is likely to be an alias. If John was indeed a spy, he would use whatever name suited the moment. Perhaps your vicar misunderstood that."

"The man was reported to have been a player in London, so he may actually have known Shakespeare and used his name to hide his real identity," Mercedes mused. "But why did he want the script returned to Shakespeare? And why is the vicar's book so important?"

"Are you sure it is?" Rankin gently laid the facts before her. "You're afraid people were killed for the book. If we suppose the killer wanted it, why would he kill this Paul after the book was recovered? I must be candid. Though it's interesting to sit here and discuss the historical possibilities, there's little likelihood the book is genuine. There's no signature. It purports to be written from an original document which is no longer available. And the stories of Drake's treasure have been thoroughly investigated. Nothing has ever been found. I'd guess someone was planning to perpetrate a hoax then thought better of it."

"But a vicar?"

Rankin smiled ironically. "You'd be surprised at who dreams of achieving fame through bogus history. The 1800s were full of such incidents. It went on in the 1900s as well, until carbon dating and other authentication techniques made it more difficult to fool scholars." He raised unruly white eyebrows. "It goes on still, because some people are eager to be hoaxed."

"Then how do you explain the murders?"

His face softened, and she saw in it regret that he had to disagree with her conclusions. "It sounds like the work of a madman to me. Maybe the notebook has some connection, but I doubt it. He could have stolen the book without killing anyone, simply by slipping into your hotel room and taking it, as he eventually did." Rankin sat back in his chair and shook his head. "As an academic, I'd love to get my hands on it, but it's not worth killing for."

Mercedes was silent. She wouldn't argue with this kindly man, but she felt sure he was wrong. Sensing her disagreement, Rankin softened his earlier response. "If you leave me a way to reach you, I'll do some more research and contact you when I've seen what I can find."

"My cell phone was stolen too. I haven't picked up a new one yet."

"Well, then, you might call me in a day or so. I won't be in the office, so you'll have to call my home. I have a card somewhere." He rummaged through his desk to no avail.

After a few moments she reached into her purse and pulled out a piece of paper. "Here. Write the number on this."

Rankin scanned the paper briefly, turned it over, wrote the number, and handed it back. "I do hope you stay in contact with the police in regard to this business. There is no sense taking chances with a madman around."

"No one knows where I am," she assured him. "I'll be fine." Rankin didn't seem convinced, but she thanked him and rose to go. She was sure he had her interest at heart, but her need to unravel this puzzle stood in the way of taking the professor's advice. The vicar's journal was real. If Rankin had seen it, he'd sense its authenticity, as she did.

***

When the woman was gone Professor Rankin tried to return to his editing, but instead he sat staring at his computer screen. After a few moments he picked up the phone and punched in a number. "I've met your American, the one you told me about."

"Really."

"Apparently she's mixed up in this murder business. She had a journal that purported to lead to treasure, and she thinks that's what the killings have been about."

"Had a journal?"

"It was stolen, she says. But she read it and believes it's authentic."

"Could she be correct?"

"Doubtful, but I'm afraid she's flirting with danger. Even if this murderer doesn't care about an old book, from what they say on the news, he isn't one to be trifled with."

"Yes. In fact, there's been a fourth murder, a librarian in Dumfries. She was found dead in the stacks, her hands cut off."

"Horrible! You don't think Miss Maxwell is the sort to be involved in murder, do you?"

"No. I spoke with her minutes before the old woman's body was found. She gave no sign of distress, in fact she was...charming."

Rankin grinned at his nephew's word choice. "Well, today she was unsettled, but she is convinced this book is the reason for the crimes."

"The news reports haven't mentioned a book or a treasure hunt. That may be the part she's imagining."

"But that's just it, you see. There was a ship lost in 1595, the *Madre de Dios*. And the story of the dying sailor's claim to have hidden its treasure is well known. Searches were made, but it was never found."

"You're saying this account could lead to treasure?"

"It's probably pure fiction, but if someone believes it, and if they believe this young woman stands in the way, she's in danger. I should have encouraged her to go to the police."

"Yes, she shouldn't be wandering about on her own," the nephew agreed. "I don't suppose you know where she's headed."

"I saw her hotel bill, quite by accident. She's at the Motorway Inn in Larkhall. I believe she plans to visit Kirkfort tomorrow. I asked her to call after she's seen the *Macbeth* manuscript. When she does, I'll suggest she go to the Glasgow police with her story. It seems she distrusts the fellow in Dumfries."

If it's not too late for her, the nephew thought, but he said aloud, "It's always good to talk with you, Uncle Allan. I'll call again next week."

CHAPTER TWELVE

As Mercedes left the Professor Rankin's building, she was surprised to recognize a person coming in. "Oh, good, Miss Maxwell, I've located you."

It was Sergeant Graham, from Kinready castle. "What are you doing here?" She grinned and slapped her own face. "Sorry, typical American lack of tact."

"That's all right," he assured her. "I am a bit out of my area. We needed an expert to authenticate a document, and after your phone call last evening, I volunteered to bring it up, kill two birds with one stone, as it were."

"A document?"

"Nothing interesting, in fact, dull as dishwater, but it has to be done. He waved a folder. "If you wouldn't mind waiting a minute or two, I'd like to take you to lunch at my favorite place in Glasgow."

She considered. She had to eat, and the sergeant was nice to have come in person to see that she was all right. And handsome as well. "That sounds lovely, Sergeant."

"Call me Jared, please."

Graham was gone less than two minutes. "I told them I'd be back for the information at two." From his grin she gathered this wasn't the way he'd been told to do it, but he led the way to his car. He was stealing time from work to be with her, which was flattering. And it was nice to see a familiar face.

The "favorite place" in Glasgow turned out to be an open-air deli situated on a major crossing of the city streets. People in business suits stood three or four in line in several places at the counter, shouting orders to four overworked waiters. Once he'd gotten their order, Graham led her across the street to the Clyde Walkway, where they sat on a bench overlooking the river and ate wonderful sandwiches stacked with thinly sliced meat, cheese, and vegetables. Inside each wrapper was also a crunchy pickle spear in a narrow waxed paper envelope. Jared had bought a soda and a bottle of water and offered Mercedes her choice. She took the water.

They chatted amiably as they ate, telling each other their backgrounds as new acquaintances do. She avoided mention of the murder at the castle, and Jared kept his efforts centered on making her laugh at stories of eccentric criminals and crimes. His crinkly eyes were as nice as she remembered, and she liked the way the muscles in his arms rippled as he moved. When he mentioned lifting weights, she remembered the feel of calluses on his palm when she'd first shaken hands with him.

"I was overweight as a lad, never liked myself much," he confided. "When I began working with weights as a teen, it changed my appearance, gave me a sense I was as good as anyone else." Jared's dark, reddish hair stood up a bit at the crown, making him look younger than his years. Boyish and built. Not a bad combination.

"It's hard to picture you as a shy kid needing a boost in self-image. You seem capable of whatever you set your mind to."

Jared blushed slightly. "Well, then, I'm half-way there. If I convince others, I'll believe it myself someday."

When they'd finished eating, the two walked along the Clyde and then into the East End, Jared pointing out landmarks and explaining the layout of the streets in typical masculine fashion. She lost track after the second or third "to the northeast/west/southwest," but she let him go on, enjoying the sound of his voice and the sights of Glasgow's somewhat grimy industrial past. The day was bright, and the dark old buildings seemed to lighten somewhat, throwing off their soberness in the summer warmth.

They crossed Glasgow Green, where a group of pipers practiced. Dressed in jeans and t-shirts, they moved forward and back, turned left and right, as the leader indicated with his baton, all the while droning and piping. It had to be tricky. She watched for a while, thrilled with the serendipitous concert. Finally the group broke up and the park became quiet, with only squirrels for company. Jared asked mildly, "What did you learn at the University?"

It was the perfect time to enlist his aid. He was with the police, he knew she wasn't loony, she felt that he cared, and he appeared willing to listen. If she told him everything, he might help—or would he insist she return to Dumfries and to Callard? Could she tell Jared, a policeman, she didn't trust a brother officer and preferred to stay away from him?

Even if Jared liked her, his job had to come first. Admitting she'd lied to Callard would put him in a difficult spot, and it wasn't fair to ask him to cover for her. In addition, she was reluctant to tell the story again. Professor Rankin had discounted any connection between the book and the deaths of three people. She believed in the vicar's honesty but realized those who hadn't seen the book were naturally more skeptical.

"I didn't mean to sound dramatic," she finally answered. "I thought I knew something about the murders, something I would have shared with you, but it turned out to be nothing."

"You were going to tell me something you didn't tell the Dumfries police?"

"I'm afraid I didn't have a good experience there." She added, "I neither like nor trust Inspector Callard. But it turns out there was nothing to tell anyway."

His cell phone rang, giving Mercedes a chance to recover from the blush that always accompanied telling a lie. Jared excused himself and stepped away for a few moments. Mercedes waited, noting that he mostly listened and was not pleased with what he heard. When he returned, his handsome face was sober. "They've put out the word to arrest you on sight."

"What?"

"Four people are dead, and you're linked to each one."

"Four!"

"A librarian was found dead yesterday in Dumfries. You'd been there, hadn't you?"

Her mind spun. "Yes, but—"

"Inspector Callard says you concealed evidence, claims you altered the crime scenes."

"I didn't touch anything," she protested. "I was terrified in both instances, and I simply ran for help."

Jared smiled grimly. "I don't think you killed anyone, but he's convinced you're involved somehow. He's a determined sort."

She recalled her impression that Callard made up his mind first then shaped the evidence to fit his theory. "That's ridiculous."

"It is to anyone who knows you."

"So what do I do? Give myself up?"

Jared scanned the area as if looking for the right answer. It took him a long time to find it. "I should say yes," he finally replied. "In fact, it's my duty to, but I don't think it's a good idea. The inspector is—well, he isn't being rational about this. Perhaps he needs time to think things through." His gaze came back and held hers, strong warning in his eyes. "Does he know where you are?"

"I don't see how he could."

"Then I say wait a few days. If we catch the killer, you'll be cleared. If not you'll be no worse off. Claim you were in the north and didn't hear the news."

"What do I do, change my looks? Wear a disguise?"

"It will be a quiet search, no all-points bulletins or the like. Do you have cash?"

"Yes."

"Then remain out of sight until we catch this man. You'll be safe once it's all sorted out. You can stay in touch with me, and I'll keep you informed of our progress."

Her inclination was to do as he said. She didn't trust Callard, and Jared apparently doubted his own organization's ability to treat her fairly. Once again, though, she thought of Jared's position. Lying to his superiors would not be good.

"I don't want you to get in trouble. It's better if you don't know where I am."

"You must stay in contact with someone." He put his hands on her arms, and they felt strong and supportive. "You need someone on your side."

Mercedes felt relieved. Someone intended to look out for her, a sense she hadn't got from Callard. Jared was putting his job in jeopardy, giving her advice contrary to his official duty, because he wanted her to be safe. She'd see he didn't suffer for his actions.

A clock over the street chimed the quarter hour, 1:45. "You're supposed to be back at the University at 2:00."

He released his hold on her, obviously reluctant to do so. "So I am." They stepped up their pace, reaching Jared's car in only a few minutes, and made their way back to the lot where Mercedes' rented Chevy was parked. He maneuvered into a parking spot, seemed about to suggest something, but instead got out of the car and came around to help her out. Old-World chivalry. Wow.

"Old World" reminded her of the morning's research. "My notes! I had a pad of paper with information I found this morning. Now I don't know where I left it."

"I didn't see it earlier, when we met."

"It must either be in the library or in Professor Rankin's office." She faced Jared resolutely, determined to keep him from further involvement in her troubles. "You need to get back to work. Thank you for lunch, and for your kindness. I appreciate it."

"Will you call me, let's say at nine each evening? I'm usually home by then, and I can keep you apprised of the situation."

"Yes, that would make me feel better."

"I'm glad I got to see you again." It appeared for a moment he might kiss her. His eyes sought hers and his hand rose toward her face, but he stopped short, allowing himself only the briefest caress. Then he took his leave, walking away with the roll of his shoulders she'd noticed earlier, a movement that forced them to relax. A leftover nervous tic from a man who hadn't liked himself much as a kid, she decided.

The notepad was at the front desk of the library, and the nice woman who'd given her directions earlier returned it with a smile when Mercedes apologized for walking off without it. "It happens all the time, dear. We're just glad you remembered it in time."

Glancing at her notes, she had second thoughts about refusing Jared's offer of help. If she told him everything, he'd take charge of the situation, and she wouldn't be on her own any more. She stopped, both mentally and physically, as she tried to decide what to do. In the end, the reactions of Callard and Rankin stopped her. Though one had been kind and the other had not, she didn't want to see that same disbelief in Jared's eyes. He had demonstrated faith in her and warned her of Callard's intentions. She'd seek out evidence, something he could take to his superiors to convince them the vicar's book was genuine.

As she rounded a corner, Mercedes saw Jared headed for his car, a folder under his arm. A man who stood out from the purposeful flow around him watched Jared go. If he wanted to be noticed for his appearance, he was.

The man was youngish, with pants worn so low as to be almost useless. His pant legs had been cut off below the knee, apparently with hedge trimmers. On top he wore the vest from a vintage, pin-striped suit decorated with a collection of badges. His shoes were battered high-tops, and his chin-length hair was dyed blue.

The sartorial specimen was regarding Jared with interest. A panhandler, she guessed, looking for a likely victim. She wondered briefly if such people were called something else over here. In the end he must have decided against approaching Jared, who got into his car and drove away without looking back. Once the car had disappeared, the youth glanced over and saw Mercedes standing beside her car. Looking away quickly he moved off, pant-legs flapping. Apparently she didn't look any more likely to give him a handout than Jared had.

It was tricky getting out of Glasgow at midday, but she managed to reverse the morning's route, concentrating on the unfamiliar feel of traffic on her right side. Mindlessly obeying the directional commands of her satellite pilot, Mercedes re-examined her original opinion. Despite the professor's doubts, the murders had to be related to the notebook. Someone thought it held the key to Drake's treasure. Did whoever had it now know she had the last page? With any luck he'd assume it was lost over the last one hundred plus years. However, he didn't mind leaving corpses behind, and the librarian's death indicated he was trailing Mercedes. The woman had known where she was going, and she'd mentioned Professor Rankin by name. Mercedes vowed to call Rankin and warn him at the first opportunity.

Jared Graham had said Sylvia Tate hadn't been a particularly upright citizen. Had she been the killer's confederate? One of them must have double-crossed the other. If Sylvia hid the book in Helen's bag, she'd probably died because of it. But Helen Flowers hadn't been a conspirator. She doubted Paul had been, though she'd seen only his public persona. As far as Mercedes knew, Paul was unaware of the book. So why was he killed? And why the innocent librarian?

When she reached the outlying town of Larkhall, where her hotel was located, it was only 3:00. Too early to go back to her room and do nothing. She should have returned to the University Library and done some more reading. On impulse, she asked the clerk for directions to the local library. It wasn't far away, and she decided to spend the rest of the afternoon there. If the place had access to the Internet, it didn't matter how small it was. Besides, every library in the English-speaking world has a copy of *The Complete Works of William Shakespeare*.

CHAPTER THIRTEEN

Late in the afternoon, as the sounds of a busy organization buzzed, hummed, and squawked around him, the man who years ago been dubbed "Bubble" stared unseeing at the fly-specked notice board across the room. The American woman knew something, and it was likely Vincent was after her. That meant danger for her, but he was philosophical. He had no control over what the madman did to get what he wanted.

Vincent was evidently free to chase Miss Maxwell across Scotland, while he was not. He wasn't worried though. Once Vincent had the book, he'd head for Kirkfort. There he'd be vulnerable, focused on finding the treasure and unaware he was under scrutiny. That was where he'd be located and thwarted. A sharp crack rang out, and the man jumped. It wasn't a gunshot, only something that was dropped hitting the floor. Settling in again, he acknowledged he was a bit nervous about the whole thing with Vincent. The image of Paul's bloodless corpse served as a warning.

His brow furrowed. Kirkfort was the general location, but where exactly? The journal said it was near a river or stream, but there were plenty of those in the area. And did one look underground, in a cave, or up a tree?

He imagined finding Drake's treasure. Under Treasure Trove Law, the finder was offered fair market value of such discoveries. But there were places where he might do better than that, collectors who'd ask no questions in return for ancient Spanish gold. No need to report the income that way. He had someone who knew a bit about that end, someone with historical background and connections to people able and willing to pay for such things. Squeak had become some sort of expert. Squeak, of all people.

Should he try to get his cousin interested? Squeak had long ago dismissed the idea of Drake's treasure being hidden in Scotland. If he brought the subject up, he'd probably get that look that said he was an idiot. But the book had resurfaced, and Paul was dead. Squeak would have to take that seriously.

He remembered it vividly: the musty attic with the dust motes floating in the spear of sunlight from the octagonal window, the weight of the homemade book in his hands, and the authentic feel of the story, the ring of truth as Vincent read like a seasoned troubadour. Four of them had spent their afternoons up there the year his cousin came for the summer. He'd always been called Bubble, so Paul dubbed his cousin Squeak, a reference to traditional dish of fried leftover vegetables. Neither cousin had appreciated the nicknames, but Paul thought pairing them as Bubble and Squeak was hilarious.

They'd had the key to John's code that summer but hadn't known where to begin. Now, with Squeak's expertise and his resources, they might do better. Of course, spreading a bit of money around might help. Squeak's latest significant other could help with that.

A newspaper lay before him, the article describing the death of the Dumfries librarian on the front page. Why had Vincent killed the woman? Surely mutilation hadn't been required to elicit the information she had. The answer was unsettling, and he had a moment's doubt about involving his cousin. Killing those people wasn't a question of need, he realized. Vincent had discovered he enjoyed it.

***

In the tiny, floor-wax-scented library, Mercedes first read general information on Shakespeare's plays: when they were written, what they were about. There was the inevitable book on who else might have been the genius. This time Francis Bacon was credited with writing plays as well as devising the scientific method. In other works, the theory of Bacon's being a secret playwright had been pretty much disproved, since the origin of the claim was a 19th century American school teacher named Delia Bacon.

A book titled *The Genius of Shakespeare* held her interest for some time. The author, Vincent I. Parks, conveniently summarized all of the Bard's tragedies then made exhaustive comments on each. Here she was able to confirm her recollection of Gloucester's blinding by his enemies.

In the *King Lear* summary, she found a reference to Gloucester's eyes being gouged out.

> The play's main theme involves parents and children, the duties of each to each. Gloucester trusts too easily in his false son's integrity. His reward is betrayal, and he suffers loss of his eyes, becoming able only then to 'see' the truth. In Shakespeare's view, fathers are overthrown by their children when they abuse their power over them. Some pay for it with their lives. Although Gloucester is saved in the end by his true son, Lear brings about his own ruin by rejecting his faithful daughter. It is a lesson for fathers everywhere.

Mercedes frowned. She'd only read *Lear* once in college, but she'd never thought of Shakespeare as an Aesop, telling fables. He was more prone to open topics such as family dynamics and filial duty through a scenario and then let the story go where it would. Paging through the book, she found other instances where the author claimed that Shakespeare was "teaching" the readers or viewers lessons of life. Again she disagreed with the absent author.

"Great writers don't teach, Mr. Parks," she murmured. "They explore life, and in life there are no correct answers."

Turning to the *Complete Works*, she found and read the scene of Gloucester's humiliation and torture. How could one forget Cornwall's gleeful "Out, vile jelly!" as he blinded an old man?

The picture of Helen Flowers' bloody face rose in her mind, and Mercedes sat very still for a moment, the silence around her complete except for a buzzing fluorescent fixture somewhere at her back. Paging through the book, she found *Titus Andronicus* and turned to Act V, where Titus avenges himself on Tamara's wicked sons by slitting their throats. His daughter Lavinia, whose hands and tongue have been lopped off by the same men so she can't identify them as her rapists, catches their blood in a basin.

Paul's throat had been slit, and a bowl found on the floor beneath it had collected his blood.

She had noted the similarity between Juliet's death and Sylvia's. Now three other murders imitated events found in Shakespeare's works. Suddenly Mercedes wanted to be away from here, away from why, away from a killer who made dramatic theatrical moments into actual death.

Her dread recalled the resolve to warn Professor Rankin. Finding a public phone, she punched in the number he'd given her. A cordial, politely-phrased recording allowed her to access the professor's voice mail. "This is Mercedes Maxwell. I know you don't believe my theory about the book I found, but please be careful until the killer is caught. I think he murdered someone just after I spoke with her. I know it sounds crazy, but I don't want anything to happen to you." She hung up, feeling hysterical and foolish, wondering how the message would be perceived. Still, she'd had to try.

She left the little library, thanking an elderly man who sat behind the counter reading Clive Cussler. He nodded, barely aware of her departure in his intent deciphering of Dirk Pitt's adventures. An eerie feeling she should warn him to be careful of strangers gripped her. Death seemed to follow her, and she had no idea how to deal with it.

What should she do? Suddenly the answer was clear, and her stupidity earlier in the day amazed her. Jared had offered to help her, but he had no idea there was treasure involved. He was someone she could trust, and he wasn't a dusty old academic with an inability to conceive of greed and murder. She'd tell him the whole story. Returning to the phone she'd used before, she dug out the card he'd provided and called.

This is Graham. I'm not in right now, so leave a message and a number where I can reach you. Well, that wouldn't do. She hung up the phone and left the library again. This time the elderly man looked up, putting his finger in the spot where he left of reading, and gave her an inquiring glance. She waved and left without comment.

The plan was on hold, but it was still a good plan. She'd return to her inn, lock the door, and stay out of sight until she could leave the area. Later she'd call Jared Graham again. He knew her well enough at this point to trust she wasn't giving in to hysterics. Jared would protect her.

Mercedes was barely aware of movement at her side before she was pulled roughly into a narrow alley. Automatically she raised an arm to fend off a blow, but instead something was slipped over her head and around her neck. As her air supply diminished, she realized dimly it was a rope, its ends held by someone who intended to choke her to death. Only the fact she'd raised one hand to her face kept her from strangulation. The hand protected her throat just enough to allow tiny amounts of air as she struggled to pull the cord away. She fought frantically, kicking and squirming so the man could hardly hold her and could do no more to subdue her.

Desperately Mercedes looked around, searching for possible help. The alley was blind, the stone walls on either side were blank except for one boarded window. She'd seen no one on the street ahead.

It was more and more difficult to breathe. The hand caught in the garrote throbbed with pain as the rope cut into the flesh. *Don't black out. Keep fighting!*

Raising one foot, she braced it against the wall and pushed with all her strength, sending her attacker reeling backward. His grip on her didn't fail, and she was dragged along until he struck the opposite wall with a grunt. He regained his balance quickly, but the pressure on Mercedes' throat released for a few seconds. She gulped air hoarsely. Her lungs ached. *Must fight!*

There was nothing within reach now, and the pressure tightened again. She slid her fingers up and gripped the thin rope, trying desperately to keep it from crushing her windpipe. But she felt her strength waning. Her struggles grew more and more feeble.

Suddenly the iron grip was released, and the man who'd held her let out a groan of pain. Still tensed in resistance, Mercedes fell clumsily to one side once there was nothing to fight. Pain shot down her arm as her shoulder hit the stone wall. Dazedly she crouched on the cobblestone, trying to discern what was happening. Tensed to fight again, her vision remained dim, as if filmy curtains had dropped over her eyes. No new attack came, though, and she lay on the hard stone, collecting her reserves. As her sight cleared, she saw two men struggling, a tall one with a nylon stocking over his face and a shorter, fair-haired man who seemed all spirit and sinew.

The match might have been uneven, but the smaller man fought fiercely and with intelligence, using his opponent's height to his advantage. He ducked quickly at his adversary, delivering body blows and then dancing back before the other could respond. It worked for a while, but her attacker was no fool. He figured out the strategy quickly enough and began making adjustments. His longer arms were dangerous, and finally he delivered a strong blow to the side of the other's head, making him reel for a moment. Seizing his chance, the taller man turned and ran. The blond took a few steps after him but, realizing the threat to Mercedes was over, returned to her side.

"Are you all right?" His rolled *r*'s made a gentle growl in his throat.

She sat up, checked herself, and croaked, "Bruised, but not broken."

He seemed familiar somehow. Squinting in the dimly-lit alley, she realized they'd spoken briefly at the inn in Dumfries. It was Professor Rankin's charming nephew.

"What are you doing here?" That sounded rude, and she rephrased. "I mean, thank you, I'm very grateful, but how did you happen to be here?"

"I believe I mentioned when we met that I live in Glasgow. I should have said outside Glasgow, in Larkhall." Her rescuer picked up the short strand of plastic-coated rope the attacker had dropped in his haste. "That chap meant to kill you."

"I'm sure he did." She touched the raw line across her neck and flexed bruised fingers.

He tested the strength of the rope. "Simple but effective method."

"If not for you, they could ask for me tomorrow and find me a grave woman."

He chuckled. "Misquoting Tybalt! Now that's a sin."

She shivered. "Gallows humor, probably from dwelling too much on Shakespeare today. Once again, I thank you and your white horse for the assistance."

"I sold my horse for a kingdom, but it isn't every day one rescues a beautiful maiden. You are a maiden, I hope, in the sense of not a Mrs.?"

She found herself chuckling despite her recent scare, or perhaps because of it. "Miss is correct. I'm Mercedes M-Martin."

The twinkle in his eye was not diminished by his recent effort. In fact, she got the sense he was exhilarated by it. "Pleased to meet you Miss M-Martin. My name is Colm Kennedy. No relation to the others you've heard of, I'm afraid." He helped her up from the ground then considered his bloodied knuckles with a grimace. "I don't know who the fellow was, but he had bones of stone and fists of steel."

"I don't know who he was either," Mercedes said, only half truthfully. It was fairly certain the killer had found her, and she was lucky to have escaped his attack. If Kennedy hadn't been here, what would have happened to her? Her knees threatened to buckle, but she managed to remain erect.

"If you're all right I'll go and find a policeman."

"No, please don't do that!" Calming herself, she explained lamely, "Since I'm unhurt and in possession of my purse, there's no need for the police."

He shrugged. "I suppose it's up to you."

She put herself back into order as best she could. Her slacks

100

were slightly torn, her hip was beginning to burn where the skin had been rubbed raw, her hand ached where the cord had cut across the palm, and the arm would turn black and blue for certain, but she was alive. "Again, thank you, Mr. Kennedy. I—"

He waved away the rest of her speech. "You were doing well for yourself. If he hadn't caught you by surprise, you'd have taken him easily." It was a lie, of course, but she appreciated it.

Seeing something behind her, he bent down and picked up a silken scarf. "Is this yours?"

It was pale yellow with a screen-printed logo: *Glasgow University*.

"No. He must have dropped it."

"Why would a mugger bring a scarf with him when he already had a rope?"

Thoughts of her day's reading spun in her head. Desdemona, the pitiful wife in Shakespeare's *Othello*, was strangled with just such a piece of cloth. He'd used the cord for efficiency but meant to leave the scarf for dramatic effect.

How had the killer found her? Both Professor Rankin and Jared Graham knew her general location. One of them could have followed her from the college. Still, neither man seemed a likely murderer. Jared was a cop, and she'd gone with him in his car in perfect safety. And the professor—could the cherubic old man have known more than he admitted about Drake's treasure and seen a chance to get it for himself? Improbable. He didn't even believe in the treasure. And his nephew had just saved her life, which argued that both of them were on the good guys' side.

Colm peered down the street again. "You've no idea who he was?"

She was evasive, being no good at outright lying. "My purse, maybe? Rich American tourist stands out all over me, right?"

He looked at her critically then brushed alley debris from the back of her shirt. "Americans do stand out, and lord knows they've too much money for their own good."

Before she knew she was going to say it, Mercedes heard herself ask, "Since I've so much money, could I buy you dinner by way of thanks?"

"I don't know if my masculine pride could survive letting a woman buy my sustenance." He paused comically, apparently in deep thought. "Since I'd give up a lot to spend more time in your presence, I'll wrestle my conscience on the money part of it."

His voice was rich and low-pitched. Something about his manner of speaking was unusual, too, somewhat larger than life. After a moment he broke the pose and declared with a grin, "The match is over, and desire to be with you has won over male pride. Shall we dine, m'lady?"

CHAPTER FOURTEEN

They eventually agreed to split the bill at a charming pub Colm chose called The Laird and Master. Pictured on the sign was a noble-looking man being hit on the head by his "master," a peevish-faced woman. Inside, the place was dark and low, with square, dark support beams obscuring the view of the large room somewhat. Tables lined three walls, and an elaborate bar ran the length of the fourth. One corner was taken up with a fireplace, cold and clean now but with blackened edges that indicated its usefulness at cooler times. It was early for the dinner hour, and the room was deserted except for the publican. Muted sounds of explosions emanated from a corner, where a video game console flashed *Game Over,* a jarring departure from the aged patina of the rest of the furnishings.

The bartender greeted them with a nod, and Colm seated Mercedes then went to the bar to order drinks and get a menu. Once they decided, he returned and put in their order, picking up the drinks at the same time. The piney gin and tonic both cooled and burned her battered throat.

They ate whole salmon poached in bouillon and vegetables, with Hard Bonnet and Bonchester cheese slices as accompaniment along with chips and the ever-present Scottish peas. She chose to forego the haggis, which Colm seemed to enjoy very much, and they finished with Dundee cake. After dinner they were served whiskey in quaichs, replicas of traditional round, flat, drinking vessels of yore. The whiskey warmed her insides but was less harsh than any she'd tasted before, having a smoothness to it that brought a relaxed, contented feeling.

They spoke of generalities: her appreciation for Scotland's beautiful scenery and his desire to see the Grand Canyon one day. Mercedes told him of her recently obtained degree and her teaching job in the fall. As she spoke, she rearranged the condiments on the table, setting them so the effect was balanced and neat. Then she took up a tray of jellies, sorting them into kinds and stacking the packets into the correct section. When she caught Colm looking at her good-humoredly, she blushed.

"I have this thing," she confessed. "I have to make things right. 'Neat and complete,' my friends tease me."

"Not a terrible habit."

"No, but I drive some people crazy. In fact it recently drove a certain person out of my life entirely."

Colm raised an eyebrow. "No."

"He said I was compulsive." She smiled, but her eyes reflected hurt.

"I'd guess he was a slob, probably every bit as compulsive about leaving dirty socks on the backs of chairs and empty dishes in the refrigerator. Am I right?"

"Well, yes."

"Then you didn't drive him away. Your differences simply made you an incompatible couple." Colm waved a hand at the table. "I find neatness an admirable trait. I could watch other people clean for hours."

She laughed then, the first genuine laugh since she'd been attacked.

"I was an idiot that first night," he said suddenly. "Blathering on about the fire and Scotland and architecture. What I really wanted to say was that you were the most enchanting woman I've

104

ever seen."

Mercedes was surprised into equal honesty. "And I couldn't get out two words that went together, but I thought you were absolutely charming."

The thought of that night brought back Helen Flowers' murder, and she sobered. "Do you know about what happened that night? At the inn?"

"I heard about it later, when I'd finished my night's work. I'm very sorry."

"Thank you."

There was a little silence, and she guessed he was trying to judge whether she was ready to answer a question. His fingertips beat a tattoo on the table that signaled more tension than he meant to reveal. "Why did that man attack you?"

She looked down at her lap. "Not an old lover or anything like that, if that's what you're thinking." Colm waited, as if he sensed her reluctance to speak of it. If she asked him to drop the subject, she guessed he would. As she considered whether to continue, she stacked their dishes neatly and wiped the table between them clean with a paper napkin.

Why did she feel like telling him the story she had denied Jared Graham? Maybe because he was nothing to her and knew nothing about her. Maybe so she could look into those direct green eyes for a while longer. She couldn't decide, but she told herself it would help to see a disinterested observer's reaction, to have him say whether or not it was wrong to avoid the police. The Professor hadn't believed her, but Colm had seen the attack and knew she wasn't imagining things. In the end she told him almost everything

He sat quietly, watching her face and reacting expressively but silently as she described the gruesome deaths of four people. After recounting the murder of the librarian she said, "Because he's after me, he killed that poor woman. It's my fault she's dead."

"No, it's not," Kennedy said firmly, putting a warm hand over hers and giving an emphatic squeeze. "It's his fault, and his alone. Now tell the rest."

Timidly she laid out her belief the murders were somehow tied to Shakespeare and a book she had briefly possessed. The only things she left out were the same ones she'd neglected to tell Colm's uncle: the page she'd found after the book was stolen and the fact that the police were after her. If people were dying for the vicar's book, it wasn't wise to admit she had part of it, and she didn't know Colm well enough to judge whether he'd turn a fugitive in on principle. Of course she didn't mention Jared Graham's offer of support that afternoon, either. No sense getting him into trouble.

When she was finished, Kennedy sat silent for a few moments. A group of men came into the pub and began a friendly banter with the barman concerning his choice of television station. Mercedes thought she could read Colm's thought: *I've rescued a schizophrenic American. Now what do I do with her?* She wondered what to do next. Try to explain more convincingly? Say it was her goofy idea of a joke? Walk away? Why had she told him, anyway? She'd known him less than an hour, knew nothing about him.

When he finally spoke, his words were a complete surprise. With a flick of his fingers against his glass that made a crystalline sort of fanfare he said, "Fate brought us together, Mercedes Martin. Not to be too modest on the subject, I'm somewhat an expert on Shakespeare, both the man and his works. And I think I was put here at this moment to help you out."

He was only half kidding, it turned out. Colm was a Shakespearean actor, starting, he said, "When I was only thistle high. My parents were on the stage, and my father eventually began his own company, directing while my mother played the various female roles Shakespeare paints so well, Portia, Rosalind, Imogen, and Viola, Mother loved them all. Naturally, when a child was called for, I was handy, so I grew up lisping the lines, so to speak, of Macduff's eldest son or Brutus' servant boy Lucius."

"Interesting."

Colm smiled. "At times, yes. My parents tried to give me a decent education, but I fear it leans heavily away from nano-technology and toward the humanities. I've been attempting to correct that somewhat by taking classes toward a degree."

"In theater?"

"In history, actually."

A shout went up as a goal was either scored or not on the set above the bar. Mercedes leaned across the table toward Colm. "Do you know anything about Willie Reid?"

"Only what you've told me. I'm originally from St. Andrews, on the other coast, and he isn't one of Scotland's favorite sons, I'd guess."

"True. No Rob Roy was Willie."

"Perhaps Rob Roy was no Rob Roy either, had we known him." Colm leaned forward now too, conscious of possible eavesdroppers. "I have heard of the lost treasure ship. Every few decades there's an attempt to find it, but no one ever has. I'd guess the entire coast of western Scotland has been thoroughly searched by now."

The barman came to remove the remains of the meal, and Mercedes sat back again in her chair until he was gone. "I'm not interested in treasure, not really. I feel sorry for the prisoner, who must have wanted badly to reach someone with his message. I'd like to know who he was and why he was sent to Kirkfort."

Colm toyed with his empty glass, rapping it absently against the table surface in a rhythmic cadence. "If you want my theory, formulated at a moment's notice, it's this. The prisoner was an agent of the Crown, sent to Kirkfort to find Drake's treasure. When the old queen died and James took over the throne, there would have been a combining of information. Something led them to conclude the dying sailor's story was real. If they'd been looking in the wrong place and suddenly discovered the treasure had been unloaded somewhere else, they'd have been anxious to track down the new lead."

Mercedes followed his logic. "Elizabeth's men might have known where John was, and James' ministers might have known Reid well enough to suspect him of foul play."

"Right. The prisoner—John—writes his coded message, which Reid is left with when he dies. Reid can't decipher it but keeps it in his journal, hoping something will shed light on it."

"But nothing does."

"Correct again. Two hundred years later, the vicar finds the journal as Reid's house is demolished. He takes an interest in it."

"He claims to have researched the two documents. By then it may have been possible to read Cecil's papers and find out that John truly was a spy."

"Since you no longer have the book, we'll have to consult those records to see what we can find." Colm set the glass down with a final clunk.

She raised her eyebrows in surprise. "We?"

Colm grinned, took one of the two complimentary chocolate mints from the tiny tray between them, and ate it. "Now that I've begun this knight in shining armor role, I think I should see it through, don't you?"

***

Mercedes didn't make her decision that evening. As they left the pub and stopped on the skimpy sidewalk, she asked, "Can you just take off like this? Surely you have to be somewhere."

He shrugged it off, waiting to answer until the roar of a delivery van faded behind them. "I have rehearsals, but if I promise to be back by Monday next, they'll be satisfied. The director said only yesterday he needs some time with the fairies." His grin in the lamplight challenged Mercedes, who took only a second to get it.

"*A Midsummer Night's Dream?*"

"Nick Bottom, at your service." He bowed comically, a hand almost brushing the floor. But do not think to—"

"—Make an ass of you? I won't. If you give me a number, I'll call to let you know what I decide to do." Colm ducked back inside for something on which to write his cell number. The burst of music and laughter that accompanied his departure contrasted with the threatening loneliness of the street, and she was relieved when he returned.

"If I had a brain, I'd take the next plane for home," she told him.

"That's probably true," he replied, handing her a slightly damp cocktail napkin with a number written neatly in pen across it. "But

109

I think you're intrigued by this puzzle, and you said yourself you don't fancy things left in a snarl."

He was right. People were dying, and she might hold a four-hundred-year-old key to why. Handing the coded page over to the police was an option, but Jared had said they believed she was somehow involved in the crimes. If she were arrested, she wouldn't be able to determine if the vicar's work was genuine. On her own she might, which would clear her of suspicion and perhaps help the police find out who'd killed Mrs. Flowers and the others.

Though she knew it was silly to suspect everyone, Mercedes didn't tell Colm where she was staying. He made no argument but insisted that she go directly to her room and lock herself in until morning. "I think we scared him off for tonight," he said, "but there's no sense taking chances."

As she disappeared in the little red Chevy, Kennedy stood on the sidewalk until the car turned a corner then took out his phone. The first call was the most difficult, and there was a short argument that ended with Colm insisting, "No, it isn't going to be easy to get away, but I think you'll agree, I have to spend the next few days very close to Mercedes Maxwell."

***

Locked inside her room, Mercedes again called the cell phone number Jared had provided. He answered quickly, and she wondered if he'd been waiting for her call.

"Jared, it's Mercedes."

"Hello!" He sounded pleased and surprised. "Where are you?"

"In a hotel outside Glasgow."

"Are you all right?"

"No. I mean, yes, I am, but I was attacked. A man tried to—"

She stopped as the nervous reaction delayed by Colm's comforting presence threatened to overwhelm her. Knees trembling, she sank onto a chair, palms sweating and heart racing.

Jared seemed to feel her fear across the distance. "It wasn't a good idea to let you go off on your own. I'll come and get you right now, tonight. We'll deal with Inspector Callard together. I will convince my superiors you're not involved, whatever he says."

Forcing herself back under control, Mercedes tried to think. What did she want? On her own she was vulnerable, but could Jared protect her from a superior officer who could use his position on the force to learn her secret? Jared didn't have the cloud Callard did. And was it fair to ask for his help? Sooner or later he'd be forced to choose between his job and her needs.

"I'm fine. I was frightened, but it's over now."

"Are you sure? If you tell me where you are I can drive up. We can talk it through and decide what's right."

She had already decided. "You need to work on catching this guy, and you don't need me to worry about. I'll be fine. I'll do as you suggested and get lost for a few days. Inspector Callard knows everything I know." *Well, almost,* she amended silently. "I don't want to see him again, but I'll keep in touch." With that she ended the call.

Her legs still felt weak, but she'd argued herself back to her original course of action. Only she believed in the vicar's notebook. Who else would follow up on it if she were in police custody? She had to stay mobile, had to see where the book led. She had Colm Kennedy's offer of help, and at least for a while, she'd accept it.

And Jared? It was probably a mistake to refuse assistance from someone with connections to law enforcement, but as long as she was a suspect, she felt more comfortable keeping her distance from all policeman, even ones with dreamy brown eyes and biceps hard as eight-day-old scones.

CHAPTER FIFTEEN

They were halfway to London the next morning when the skies opened like sluice gates. Mercedes had called and agreed to travel with Colm under conditions that were slightly embarrassing to mention. She needed to know first of all that it wasn't the prospect of a sexual relationship that motivated Kennedy. He had, after all, tried to pick her up at the inn in Dumfries. She didn't need that particular complication at this point.

He'd laughed good-naturedly when she stipulated they occupy separate rooms. "I'll behave myself, promise. I'm grateful you don't think me the other sort, knowing my profession." He'd showed up at the inn within the hour and followed her to a rental agency where they returned the Chevy and then headed south in Colm's dark green, slightly battered Aston-Martin.

Mercedes wasn't sure why she'd accepted Colm's offer. There were at least a dozen reasons why she should not, and after they'd ridden in silence for a while she asked, "Why did you want to go off on this unplanned, probably crazy search with me, Colm?"

"I suppose I've fallen under the spell of John Romeo's story, just as you have," he replied. "I'd like to find the truth of it." He turned, and his green eyes met hers as he added, "You won't give it up, I can see that. I figure you need someone who knows a bit about the territory. I'm your man—your strictly-hands-off man, of course."

She blushed, studying the road ahead rather than rising to the jibe. After a few minutes more, he asked, "It's that neat streak of yours, isn't it. You have to tie up the loose ends and hand it over to the police in a neat package."

She shrugged. "Order is good."

He turned businesslike. "Well, we need information first. You've looked at what's readily available in print, but there are people who've spent their lives studying the times we're interested in. They might be able to put things together more easily than we can by reading a bit here and a bit there."

"You know experts in Shakespearean history?"

Colm gestured expansively. "In my slow but steady progress toward a university education, I've taken classes wherever I happen to be. I have a few connections in both England and Scotland."

When the rain began, it wasn't a wet Scottish mist but a full downpour that blanketed the windscreen. The wipers were useless, and there was nothing to do but stop for a while. They found a comfort station filled with depressing furniture and depressed tourists, and Colm fetched tea while Mercedes attempted repairs in the ladies' room. Outside the entry were telephones, and she remembered that she'd promised to call Professor Rankin. He might have found more information for her. The secretary recognized her voice and put her through.

"Miss Maxwell, are you well?" His voice sounded different, sharper.

"I'm fine. Did you find any more about Willie Reid?"

"I tried all my resources, but there's no further mention of the man. There's another reason I hoped you'd call. I appreciate your warning to me, and I have one for you."

"A warning?"

"Someone came into my office and snooped in my computer files."

"What?"

"After you left yesterday, I went to lunch. My secretary got a call there was a package she needed to sign for, but when she reached the entry there was no one there. She returned to find a man leaving my office. He said he was your traveling companion and you'd left a pair of glasses behind in my office. After showing her the glasses, he left. She thought no more of it."

"Except I don't wear glasses, reading or otherwise."

"I'm old, but I'm not blind, my dear," Professor Rankin said dryly. "After she mentioned the two incidents, I looked around the place. Nothing was missing, but I think someone used my computer, perhaps to see what sites I'd visited recently. Though I'd looked at several other sites after you left, the history showed the last site visited was one you and I looked at together. In addition, the screen was tilted higher than I'm accustomed to, as if a taller person sat in my chair." He paused in confusion. "Why would anyone want to know what sites we looked at?"

To figure out where I'm going next. "Did your secretary say what the man looked like?"

"Tall, she said, with dark eyes and one of those chin beards one sees nowadays."

Mercedes thanked the professor, promised to be extremely careful, and replaced the handset. The man who'd attacked her had been masked, but he had been tall and dark-eyed. She was lucky Colm had been nearby.

An oddly familiar figure caught her eye as she exited the phone station. His back was to her but the blue hair, pin-striped vest, and ridiculous trousers struck a chord. She'd seen that outfit the day before, in the university car park.

Scanning the crowd anxiously, she found no sign of Colm. When she turned back, the oddly-dressed man was gone, too.

Stop being paranoid, she told herself. More than one outfit like that could exist in the British Isles. After all, those who ostentatiously reject society's fashion norms are often pitifully uninspired in creating what they think is a different look. The outfit probably aped some bass guitar player she'd never heard of.

Colm came toward her, his grin flashing when he picked her out of the crowd. What a relief to have him with her, to know that someone was watching out for her safety.

The drenching wore itself out fairly quickly, leaving bright sunshine that glistened off wet leaves and sparkled in the puddles. There was a general exodus from the shelter, a busy slamming of doors and grinding of starters that signaled the return to moving on. As Colm led the way to the car, Mercedes reported on his uncle's surreptitious visitor. "I warned him to be careful," she finished, "but I didn't mention you were with me. Did you tell him?"

"No. I'll do that in a day or two, when we know something."

He was taking her, he said, to see Arthur Fairbanks, a man whose historical interest centered on the Tudors and encompassed a wide range of information within that era. "You won't like him, though," Colm predicted with a grin.

"Why won't I?"

"He's one of the anti-Shakespeares."

She grimaced. "Shakespeare didn't write Shakespeare?"

"Exactly."

"Is he for Bacon, Marlowe, or deVere?"

Colm glanced at her obliquely. "Would you believe all of the above?"

***

"It is most likely that the Shakespeare works resulted from collaboration." Dr. Fairbanks spoke in stentorian tones, jutting his lower lip like a Winston Churchill wannabe. "I could cite a dozen examples to demonstrate it. For one, why does Macbeth hire two murderers to kill his friend Banquo, yet three show up to do the deed? That's something one author would keep straight, but a group, with everyone tossing in ideas, might miss the mistake."

"I thought the third murderer was Macbeth himself," Mercedes offered, quoting some past literature teacher.

Fairbanks smiled condescendingly. "I've heard that argument, but why hire it done if he planned to be there? He'd killed Duncan; he could have killed Banquo as well."

"He didn't want to do it, only to assure it was done."

Fairbanks leaned back in his chair and ignored her argument, instead steepling his fingers and continuing his lecture. "Most of mankind's great leaps forward are made not by one person, but by several, sometimes working together, other times working separately but benefiting from each other's successes. Why should the writing of a great body of superior drama be any different? Even television writers work in groups."

Biting her tongue and placing a knuckle firmly over her mouth to keep it closed, she glanced around the tasteful if somewhat characterless room, refusing to appear interested in Fairbanks' pedantry. The place was obviously the den of a very self-satisfied lion, a recognized expert who had succumbed to the accolades of his colleagues and now had no doubts as to his supreme authority.

117

Framed certificates hung everywhere, citing Fairbanks' contribution to the study of history. Books and magazines lined a shelf behind him labeled *Published Works*, colorful ribbon markers cascading from each, presumably marking the mention of his name. The desk was the opposite of Professor Rankin's, which had overflowed with items of interest to him at the moment. Fairbanks' desk was Spartan, each item there apparently required to demonstrate imminent usefulness and sit precisely in its allotted position. Mercedes admitted to being a neat-nik, but she guessed Fairbanks was the sort who could cite how many paper clips were in the right front desk drawer, how many sheets of paper would be required to print his next article.

It was typical of a person of limited genius to refuse to admit genius in another, she thought, to pronounce Shakespeare's body of work to be a group project, like skits concocted by high school students. So many counter-arguments came to mind that Mercedes paused to sort them out before continuing. Leonardo? Mozart? Geniuses had assistance, certainly, but it was their unique creativity that lifted them above the rest. Shakespeare understood human nature, capturing both its best and its worst moments. That came from what might be called "soul," and it couldn't be accomplished by committee. She opened her mouth to argue, but a glance at Colm's quirked eyebrow reminded her she wasn't here to dispute theories.

"What Miss Martin is really interested in is Queen Elizabeth's spy network," he said smoothly, diverting Fairbanks from further comment on Shakespeare.

"I'm writing a book," she put in, as she'd been prompted. "A novel of the time, and I'd like to put Walsingham or Cecil in it, and a bit about the spy network for historical interest."

Fairbanks' hawkish nose lifted somewhat at the word *novel*, but he managed to continue without sneering. "Walsingham is the more famous, of course. Brilliant chap. He had some blind spots, hated Catholics and particularly Mary Scots, but to build and maintain the network of spies he had and serve his queen's interest so unswervingly is admirable." His tone implied the long-dead Walsingham should be grateful for Fairbanks' favorable opinion.

"I know Christopher Marlowe was one of his spies."

Fairbanks lit a briar pipe, an affectation if she'd ever seen one, and worked futilely for some seconds to get the thing to draw. "Briefly, yes. Marlowe was one of many."

"Is there a list of the names of the agents?"

Fairbanks shook his head. "I doubt there ever was. He'd have kept it all in his head."

"But when Walsingham died?"

The pipe finally took off and a not unpleasant smell reached Mercedes' nose, though she doubted the taste of burning vegetation was equally pleasant. "As you're aware, Robert Cecil was the next spymaster of note, the son of William Cecil, who is much better known." Mercedes recognized the name of Elizabeth's most trusted councilor. "Robert was intelligent and trustworthy, like his father. He later served James I, and it was he who discovered the Gunpowder Plot."

As Mercedes tried to figure out how to get Fairbanks around to the questions she wanted answered, Colm put in smoothly, "Miss Martin thought of making her spy a young actor come to London to try the stage. He'd be recruited by Walsingham but continue to act as his cover."

The Great Man forgot his superior reserve as the suggestion triggered a memory. "That actually happened. A young man who'd been in a London company for several years decided to seek a life

119

of adventure. He sailed with Drake, acquitting himself well at the defeat of the Spanish Armada. Elizabeth herself came on board the Golden Hind afterward, and Drake served her a banquet." Fairbanks' ruddy face took on the look of one who's envisioning his tale as he tells it. The pipe lay forgotten on a ceramic plate at his side.

"Of course Drake went to the limit to impress his beloved queen, and Elizabeth loved every second of it. During the course of the evening she was introduced to the young man, who'd been slightly wounded in the battle. Drake praised his courage and mentioned his background on the stage. The queen said something to the effect that England had need of such men as he. Perhaps more was said, who knows, but shortly afterward, Walsingham makes mention of a 'certain sailor' who has become part of his network."

"So the queen mentioned him to Walsingham and they recruited him?" Colm had shifted forward in his chair, hands resting on the desk.

"He was perfect for their purposes. They put it out the sailor's wound had festered and he died. Once he no longer existed to those who had known him, he went through training with Walsingham himself, learning cipher and how to disguise his handwriting. Once he was trained, he'd have been used in various capacities, slipping in where needed to observe and report. Either a sailor or an actor might come and go without much notice taken, since the jobs were fairly transitory."

"But what if people recognized him?"

"I would guess he disguised himself," Fairbanks replied. "Walsingham refers to him as 'the Player' and is pleased with his acting abilities. He could travel with various troupes or serve on board a ship as the occasion arose. A very versatile spy. References to him are frequent in the papers of Walsingham and Cecil."

Mercedes gripped the arms of her chair to keep herself rooted in reality. Could the Player be John Romeo?

Fairbanks concluded what he knew of the man's history. "The Player was very useful to Cecil, but he disappeared on a mission somewhere after—oh, let me see—" He swiveled his chair to a file cabinet at the end of his desk and pulled out a folder. There was a moment of silence as he leafed through some papers, and then he nodded triumphantly. "Here it is, 1608." He set the folder on the highly polished mahogany desktop and went on. "They weren't worried at first, because the Player went about things his own way and was often out of contact for some time. But after a year, they concluded something or someone had ended his career."

"And what was his last mission?"

"Something in Scotland, I think." He scanned the folder as the conversation continued, running a finger down the center of each sheet before laying it aside.

"If we wanted to look at Cecil's papers, are they available to the public?"

"That depends on what you mean by available. They're in the private collection of one of his descendants. The man has the reputation of a misanthrope, though he has allowed access to the works so that historians could make copies for study."

"And these copies would be found where?"

"At the National Archives in Kew."

Colm and Mercedes exchanged glances, confirming their intention to visit the place.

"Have you spoken with Aletha about this?"

Colm's reaction was surprising. A flush spread across his face and he lowered his gaze to his knees. "No, I haven't."

"She'd be the one to ask, but you know that." Fairbanks seemed unaware of Colm's discomfort. "I saw her not two weeks ago, and she gave me her most recent phone number. Now where did I put it?" He searched the desk drawer noisily, shoving aside various metallic objects, and came up with a business card. "I'll give her a call. She'd be more than willing to help you."

The call produced an invitation for Colm and his friend to visit her at home in the morning. "I was right," Fairbanks said proudly. "She's intrigued by your interest in Shakespeare and spies, and she says you know the way."

Unlike Fairbanks, Mercedes was tuned in to Colm's reaction, and the best word for it was *reluctance*. He hadn't intended to ask this woman's help, but now he was stuck. If Ballert was an expert and an acquaintance, why had Colm chosen Fairbanks instead, a knowledgeable source but a bit of a blowhard?

Fairbanks had returned to his folder of notes, searching for the Player's last assignment. "I'm surprised I've remembered as much as I have. There were so many nameless spies at the time," Suddenly he jabbed a finger at the paper before him. "Here. I knew I'd made a note. Cecil records that the Player went to Scotland to find Mary."

"Mary Queen of Scots, perhaps?" Colm asked.

"She was long dead. I'd guess it was a contact who monitored the state of affairs in Scotland. Always a rebellion brewing in those days."

Mercedes' thought went in a different direction. Thinking like a spymaster who often used codes, she said, "The mother of God: *Madre de Dios*."

CHAPTER SIXTEEN

Colm and Mercedes sat at a roadside table, eating meat pies still warm from the oven of a little shop they'd almost passed without noticing. The flaky crust was a perfect opposite to the meat-and-vegetable mixture inside, and she ate heartily, brushing crumbs from her lap as they fell.

They discussed Dr. Fairbanks' information, trying to fit together the pieces of what they knew. "If Walsingham's spy was an actor, he might have known William Shakespeare, might have even acted in some of his plays." Mercedes took an enthusiastic bite.

"You're thinking he went to find Drake's treasure and was captured by Reid?"

"Why would they send a Londoner to Scotland? Surely they had spies in the north who'd be less conspicuous."

"Maybe he wanted to go for some reason."

They took rooms at a bed and breakfast for the night, at which she paid cash and they used false names. Colm did the talking to conceal Mercedes' American accent. Before they crossed the border into England, she'd confessed the police were looking for her, feeling guilty about involving him in her flight from the arms of justice.

"I've heard nothing of a hunt for you on the news."

"I was warned by a friend—an acquaintance, actually—on the force." Colm raised an eyebrow at that, but made no comment.

The evening's conversation was a rehash of everything they'd discussed already, but the story was less and less story, more and more fact. At ten Mercedes wished Colm goodnight and went to her room. She'd exhausted her supply of clean clothes, and she needed to do some housekeeping tasks.

The bath was down three steps, across a landing, and up three steps opposite. She spent a few moments washing out a blouse and some underwear, rolling them in a towel to dry them as much as possible. Her actions were quiet, which is how she happened to hear a telephone conversation.

"She's very smart," caught her attention. It was Colm's distinctive voice, perfect for the theater but too resonant for secrets. "But I'm doing my best with my charming accent and boyish grin."

Was Colm talking about her? Rude to eavesdrop, but still...

"We went to see Doctor Fairbanks today," he told his listener. "...I know he's a crank, but he knows his Elizabethan history...Are you doing as I said?...Good. You must be careful."

Easing her way out of the bathroom with her damp laundry wrapped in the towel, Mercedes tiptoed back to her room. Had Colm told someone about her? If so, it was a betrayal. For a moment she wondered if he'd followed her to Larkhall and set up the attack on her so he could act as rescuer and gain her trust. Was that possible?

No. Colm's anger at her attacker had been real, she was sure of it. As to the phone call, he might have been talking to anyone—a friend, a co-worker, a relative—about any woman. Because of her situation Mercedes had become paranoid, making bizarre conspiracy theories out of every encounter. She was sure Colm Kennedy was just what he appeared to be, a charming man who'd become interested in helping a woman who was alone in a place strange to her. She admitted it was possible he'd done so because he wanted to get close to her, but Mercedes had to admit she wouldn't mind getting closer to Colm either.

***

Five dead, all made into tributes to Shakespeare's genius. The historian had brought Macbeth to Vincent's mind, a proud and commanding exterior but wimpish underneath. It was Friday. With any luck the man's body wouldn't be found until Monday, maybe later. He'd left the head upright on the polished, pristine desktop. After all, he was no Macduff to go carrying it around with him. The police were in pursuit, but they had no idea why, no likely places to search. His old friend on the force had kept quiet, proving he had his own agenda. No one else knew about the book, then. As soon as he got from the woman what she knew, he'd see no one ever did.

The historian hadn't known where the girl was headed. London, he thought, but he had revealed the identity of the companion. Colm Kennedy was an actor fairly well known in Scottish theater. He specialized in comedy roles, being a shade too short for a tragic leading man, but he'd been noticed in London last season, playing both Petruchio and Benedict with some success. Vincent had seen one performance, though he doubted he'd have recognized the man if they'd met on the street. Well, they had met, but it was dark then.

What was he doing with the Maxwell girl? He'd watched in fury as the two dined together after Kennedy's interference. When they parted, he'd decided to shadow the man. It paid off, because Kennedy and Mercedes left together in his auto. It made Vincent so angry he'd almost broken his fist against the dashboard.

In a driving rain and with great difficulty, Vincent followed them southward, waiting impatiently in his car whenever they stopped. He noticed but took no note of the rusty, cream-colored caravan that pulled into the comfort station along with the Aston-Martin and left at the same time. He spared only a glance at the blue-haired freak who slunk out of the driver's side, slamming the door twice before it stayed shut, and went inside. All sorts of creatures appear when it rains.

When the weather cleared, Vincent followed the couple to Fairbanks' home and waited until they left. Now he had a dilemma. Should he follow them or question the professor? In the end he trailed Mercedes and Kennedy to an inn, where they settled in for the night. He dealt with Fairbanks while they slept, and the information gained was quite satisfactory. The woman's determination to discover all she could about John Romeo convinced him she had the missing journal page. He could not lose track of her. With Kennedy's help she might even solve the puzzle the Player had devised. It would be easy then to step in and dispose of both of them. Drake's treasure was his, and he intended to have all of it.

***

At a pub three times longer than it was wide, Colm led Mercedes to a table at the back, where they were away from the noise of the place. The menu offered steak and she was tempted, but Colm warned against it. "Stick with what we do well on this side of the pond," he advised. "Steak isn't it." She chose shepherd's pie instead, which turned out to be a good decision.

Mercedes had begun to look forward to meeting another historian. "Maybe this other professor can give us specifics on Shakespeare's life that might help us connect him to John Romeo."

"Yes." Colm's expression was hard to read.

"What's wrong with her, Colm? Why don't you want to see

her?"

Colm stared at the menu card he'd picked up from the bar. "She's very knowledgeable. I just thought Fairbanks would have the information we needed and we wouldn't have to bother Aletha."

"Is she a prickly old maid? Will we have to answer three riddles before she'll help us?"

"I wouldn't say old maid is the correct term," Colm said vaguely. "Though last I knew she wasn't married." He changed the subject, not as smoothly as he wanted to, she suspected. "So what will you do with this treasure if you find it?"

"I never thought about it. I only want to prove to the police this whole mess is connected to the vicar's journal. Then they'll be able to find the man who killed all those people, and they can stop thinking I had anything to do with it."

"And what happens if they catch him? Will you still want to solve the puzzle?"

Something in his tone had changed, and she wondered what he was asking. "I don't want the treasure, if that's what you're asking."

"But you do want to see if you can find it." His eyes were intent. Something burned there, but she couldn't say what it was.

When they'd finished their meal, they walked along the street of the village until they came to a well-worn path into a copse of trees. "Explore!" Colm exclaimed playfully as he led her off the sidewalk.

It wasn't much of a discovery. The path led to a field surrounded by a stone fence. They sat on the wall for a few moments, watching the sky darken and the stars appear, one by one.

"Why did you come with me?" she asked suddenly.

Colm hesitated, and then instead of answering pulled her to him in a kiss that sent her head spinning and her senses tingling. She slid her arms around his neck without conscious choice, narrowing the distance between them until there was none.

When they finally separated he gave an embarrassed laugh. "There. I've broken my promise. I'm a man who can't be trusted."

Mercedes glanced around the deserted area. "You promised separate rooms, and we have them. I don't recall that woodsy encounters were part of the discussion."

This time his laugh was not embarrassed in the least. He pulled her farther into the trees, where shadows darkened their faces. Their second kiss was better, and Mercedes felt as if her whole body had gone soft. There was nothing but the feel of him against her—and something rough and wet on the back of her hand.

She jumped back, startling Colm. The rough caress resumed, and she looked down to see a collie licking her hand, apparently entranced by the scent of her recent meal.

A voice called from the path. "Milton! Milton, come back, naughty dog!" Within seconds a face appeared, followed by a man bent low to make his way under the branches. He stopped short when he perceived the two before him. "Oh, hello there."

"Hello," Colm replied, his voice even lower than usual.

"I'm so sorry if Milton's interrupted—I mean, he's not usually the sort to take off like that, and I'm—" Finally the elderly gentleman gave up. "I'm sorry."

Me too. Aloud Mercedes said, "It's quite all right. We were just

128

leaving." She bent to scratch the collie's ears for a moment, holding him back from applying dog kisses to her face. They wished the man a pleasant evening and went back the way they'd come.

What would have happened if they'd been uninterrupted? She could still feel the heat of the moment between them. When they got to the inn, Colm wished her a pleasant night's rest and kissed her hand in a comic, cavalier gesture. Was he acting now, or had he been acting then?

***

By eight the next morning, the police station at Dumfries was abuzz with activity. Maps had been marked with pins for the location of each victim, and supervisors spoke with other supervisors. Disappointingly small amounts of evidence trickled in. The victims were not necessarily acquainted, and those who were had no obvious connection other than proximity. Paul Prescott had known Sylvia Tate in school, years ago. Sylvia's friends said they sometimes "got together" when Paul's tours came through Canready, but nothing more was known. Paul had not gone inside the castle, remarking to the bus driver he'd "seen the bloody place ten times too many."

Mrs. Flowers' only connection to Paul was as one of his flock. The librarian in Dumfries was connected to none of the others. The woman had lived a quiet life, staying among the books she loved, eschewing husband and family. The only person who admitted to being in the library that morning had seen a lone woman sitting at a table full of books. She was a stranger, and the witness had assumed she was working on a research paper for some university class.

She'd been working on something, Callard thought, but it wasn't a college project. The woman was Mercedes Maxwell, the link that connected all the others. She'd been there when Sylvia died at the castle, when Mrs. Flowers died in a Dumfries hotel, and just before the librarian died a horrible death. She couldn't have killed Prescott, but she had to know why he died.

A young policeman stuck his head in the door. "Sir, there's been a murder in Birmingham, a professor of history. It looks like the same sort of thing."

After hearing the details, Callard made a phone call. When it was answered he said, "Callard here. I think we need to get together, to discuss these murders." He paused. "Yes, I can meet you there. I'll leave here around two." As he hung up the phone, he frowned. Mercedes Maxwell hadn't called in two days, and he wanted very badly to locate her.

CHAPTER SEVENTEEN

Colm was subdued at breakfast the next morning. The closeness of the evening before evaporated, and he seemed to have had second thoughts about their visit to the English professor's home as well. "I'm not sure Aletha can help, and it's out of our way if we're headed to London." He stared at his breakfast, refusing to meet Mercedes' eye.

She retreated to a businesslike attitude. "If you don't want to go see this woman, that's fine. Give me her address and I'll rent a car." He said nothing for a moment and she added, "I understand if you've changed your mind, Colm."

She didn't understand, not really. It was what one said when she felt a relationship slipping away. Maybe what happened last night had scared him off. Or maybe it hadn't been as wonderful for Colm as it had been for her.

"Oh, I'm going if you are. I'm not breaking any more promises."

She was impressed a few hours later when he turned the Aston-Martin into a long drive that swept in a large semicircle down toward a clear, shallow river. From the drive's entrance, guarded by a gate he had to open before driving through and close behind them, the house could not be seen, but as they descended the hill that was really an extended riverbank, the rhododendron bushes parted and the house rose before them. It was stone, of course, with the ultimate frippery of older days, rows and rows of windows. The massive front door was overshadowed by a roofed entry topped with a cupola of antique brass. The front garden was a riot of color, revealing the hand of either a hard-working amateur or a well-paid professional. When the door opened and she saw her hostess, Mercedes immediately concluded that the gardener was hired.

While Doctor Fairbanks had been much as expected, full of useful information but pedantic and stuffy, Aletha Ballert looked more like Miss July than a professor of history. Dressed in turquoise capris and matching blouse, she had added gold jewelry that dressed the outfit up and made Mercedes feel grubby in the navy pants and striped T-shirt she'd worn for two days now.

Aletha's black hair, dark eyes, and the curve of her features showed traces of foreign heritage. Probably Great-grandfather Ballert had brought home an Indian wife in the days when the sun never set on the empire.

This woman was no retiring flower of yesteryear. When she opened the door it was clear a visit from Colm was a joyful occasion. When she saw Mercedes beside him, however, there was in quick succession surprise, confusion, and something like anger.

"Aletha, this is Mary, a friend who'd like to talk with you about Shakespeare."

She was not obviously not pleased that Colm's friend was female. "Please, come in." The words so contradicted her body language and tone of voice that Mercedes had the urge to blurt out a disclaimer to any relationship between her and Colm. She sensed it wouldn't help.

The house was as impressive inside as out, the furnishings authentic antiques, well-preserved. Crazed patterns of age showed in the vases, and the wood had developed the soft patina so prized by lovers of such things. What was modern, the sofa, chairs, draperies, and lamps, had been chosen to blend seamlessly into the ambiance of the place so as not to detract from ancient elegance.

Colm insisted, to Mercedes' discomfort, that she receive a tour of the house. He probably meant to allow Aletha a chance to show off, but his familiarity with the place only made it more obvious he'd spent time here. Obligingly but coolly, Aletha narrated as she led them from room to room. The kitchen was large and open, with utensils hanging from a frame centered over the workspace. A large antique cook-stove had been left in place for effect.

"This place was once a manse," she explained. "The kitchen was used for all sorts of community purposes, directed, of course, by the parson's wife, who fed the poor as well as her household and served as hostess for visiting clergy and various church functions." Hard to imagine Aletha cooking for anyone, including herself.

There were enough bedrooms upstairs that Mercedes lost count, each furnished in a dominant color and referred to by that convenience: the pink room, the lavender room, and so on. Last Aletha showed them her small but impressive wine cellar, where she said to Colm in a familiar, teasing tone, "I remember you found this spot interesting the last time you visited."

His face flushed, and for once he had nothing to say. Aletha, with a sly look from under her lashes, suggested they return to the main floor.

They took seats in a room that proclaimed its owner's specialty. Bookshelves ran from floor to ceiling along two walls, many of them dealing with Shakespeare's life and works. The third wall was a stone-faced fireplace, scrubbed so clean that the brass andirons shone.

Colm sat next to Mercedes on a sofa along the fourth wall. She was irritated that he chose to put himself next to her, oblivious to his hostess' flash of animosity. The sofa, chosen to match the room, illustrated that style doesn't necessarily translate to comfort.

Aletha faced them, seating herself gracefully in a leather chair and regarding them across a marble-topped coffee table. Or did they call them tea tables over here?

"I understand you need my help, Miss Martin?" Get it over with, her expression said.

"I'm looking for information on Shakespeare's family. Might he have had a brother no one's heard of?"

Aletha showed immediate interest. "Why do you ask?"

This was the tricky part. How much truth should she tell? "I found a document claiming Shakespeare had a brother who died at the hand of a Scottish outlaw."

The cool reserve evinced thus far was replaced by something else. "What document?"

Mercedes was careful, though she didn't know whether it was from fear of betrayal or of being told again that she'd been duped. "It's a second hand account, and I no longer have the document, but I believe the author thought he was telling the truth." She returned to her point. "Is it possible that Shakespeare had an unknown brother?"

Examining perfectly groomed nails, Aletha ran her thumb along the edges to test their smoothness. "Actually, I've done some work on that subject myself. It makes sense to me that William had a close relationship with someone who fed him information on certain subjects."

She sat back in her chair for a moment, her perfect face concentrated on putting the arguments into proper order in her own mind before beginning. "For centuries it's been argued that such a vast body of work as Shakespeare's couldn't come from one man. His command of the language is amazing, and when he can't think of the proper phrase, he invents one perfect for the situation,

134

like Lady Macbeth's claim that her husband is 'too full of the milk of human kindness.' Scholars question one person's ability to produce so much that's excellent, but can't the same be said of Mozart or Leonardo?"

Mercedes was pleased that she'd made the same argument as an expert on the topic.

Aletha went on, her iciness thawing as she spoke. "It isn't fair, but nature sometimes creates a person who puts the work of all his or her contemporaries to shame."

"Benjamin Franklin," Colm murmured. "American Renaissance man."

Aletha wasn't about to get sidetracked by rebellious English subjects. "Of the arguments that Shakespeare couldn't have written the works attributed to him, one of the strongest is that he didn't know enough about the world. He was born and raised in a small town and had a limited, very basic education, yet his works span history, cultures, class and even gender. How could a man so provincial know so much about things he'd never experienced?"

"Didn't Isaac Asimov make an interesting argument on that topic?"

Aletha looked at Colm fondly, proud of her clever pupil, but a little like a cat at a bowl of cream, too. "He did. Asimov said there are enough mistakes in the works to demonstrate that Shakespeare did write them. Those very mistakes show an un-traveled, under-educated man whose talent was great but who was more interested in drama than in historical accuracy. For example in *Julius Caesar*, Brutus' clock chimes, and the conspirators know it's time to depart. But sundials don't chime."

Mercedes had read the play in high school and not even

noticed the anachronism. Neither had her English teacher, apparently.

"There are other examples as well. The language soars, the action grips like a vise, the drama is matchless, but once in a while, the lad from Stratford bollixed it up."

"So what are you getting at?" Colm asked.

The professor smiled archly. "What if Shakespeare had a close connection to someone who had seen more of the world, someone he knew well and saw often?"

"His brother?"

"I have no concrete evidence to support it, so I've never publicized my idea." She regarded them both, a challenge in her eyes. "I don't care to be a laughingstock, but since you brought it up—" She ticked her points off on her fingers. "First, the baptismal entry documenting the existence of William Shagspere, spelt various ways in various documents, child of John and Mary, is preceded by an entry that has been blotted out."

"A mistake?"

"Possibly. But what if it were another child, one who was later erased?"

"A brother?"

"A twin brother."

In an instant, names flooded Mercedes' mind. *The Comedy of Errors, Twelfth Night*— There was ample evidence in his works that Shakespeare had experience with twins.

"Why would evidence of his birth be erased?"

The woman's perfect face creased in a frown. "This sounds

strange, but I think John Shaksper became involved in—" She stopped, probably unwilling to commit herself.

"—Spying?" Mercedes supplied.

Aletha frowned. "I'd like to know more about this document you mentioned."

"That will come later," Colm assured her. "Right now we need you to tell us what you know, to see if we're headed in the right direction."

Aletha paused for a moment and then took up Mercedes' last question. "Spying, exactly. Here's my theory, which is impossible to prove, I admit. The Shakspers have twin boys, naming the older one after the father. They are identical and probably loved fooling people, as twins often do, by trading places. The boys grow up, they go to school, they help their father in his business dealings, but they're very different in personality. John is adventurous, William studious. John loves attention and acclaim, William is modest and self-effacing.

"As the boys reach manhood, two things happen. One we know from records, the other from legend. First, William marries Anne Hathaway, several years his senior. Anne, whom they'd known all their lives, was a nice girl in an unfortunate situation. Her mother had died years before and her father had remarried, and now he too was dead. Anne was left in her stepmother's home, an apparent spinster. Suddenly she and William get married, and only a few months later, a daughter is born."

"He saved her good name," Colm commented.

"The odd thing is that the day before they applied for a license, Will Shakespeare applied to marry a girl named Anne Whateley. No one knows what happened to this marriage. Is it a mistake?

137

Why two licenses, two Annes?"

"So was it really John who applied to marry the other Anne?" Mercedes asked.

"We'll never know." Aletha sighed. "Suppose it was a clerk's mistake. He meant John, but John backed out at the last minute, leaving his Anne single. But Will did the right thing by the woman he'd wronged. It's even possible that John, the wilder twin, courted this other Anne using his brother's name. She was from another town and might not have known the difference. John tells her they're to be married, even goes so far as to apply for a license, using his brother's name. Stranger things have been done to convince a woman to have sex with a man."

Colm took a different view. "It's also possible that John was the father of Anne Hathaway's child, and William married Anne to save her name and his family's. That would explain the apparent lack of love between them and why Will left Anne in Stratford for twenty years while he pursued a career in the theater."

"You may be right, though it's clear Will loved the daughter, Susanna. He left the bulk of his estate to her and her husband, John Hall."

"Another John?" Mercedes moaned.

"There were a lot of them."

"You said there was a second event."

Aletha took a pedantic tone. "Why did Shakespeare go to London?"

"Rumor has it there was trouble with the local law officers over his killing a deer."

"Right, only I'd say that sounds much more like John than Will. At that point, Will should have been settling down with his

138

wife, who was due to have twins."

"A genetic clue," Colm put in. "Twins run in families."

"But why would a family man go out and hunt illegal deer? They weren't starving."

"So it was John on a lark?"

"Again, my take on events. John goes to London because he, not Will, is in trouble. He joins a troupe of actors, not exactly a prestigious occupation. Players were generally not respected or well-treated, but acting jobs were easy to get, since the theater was on the rise as an entertainment form."

Colm played historian for a moment, showing off his knowledge of the era. "Elizabeth's policies had increased the financial stability of the nation, bringing it back from her siblings' mismanagement and her father's excesses. People had leisure time and a little money, so plays were produced that appealed to general audiences."

Aletha sat back, pleased she had two converts to her pet theory. "Not being the shy type, John was probably a fairly good actor."

"Why doesn't his name appear on any bills?"

"Because he wasn't using his own name. He was in legal trouble, remember?"

"So what about Will?"

"Keep in mind I'm guessing here." She glanced at the array of works around her as if communing with the Bard himself, willing him to reveal his secrets. "Bookish Will has always wanted to write, always loved words. Once his brother is established in London, he goes to visit and is bitten by the bug. He wants to be part of the theater, loves it all, so he sends word to Anne that he's staying. Not much of an actor, he serves mainly as stage manager, prompting and keeping track of props. It takes him a while to get up the nerve to show the troupe his writing, and it's seven years before his first play is performed."

"The lost seven years." Aletha's scenario seemed right in light of was known about Shakespeare. "So they're both in London?"

"Perhaps briefly, but I think John, being the adventurous one, wanted more from life than acting could provide. He left the troupe and went to sea, which was the greatest opportunity a man of limited means could have in those days. It was the age of ships, and John was lucky enough to sign on with Francis Drake, who at that time was singeing the beard of the King of Spain."

"And as Drake's man, after the defeat of the Spanish Armada, he was recruited as a spy by Francis Walsingham." Colm couldn't resist finishing the story.

"How do you know that?"

"Dr. Fairbanks knew of a spy that Walsingham called the Player. He didn't know the man was Shakespeare's brother."

"We don't either," Aletha reminded him. "Without new proof, it's a theory." She didn't look as if she doubted herself. Mercedes would have bet she seldom did.

"What gave you the idea of an unknown brother?" she asked.

The woman's face turned blank. "Oh, I don't know. I put together things I've heard in different places, I guess. If one reads everything available and keeps an open mind, certain ideas seem to emerge. Some say a poorly-educated, small-town boy couldn't achieve such greatness. I prefer to believe he could, especially if there is more to the story than we know."

"You've tried to prove what you've told us?"

Aletha nodded. "The Information Age is an amazing thing. It allows tiny bits and pieces of data, hidden away for centuries, to be thrown into a giant pool of information. If one is clever and not too gullible, something comes of it. Still, I have nothing concrete."

"How certain are you that Shakespeare had a twin?"

Aletha smiled enigmatically. "Not certain at all. But my intuition says he did."

CHAPTER EIGHTEEN

Vincent was furious with himself, hardly able to believe he'd been so stupid. Of course he'd hardly slept in days, had run on his last resources, but that was no excuse. Parked to one side of the bed and breakfast where the woman and Kennedy stayed, he'd nodded off, settling his head against the window just for a moment to rest his eyes. Twenty minutes later when he awoke, the little Aston-Martin was gone. Fairbanks had stammered two possible destinations for his earlier visitors, and Vincent had no idea which they planned to visit first.

Sitting dejectedly in front of the stately brick house, he heard the dim sound of a door slamming and sat bolt upright, scrubbing his numbed face with a pale, fine-boned hand. A woman left the side door of the house and went out of sight, presumably into the garden. She wore overalls and a large straw hat, carried a basket and some shears. Following the direction she'd taken, Vincent was pleased to see her disappear into a potting shed.

The woman knew nothing until she was knocked to her knees. There was a subdued crash as the items she carried skittered across the dirt floor, the basket coming to rest against an upturned barrow. Dazed, she caught her breath for a moment, unaware of her situation. Finally she frowned at the sound of a scrape behind her and turned to see a tall man closing the door to the shed, shutting them in. Immediately the smells of dried earth and pungent peat turned from comforting to threatening. A small sound escaped her, but he gestured with the shovel he'd used to knock her down. She fell silent.

"I'm going to ask some questions," he said, "and you are going to answer."

Terrified, she stared at him for some seconds, but finally he saw a small nod in the semidarkness of the shed. The boards didn't fit together tightly, and slits of sunlight sliced across the woman's chest like *Cut here* lines on a pattern. "The man and woman in the Aston-Martin. Where were they headed?"

Her peril was evident to her now, and she had to try her voice twice before it sounded. "London, I think."

"Where in London?"

"They didn't say. I heard—them mention taking the—05—and they said something about—stopping near Oxford." The words came out disjointedly as terror slowed her thought process.

Finished with her, Vincent brought the shovel down quickly. He was not, after all, a monster. Though his mission was pressing, he paused briefly to arrange a tribute. In the dark shed, redolent of compost and decay, Hamlet's ghost came to mind, a creature who despite death had given valuable information to a seeker of knowledge. Taking a bottle of herbicide from a shelf along one wall, Vincent poured poison into the woman's ear.

***

Aletha invited Colm and Mercedes to stay the night at her home, but she said she had a meeting and would be gone until late. After seeing the reaction of his erstwhile professor and possible lover to the presence of a rival, Mercedes was uncomfortable with the situation, but Colm accepted, more relaxed now that Aletha and Mercedes were allies if not friends. After pointedly assigning them rooms on either side of hers, Aletha left, her car shooting up the narrow drive much too fast, spitting gravel. The whine of gears faded like a disappointed mosquito.

"Come on, I'll show you round the garden," Colm offered, and they went out terrace windows into an amazing variety of flowers and plants. "She did much of this herself," he explained as their steps echoed down a stone pathway curving among carefully chosen groupings of plants. "She inherited the house from her grandfather, and it was a bit run down."

Picturing Aletha with spade in hand was difficult, but there was often more to a person than first impression revealed. Mercedes explored the flowers eagerly, sniffing the larger blossoms and naming the ones she knew. Colm wasn't much help when a variety foreign to her came up. "Not a flower sort of person," he grumbled, but he pointed upward.

"That I can name. It's a monkey puzzle tree."

She looked up at the oddest tree she had ever seen. Its branches indeed looked like the tails of monkeys, all curled in different directions with needles in a rounded, brush-like formation. "Now that's unique."

"I think it's properly called Chilean pine," Colm offered, "But that's as far as I go." Suddenly he froze like an Irish setter on point. "Did you see that?"

"What?" She was still gazing up at the odd tree.

"Somebody ducked behind that rhododendron just now." Colm pointed, and indeed there was a rustling in a wildly pink-tipped bush a few yards ahead. The leaves waggled as if waving at her, but there was no breeze to stir them.

"The gardener, maybe?"

"Why would a gardener hide from us?"

"I don't know." The bush fluttered again. The spy wasn't much good at concealment.

He touched her arm briefly. "Stay here and keep talking, like I'm with you. I'll circle round and see what's what."

"But Colm—" Too late. He was gone. Mercedes tried to keep up a running patter, but it was difficult when there was no one to talk to and someone to worry about. She'd almost resorted to reciting "Jabberwocky" when there was a shout from the rhododendron, or at least that vicinity.

She saw only flashes of what occurred. A yelp of surprise that sounded something like "Oy!" came from the bush, then bright blue hair caught the light as its owner's head moved back and forth violently. She understood why when Colm stepped onto the pathway, gripping the blue-haired youth by the vest and shaking him.

"Who are you? What are you doing here?"

The response was nonverbal and instinctive. With strength born of panic, the young man head-butted Colm ferociously. She heard the breath leave him in a woof of surprise, and both men disappeared into the shrubs again. Blue Hair wrenched free, staggering backward a few steps with arms flailing wildly before finding his balance. A glance in her direction told him that path was blocked. He turned away, vaulting a low hedge and heading toward the road at a dead run. She heard him gasping in panic, and his skinny arms pumped as ferociously as his legs.

Hurrying to where Colm lay dazed on the ground, his body outlined in dainty pansies and certainly squashing others beneath it, she asked, "Are you okay?"

He rose, rubbing his forehead ruefully where a knot was forming. "It's my pride, you see. To be bested by that!" He indicated the retreating figure. The garden had gone peaceful again. The last view of Blue Hair as he clambered over the wall was surreal in contrast.

Had the interloper meant to harm them or merely listen in on their conversation? Briefly she reported seeing him twice before. "How did he find us, I wonder?"

"Must have been following. I don't like this."

The guy wasn't much good at remaining hidden, since she'd seen him twice and Colm had spotted him lurking in the bushes. Despite his frequent appearances in her life lately, Mercedes found it unlikely that the skinny young man was a threat. But why was he following her?

***

Looking mildly professorial, Vincent visited the offices of the history department at Oxford that afternoon. He wore a corduroy jacket over a pale blue shirt, polyester trousers, and canvas deck shoes with no socks, all casually stolen from local shops.

"Perhaps you can help me," he said to the receptionist. "I'm doing historical research and need an expert to point me in the right direction."

"What sort of help do you need?"

"I'm comparing the use of spies in the Tudor era to clandestine operations of today and need help locating relevant documents."

The girl frowned. "Ms. Ballert is our expert on the Tudors, but she's taken the summer off. We won't see her till September."

"I wonder if I might call her." Vincent's smile radiated charm. "I have a deadline."

The girl smiled with no real warmth. "I'm sorry, sir. We don't supply private numbers. If you leave a voice mail at her office number, she'll get it within a day or two." She went back to her work with a second cool smile, which made Vincent want to strike her then and there, but of course there were people all around.

Swallowing his anger, he thanked her tersely and left. What an excellent tribute the snippy girl would have made, her smug look disappearing as she saw death approaching. Still, he must focus on finding Mercedes Maxwell. Only she was important now.

CHAPTER NINETEEN

Colm found a cold roast in the fridge and cut thin slices for an impromptu dinner. He piled the beef on two slices of crusty French bread which he'd covered with cheese and warmed in the toaster oven, adding sliced tomato, lettuce, and some pickles. It looked appetizing, but his familiarity with Aletha's kitchen was still somewhat disconcerting.

Topping one sandwich with a second slice of bread, he sliced it and set the finished product before Mercedes, returning to give his own meal some additional treatment. He added a second kind of cheese, two slices of bacon he'd crisped in the microwave, and a large spoonful of coleslaw he found in a deli container on the bottom shelf.

"You won't live out the year with a diet like that," she teased as he squashed the whole with a second slice of bread. She'd been writing on a small piece of paper, but she set it aside and took a bite of her own portion, savoring the warm bread against the coolness of the tomato and lettuce.

"Americans!" he scoffed. "Worried you'll die of eating, always thinning. Where's the joy in that?" He took an enthusiastic bite to demonstrate his disregard for modern medical wisdom and asked, voice muffled by the various ingredients, "So what do you think?" He tapped the list she'd been compiling with a knuckle to indicate he meant her thoughts on Shakespeare, not sandwiches.

"John Romeo is John Shaksper. I feel it. He was recruited on Drake's recommendation, as Doctor Fairbanks said, and from then onward he worked on Her Majesty's secret service."

"Sometimes a sailor, sometimes an actor." Colm took a second bite. "Whichever suited the spymaster's purpose."

Without conscious thought Mercedes rose and began picking up the plates, bottles and jars he'd set out and returning them to their proper places with an efficient clatter. "He must have been good, to last through two masters' tenure."

"Three, I think. There was one between Walsingham and Cecil, but I forget who."

She noted he'd apparently been researching on his own, probably with the laptop he didn't admit to having.

"It was a perfect system, I must say," he went on, peering under the bread with a critical frown. "They erased Shakespeare's twin from existence, and two men played the role of one. When necessary John used an alias, probably many of them, but he could always return to London and become Shakespeare the player. What have you done with the mayonnaise?"

"I put it away."

"Are you always like that?"

"Like what?"

"All over the place putting things away."

"I guess so," she said defensively. "I can't eat until I've cleaned up the kitchen." She frowned. "You said you didn't mind."

He regarded her good-humoredly. "I suppose I must do without a few extra grams of cholesterol." He took another bite. "Anyway, Will probably knew John's real profession, right?"

"They'd have enjoyed it, like when they were kids." She got out the mayonnaise and handed it to him with a ladylike curtsey, and

149

he slathered a second layer on his sandwich. As soon as he set the jar down again, she replaced the lid and returned it to the refrigerator. "Will could go home to Stratford for months at a time to be with his family if his brother sometimes took his place at the theater. John could play small parts as well as Will, knew the plays from having served as sounding board, and was familiar with the theater's organization."

"I've read references to Shakespeare having memory problems." Colm raised a mayonnaise-laden finger then licked the condiment off. "When one of them didn't know what the other had said or done, he blamed his aging brain. Convenient."

"It all fits. See here?" She turned her notes so he could see what she'd written.

1582-Will marries Anne Hathaway
1585-92-the Lost Years-Shakespeare's actions unknown
John joins the military ???
1588-the defeat of the Spanish Armada
John is recruited as a spy ???
1592-1607-Will in London, both use Will's identity
1603-Elizabeth dies and James I assumes the throne
1608-John dies at Kirkfort
1610-Shakespeare returns permanently to Stratford

"It's sketchy, I know, but the timeline fits."

"I've heard some claim Shakespeare was in the military."

"Not a likely occupation for a bookish man with a wife and three children. But with his brother John to recount battles and explain military protocol, Will could write very realistic scenes."

"And if it were John and not Will who was the soldier or sailor, it fits his personality and lifestyle." Colm drummed on the table in triumph, having convinced himself.

"Your girlfriend is right, though. It's an argument for the bumpkin from Stratford having the resources to write great plays. Will was a man of words who devoured books and knew history. He had no windows on the cosmopolitan world, but through his brother, who sailed the seas, visited foreign countries, and even hobnobbed with royalty, those windows were opened. He could write about what his brother had seen and done."

Colm had missed everything after the second word. "My girlfriend?"

"Come on," she said lightly as a blush rose in her cheeks. She finished the last of her sandwich and wiped her hands on a napkin. "Anyone could see that there's something between you two."

If looking mystified was part of his actor's art, he had it down perfectly. "Aletha? She's a friend, but—" His voice trailed off.

"You were reluctant to bring me here. You didn't want us to meet."

He folded like the proverbial lawn chair. "Aletha and I have some history, but it's nothing to me now. Or to her, either." This last was said with less confidence. "I would never hurt Aletha, but you've got to understand the sort of woman she is. She doesn't want me in particular. She just...enjoys the company of men."

"Yours in particular, I'd say."

He looked both embarrassed and frustrated. Maybe the right words won't come without a script. "We had some good times, but since I met you, Mercedes, things seem different.

Not for Aletha, I'll bet. But she was pleased at his words. Things seemed different to her, too, but there was too much going

151

on to sort out what she felt.

And it was impossible to sort anything out, because Colm took her in his arms. At his touch logic fled, and she forgot his coolness that morning, forgot Aletha, forgot everything except the feel of his lips on hers.

They jumped as a key turned in the lock of the kitchen door and a man stepped into the foyer. There was a moment's hesitation when no one knew what to do, but Colm finally said, "Are you Frederick, by chance?"

The man's face cleared a bit and he clicked the door closed behind him, apparently somewhat reassured. "I am."

He reached out a hand. "I'm Colm Kennedy and this is Mary. Aletha invited us to stay the night, but I don't think she expected you back."

The man was still wary. "I caught an earlier train." As his eyes took in Mercedes he relaxed a bit further, probably concluding that a second-story man wouldn't have brought his girlfriend along. "Do I smell food?"

She jumped to get out the meal items she'd recently stored away. A slightly edited explanation was made of their presence. Colm said merely that he was a former student of Aletha's who had come for help on a project. Frederick's presence was not explained, but it became clear to Mercedes in a few moments that he lived in the house. He asked when Aletha might be home, took his suitcase upstairs and left it in her bedroom, and then came down to join them in shirt-sleeves and minus his tie. Colm had sliced more bread and now stepped aside, allowing Frederick to make his own light supper.

Well past fifty years old, Frederick wore his age well. Distinguished white hair was carefully barbered to keep it under strict control, and a matching mustache betrayed traces of wax at the tips, which made Mercedes smile at the antique affectation. His eyes were a striking blue and his gaze direct, as if he knew the color was unique and used it to his advantage. His face was cleanly shaven and shiny, his chin firm with no trace of a droop. It was the face of a man who didn't let things get away from him, who kept them firmly under control.

"So you've heard of me then?" There was a bit of challenge in his voice. Far above Aletha's age, he might well be defensive.

"Aletha said she'd met someone who makes her happy."

"We're well suited to each other, I think. It's a bit difficult since I'm often on the road, but she keeps busy with her teaching, and of course she publishes. Lots of research to do. I know nothing of Shakespeare, was hopeless at such studies at school, but Aletha is amazing."

"She's been very helpful to the work on my novel." Mercedes wondered what Frederick's business was, but she'd learned not to ask the personal questions that are considered friendly by Americans and rude by Europeans.

Frederick volunteered the information. "I suppose one would call me an entrepreneur," he said with a smile that was a bit arch. "I seek out opportunities and follow them up. It's worked well for me so far."

Judging from the cut of his suit and the car she glimpsed out the window, he wasn't bragging. Still, the man seemed a bit of a caricature, something out of a film from the forties. Maybe Aletha was a classic movie fan.

After making himself a sandwich with the remaining beef, some cheese and a large dose of mustard, Frederick microwaved a cup of hot water for tea and retired to his room with the food on a plate, resting under a tidy white napkin. Watching him go Colm said musingly, "He's not what I pictured when they said Aletha had met an older man."

"Very attractive," she commented, keeping her observations positive. "Rather Errol Flynn-like."

"Really?" Colm's tone didn't match her approving one.

"I simply meant he's got that dashing air. He'd be able to stand up to Aletha's rather effete manner."

"Yes, I suppose so. Aletha changes men every few months, like some do toothbrushes, but Frederick seems different, less transitory. Maybe she's found the one."

Or maybe she's realized she can't stay young forever. A man with Frederick's looks, charm, and apparent wealth might be worth settling for, even if, maybe especially if, he was the sort who paid little mind to what was going on around him. Aletha might settle in for security, but if the way she looked at Colm was any indication, her settling down was doubtful.

Around ten o'clock Mercedes went upstairs to the austerely beautiful room she'd been assigned. The walls were the palest lilac and there were no curtains, extra pillows, or fluffy accessories. The decorations consisted of books piled neatly on white-enameled, wall-mounted shelves of different lengths scattered around the room, creating an overall balanced effect with artful randomness. It smelled faintly of sandalwood. She curled up on the bed with a book of poetry, paging through idly.

Once she was alone, the day's events began to bother her. Colm had brought her to a woman who made no secret of wanting to know her source of information. In this woman's garden, they'd been stalked by a mysterious man who kept showing up where she was. She wondered how he'd known where they were and what he had intended to do. And she couldn't get out of her mind what she'd heard Colm say the night before on the phone. "Be careful." Careful of what? To follow her unseen? To stay behind them? What if Blue Hair and Colm were acquainted and had set this scenario up to cement her trust in him? What was he up to, anyway?

Sleep was impossible with the suspicions that whirled in her head. At a few minutes after eleven she heard Aletha's car roar up the drive and into the garage. She hadn't heard Colm come upstairs, though Frederick seemed settled in for the night. Slipping down the hallway against the far wall, out of the light from below, she took a place at the head of the stairs where at least some of what was said could be heard.

First she heard the clink of glasses, the sound of a bottle set down, and the soft step of a woman's foot on the tile floor. A nightcap with his former lover?

Aletha's voice was a purr, and she caught only a word now and then. Colm's actor's voice was louder, and she caught a tone of denial in the words that drifted upward. "It's something I have to do," he said once. Aletha's tone turned mocking, but the words were lost. After a mumble she heard, "—I'm staying close to her." After a pause she heard, "I think she knows more than she'd told me thus far."

Her fears were confirmed. Colm was traveling with her in order to find out what she knew. Along with her feelings of betrayal, Mercedes comforted herself that at least he didn't know everything. Whether he was working with the man who'd tried to kill her or with someone else, he didn't have the clues to Drake's treasure. He didn't even know for sure that she had them.

She wondered if Frederick was aware that Colm and Aletha

were so cozy together. If he came and went frequently on business, as he'd said, he probably didn't know what his lady friend was up to between times.

Again she asked herself how Blue Hair had known where to find her. Colm had disappeared at the rest stop, maybe to check in with someone. And now he'd brought her here, to a woman who obviously knew him well. He was probably waiting for a chance to search her things. Once he found what he was after, would she be expendable? She shivered in the darkness. If Colm was working with the killer, what would happen to her? Hanged like Cordelia, perhaps, or drowned in the wine cellar like the Duke of Clarence. Mercedes moved silently back to her room. Whatever his plan was, he wouldn't get the chance to put it into action.

***

The death of the bed and breakfast owner was discovered by her sister around noon, but it was some time before the woman could speak coherently with the police.

"Were there guests last night?" the inspector asked when she was composed enough to answer questions.

"Yes, but they were gone early, didn't even wait for the breakfast."

"Who were they?"

"A brother and sister, I believe. Mary Mayhew and...Let me look." She opened a book at the table beside her. "Yes, Nicholas Nottom. A very nice young man." She described the couple. The inspector took notes.

"You say you saw your sister after they left?"

"Oh, yes, she came in and said she was going to weed the dianthus. The grass grows in around them, you know." Tears fell as the woman tried to block the image of her sister's dead body, the feeling of panicked tightness in her own chest when she inadvertently grasped the shovel, caked with dirt and blood.

"Anything else? Did you hear anything?"

"No."

"And the couple who stayed the night? Unusual?"

"No, I don't think so, although...I suppose it doesn't matter, but I heard her speaking to her brother and it struck me odd. She sounded like an American. Do you suppose they were raised separately, like those twins in *The Parent Trap*?"

CHAPTER TWENTY

Slipping quietly down the stairs, Mercedes stopped to get her bearings on the landing before continuing to the front door. She worried briefly that Aletha had a security system, but she'd seen no evidence of one. No tiny lighted panel shone near the door. Taking the chance, she eased the lock back and turned the knob carefully. The door groaned slightly, but the clock struck the hour at that moment. She stepped out and closed the door again before it finished: four a.m.

Outside was darker than she was used to. City people seldom see true darkness, and the quiet of country nights was equally alien. Behind her somewhere the river gurgled as it flowed past the house. The drive seemed much longer now that she was on foot, but she hurried along in the half moon's light. She figured it would be three hours, four with luck, before anyone woke and realized she was gone. She needed to rent a car but didn't even know for sure where she was. Outside Oxford, but how far?

The gate loomed ahead. If there wasn't security on the house, there might well be something here, maybe a bell to alert the household when it opened. She dropped her case lightly to the other side and climbed the gate clumsily, reflecting that tennis shoes would have been more suitable for this part. Still, she hadn't wanted to look like a tourist, so she'd put on her only other outfit, black slacks with a turquoise silk blouse, a paisley scarf that combined the two with splashes of yellow, and black flats. Once the fence-climbing was over, she hoped to look like a career woman whose car had broken down.

Luck was with her. Not half a mile up the road, on which she had no idea which way to go, she heard a low rumble, then the hiss of air-brakes and a bus stopped, empty except for the driver. She gave her prepared story of needing to get to London and asked where she might rent a car. He was headed in the opposite direction but said cheerfully, "If you don't mind going a few miles the wrong way, I can drop you off at Millwick. It's not a large place, but there's an old gent who owns a small garage for tourists wanting to drive to Stratford or Stonehenge for a day. You can get a car there, but it won't be new."

It was perfect, actually. The old gentleman was a garrulous, helpful sort with very poor eyesight. He asked Mercedes to read him the information on her driver's license, so she was able to transpose several of the numbers and change her name to Millicent Morgan. Three hours after she'd slipped away from Aletha's house, she took possession of a slightly ancient Mercedes, which she thought fitting. She paid cash for the rental, regretful that she would later abandon the car but promising herself the man would be reimbursed for its return. As she turned the key and listened to the soft purr of the still-superior engine, hope surged. The fact that she'd gone the wrong way might actually throw off any pursuit that might be in the works.

It was overwhelming if she let herself think of it. The police were after her, believing her to be a murderer's accomplice. The murderer was not far behind, spreading death as he bore down upon her. And now Colm and possibly Aletha too would be looking for her, seeking the key to the treasure that Mercedes wanted no part of, a clue she'd gladly hand over to the authorities if they'd only give her a chance to explain. She wished anyone but Callard had been sent to interview her. He'd probably told others she'd acted guilty, maybe even said she'd stolen the book. He could easily make her seem dishonest unless she had proof that what the vicar said was true. Unless she found the location of Drake's treasure.

Where could she turn for help? It was crazy to keep running around the UK on her own. At the next village she stopped and entered shops until she found one with a pay phone. Digging through her purse she collected all the change she could find and the number Jared Graham had given her.

There was no answer, and she checked her watch. He was probably on his way to work. She could leave a message, but what would she say? "I haven't called because I took up with a man who turned out to be untrustworthy. Now I need you again so I'm back on your doorstep." There wasn't even a number she could leave for him to return the call.

On impulse, she dug out the other card she'd been given and called Callard's office. She could at least try to explain herself to him and try to gauge his suspicions. The receiver felt warm in her hand, and she realized her grip on it was tense. Things were getting to her. She had to find someone who really wanted to help her.

When the call was answered by a brusque male she said, "Inspector Callard, please."

"Inspector Callard is not available. Would you like to speak to another detective?"

"When will Inspector Callard return?"

"Who's calling, please?" The voice sounded suspicious, and she pictured a phone tap starting.

"I'll call later," she said hurriedly and cut the connection with a tap on the cradle. Dejectedly, she stared at the receiver in her hand as if it had secrets to reveal. She was cut off from help for the moment, and she wanted to get far away from this place.

If she went on to London, Colm and possibly others would know where to look for her. Still, she needed to see Cecil's papers, to know exactly what the spymaster had said about the Player.

Then something Franklin had said struck her. Why go to London? The original papers were at Salisbury, only a few miles from here. If she could convince the Earl's descendant to let her see them, she might find what she wanted. Since no one expected her to go to Salisbury, it was relatively safe. Feeling more confident, Mercedes left the dark pub and stepped into the sunlight.

The first problem would be learning the name of the man who now possessed Robert Cecil's papers. She didn't know much about Salisbury except there was a famous cathedral there. Where there was a cathedral, there were docents, who tended to be both helpful and knowledgeable. Fortifying herself with a rather bad cup of coffee and a delicious, berry-stuffed muffin, she studied the map briefly, familiarized herself with the Mercedes' dashboard setup, and headed down the motorway to Salisbury.

The town was as quaint as it should be, the cathedral as impressive as she'd heard. From her first sighting of its lofty spire, 404 feet high, to her entry into its cool recesses, she was rapt. Inside, the sanctuary was hushed despite the number of people who roamed the aisles, peered into the corners, and sat in the pews, taking in the ambiance of the place. The huge Cloisters, the airy, sharply-pointed lancet windows, and the nave, divided into sections by polished marble columns, threatened to distract from her purpose, but she resisted the urge to explore and surreptitiously observed the staff instead. Settling on a genteel-looking man with a mustache that reminded her of the Major General in *The Pirates of Penzance*, she approached when he stood alone for a moment. The mustache was even more impressive on close observance, and he smelled of some old-fashioned hair oil, heady and heavy but not unpleasant.

"This is a beautiful place," she began, gesturing around them vaguely.

The man assumed his polite demeanor and went into the canned speech. "Thank you, Miss. The prince himself has taken great interest in restoring the cathedral over the past twenty years, and it has been a joy to see it come back to its original splendor."

"I'm a student of Tudor history," she told him. "I understand that Robert Cecil, the Earl of Salisbury, is associated with this area."

"Oh, my yes," the man replied, interested in the chance to speak on something other than the transept width and span. "A fascinating man."

"Are his descendants still living in Salisbury?"

"I wouldn't know," the man replied. In her disappointment she almost walked away, but then he added, "Of course, old Cutler has his papers." He went on to explain in his pedantic way, and it turned out that Fairbanks had been wrong. It was not a descendant of Robert Cecil who possessed his papers, but a descendant of the man who had bought the estate after his death. "Cecil left a huge debt." The docent sniffed with the superior air of one who pays his bills on time. "A large part of the estate was sold to pay it off. Cutler is the last of the purchaser's line. They're odd lot, to be blunt, but they've kept the papers together, which is to their credit." He sniffed as if to imply there wasn't much else to approve of in the family.

"I wonder if I could meet Mr. Cutler."

The man smiled. "I doubt it. The gentleman dislikes company. He does historical research, but only on his own terms." Disapproval again. She guessed Cutler didn't support causes the docent deemed worthy, the cathedral, perhaps, or the renovation of the close around it.

After she'd thanked the man and left Salisbury's dim quiet,

Mercedes found the outside oddly jarring and noisy, as if she'd lost an island of serenity in the madness of the past few days. She found the nearest phone book and consulted the listings. No Cutler was listed. Undaunted, she strolled the perimeter of the cathedral close until she found a talkative shop owner. a woman almost as broad in the hips as she was tall. Her humorous face twisted into a sneer when she heard who Mercedes sought.

"Cutler, oh, yes, everyone knows about him, though you don't see him about much. Flinty old thing."

"Where does he live?"

"All by himself, luv. Won't no one live with him." Mercedes waited as the woman enjoyed her joke. "He lives off Poultry Cross. You must ask the way from there, for it's difficult to describe. He won't see you, I've said that."

But she was already on her way.

Just before she reached the street where she'd left her car, Mercedes stubbed her toe on a rough curb and stumbled. In a typical human response, she turned to look back at the offending spot. Half a block behind her, a now-familiar shock of blue hair stood out. When he saw recognition on her face, the man's own expression registered frustration at being caught yet again. Mercedes ducked into the nearest shop and, taking the first thing she found on a rack by the door, asked, "May I try this on?"

The clerk raised her eyebrows slightly at the choice, but indicated a dressing room on the side wall. Entering quickly, Mercedes closed the door. The size XXX walking shorts she'd grabbed with the "Bournemouth Cherries" stitching on them reflected backward in the mirror.

She spent several minutes in complete silence, listening for the sound of the shop door opening. When it didn't, she peered out at the clerk, who tried not to notice her odd behavior. Calling her over Mercedes asked, "Do you have a back door?"

The clerk was doubtful. "There is, but we don't —"

"My ex-husband is on the street. He's stalking me."

She'd chosen the wrong lie, for the woman reached for the phone and squinted nearsightedly at the numbered buttons. "I'll call the police."

Fumbling for an argument, Mercedes said, "I'd rather not. There's my daughter to consider. He is her father, and I hate to get him into trouble with the law." The woman looked doubtful, but she cradled the phone against her chest and raised her brows expectantly.

"He isn't violent, only irritating, showing up wherever I am and lurking, you know? If I can go out the back, I'll go right home and call my lawyer. He'll know how to handle it." It was a terrible story, and it occurred to her belatedly that they weren't lawyers here. Was it barristers or solicitors who handled such matters as Personal Protection Orders?

The clerk stared at her for a moment then replaced the handset. "What does he look like? If he comes in I'll say you went the opposite way."

"He's very nice-looking," she ad-libbed, trying to conceal her relief. "You'd never know what a louse he is unless you'd been married to him."

The woman's face tightened. "I know the type." Opening a door marked *Staff Only,* she led Mercedes through a hallway that was a jumble of boxes, crates, and other items stacked in wild disorder, not in any condition for a visit from a fire inspector. There was a door at the end of it, however, that opened onto a quiet, oil-slicked alley where only a stray cat moved.

With a quick word of thanks to the clerk, Mercedes and the cat went in opposite directions, both furtive and hurried. By cutting through a second alley farther down, she crossed to her car without being seen from the street. Blue Hair was nothing if not persistent, and she wondered how he managed to turn up wherever she was. And what it was he wanted.

Suddenly she missed Colm, or at least the person she'd thought him to be. It wasn't that she couldn't go on alone, she told herself, it was that she'd felt so much better with him beside her. Was it Colm specifically, she wondered, or would any strong man do? Jared Graham was strong; she'd felt it in his touch. She decided it wasn't Colm she missed. It was simply the sense of security that came with companionship, with not being all alone.

***

The man to whom Drake's treasure was becoming an obsession left work with the excuse that he didn't feel well. After quickly changing clothes, he headed south to a meeting with a prospective partner. He was pleased to find the man at the small pub, waiting for him. Slipping into the bench seat opposite with a minimal greeting, he nodded to the waitress' offer of tea and ordered the lunch special without much consideration of what it was. Though the place smelled of stale beer and long-standing clouds of tobacco smoke, it was out of the way and largely uninhabited.

"Did you say you were meeting me when you left home?" he asked once the woman had plopped his tea in front of him and moved off.

"I said you had a business proposal for me. Your cousin hasn't the same interest in this affair that you have, but I find it intriguing." The eyes said more than the words did, and a mutual

165

understanding passed between the two men.

"If we pool our resources, we might all benefit. Your part will be financial, of course. We'll need historical expertise as well, but that can come later. Right now I'm tracking Miss Maxwell's progress."

"So you said on the phone. What does that mean?"

"I've got someone following her."

"I thought she'd agreed to stay in contact with you?"

"She had, but something made her change her mind."

"Kennedy?"

"Probably. I don't know why she left him behind."

"And the man you sent?"

The other looked glum as he stirred a precise half teaspoon of sugar into his tea. "Haven't heard from him today, but since you say Kennedy spoke of him, he's botched the assignment and she's aware she's been followed."

The older man puffed out his breath in frustration and absently brushed the hairs of his mustache back into place. "Where will she go if she trusts neither the police nor Kennedy?"

The waitress, who appeared to have leg pain, leaned over the counter to say their meals would be ready soon. Neither man acknowledged her. When she turned away, the policeman swirled the remains of liquid in his cup thoughtfully before replying, "Eventually, she'll end up in Kirkfort. She'll want a look at the original script."

"And will you have her arrested?"

He shook his head. "Better to let her draw Vincent out. If we step in at precisely the right moment, only we will know what it was all about."

"But you said this Vincent is likely to kill her."

He shrugged. "I'll try to get to him before that happens, but I have no control over what Vincent does."

"You'll have to kill him to keep this quiet."

The face across the table turned grim. "That will not be a problem."

***

Once Mercedes lost Blue Hair, it took the help of several townspeople to find David Cutler' timber-framed house. Well-preserved and large, the place had double balconies overhanging the ground floor and whitewashed plaster crossed in interesting patterns by dark wood. After only a moment's hesitation, she knocked smartly on the recessed double doors.

There was a rustling sound inside, then a hesitation, as though visitors were an unusual occurrence. Finally the door opened with a muted squeak to reveal an elderly woman with hands like a man's, large and work-roughened, which she wiped on an honest-to-goodness apron. Blinking into unaccustomed sunlight, she asked brusquely, "What is it?"

"I'd like to see Mr. Cutler." Mercedes spoke more confidently than she felt. "Please tell him I have information concerning Robert Cecil's work for Elizabeth Tudor. I'd like to arrange an exchange."

Something in what she said caused the woman's eyebrow to twitch, but she sniffed dismissively. Mercedes was left on the doorstep, evidently in the belief she'd soon be sent on her away. It took a long time. She considered the architecture for the first few minutes then began to wonder if she might simply have been left to conclude her visit was not welcome. Finally the door latch worked again and she turned, expecting the woman. Instead a man stood in the doorway, studying her with a disapproving glare.

He was tall and rather spare but looked fit enough for his age, which was about seventy. White hair graced his head in abundance, the color and texture so fine that few could object to such a crown. Blue eyes met hers steadily, and a strong chin met a mouth slightly down-turned, creating a daunting expression. His clothes, though well-made, qualified as vintage: a white shirt buttoned to the neck with a russet cardigan sweater over it, trousers of gray that might have been flannel, and expensive shoes of soft leather creased with age where the toes bent. Judging from his expression, he wasn't pleased to have company. Good. He was at least intrigued enough to judge her worth for himself.

"What do you know of Robert Cecil?" His tone contained no welcome, and he kept the door between them as if she were an invading Saxon.

"If you let me come in, I'll tell you," she replied, keeping her voice neither aggressive nor pleading.

"I don't take visitors."

"I don't discuss important information on doorsteps," she replied. "I know things about one of Cecil's spies that I believe will interest you. You have Cecil's papers, which I would like the chance to see or at least discuss. I'm not willing to wait or come back or stand here much longer." She folded her arms. "Your decision." Aware that it was a bit theatrical, she tapped one foot to show impatience. Colm would have been proud of that, she thought, but she reminded herself that Colm had betrayed the trust she'd placed in him. Maintaining a firm stare, Mercedes faced the man in the doorway.

She had taken the right tone. The door opened wider, and Cutler's expression showed reluctant interest. One could almost see the emotions that battled each other, curiosity versus mistrust, desire for solitude versus the need to know. His manner softened somewhat. Cutler coveted what she knew, and he apparently had no defense once someone faced down his aggressive manner. "Come in, then," he mumbled, and Mercedes, with a last cautious glance around, followed him into the house.

CHAPTER TWENTY-ONE

Cutler's house was like a museum, except everything in was it both useful and used. Chairs that had to be Queen Annes sat on either side of the entry, one with muddy boots under it suggesting a casual indifference to its antiquity.

Leading her into a small sitting room, Cutler pointed to a chair. Like the others, this room was filled with antiques so valuable that she hesitated briefly before obeying. It appeared that nothing there was less than a century old. Paintings and clocks vied for wall space while every flat surface was arrayed with objects, some identifiable to Mercedes' untrained eye, others not.

No attempt had been made to match styles or periods. Duncan Phyfe sat next to Louis XIV and Chinese vases shared space with Dresden china. It was a collector's room, in fact, a collector's house. As the docent had said, her host appreciated anything with a past. The place smelled of age and care, lemon oil, beeswax, and old, old leather.

The chair she sat on was a U-chair of Tudor design. She had a brief image of Katherine Parr or Bloody Mary sitting in this same chair and touched the wooden arm reverently. Cutler gave a curt nod of approval at her respect for his things.

A frown appeared as if he'd had a thought but couldn't grasp it. After a moment his brow cleared and he raised his voice. "Mrs. Peterson, some tea!" It was an attempt at propriety. He moved a humidor, several books on weaponry, and two rough iron shapes, rather like oversized jacks, from a table top and onto the floor with a faint thump.

"What are those?" she asked, indicating the metal stars.

"Caltrops." He took one up again and handed it to her. "Knights on horseback were the tanks of their day, and these are anti-tank weapons, so to speak. Strew them across a field and you disable the horses. Without their mounts, knights were much less imposing."

She winced at the thought of what the iron spikes, with one point always jutting upward, would do to the soft center of a horse's foot. Like modern land mines, they would lie undetected until it was too late. Shuddering, she set the caltrop aside.

Taking a seat on a leather chair that must have come from a Georgian gentleman's club, Cutler turned a gaze on her that, while not cold, couldn't be called inviting. "You say you have a story concerning a spy?"

Mercedes had decided on her approach. "Are you familiar with one of Cecil's agents known as the Player?"

The name meant something to him. He relaxed a bit, evidently satisfied he'd made a correct decision in admitting this person to his home. "Miss," he said archly, "I have studied Robert Cecil's papers for most of my life, and it is no boast to say I know as much about them as anyone living. I know the Player. The point is what can you add to my knowledge?" Eyes like icy darts focused on her, and except for the ticking of several clocks, not quite synchronized, there was silence as he waited.

Steeling herself for yet another rejection, Mercedes began. "I recently found a notebook written in the mid-1800s by an anonymous vicar in Scotland. He transcribed the diary of an outlaw who held a man named John Romeo captive until he died of starvation. I believe John Romeo was the Player."

171

Cutler was silent for a long time, searching her face for truth. She waited, sensing that he needed to absorb the information, catalog it in a brain filled with bits and pieces of information from the time. A fly buzzed in the lampshade beside her, banging its determined body over and over against the heavy paper, unable to see its way clear despite the open spaces below and above. Finally he said, "Might I see this vicar's account?"

"It was stolen." Mercedes hurried to explain, "It wasn't mine to begin with, but I became interested in the story, particularly in the Player. Do you know who he really was?"

He shook his head, his gaze falling from hers to the scuffed wooden floor. He looked stricken, as if he'd learned a good friend had died. But then, she'd already guessed that most people of significance to this man had died centuries ago.

"He was one of my favorites," he said dully. "I think Cecil liked him, too. It comes through in his letters." He rose and moved to the window, parting fine Irish lace curtains vanilla with age to stare outside, apparently seeing another century. "The Player gave them fits, coming and going as he pleased. But he always returned full measure, so they let him be."

"He began as an actor?" She tried to frame questions that brought the answers she sought while revealing little of what she'd theorized.

Cutler returned to the chair and sat down. He was silent for a time, fingering the studs in the leather, polishing them unconsciously for perhaps the thousandth time in their existence. "The Player never left the stage for good. When in London, he worked with a troupe. Sometimes they sent him out with a traveling company, which was good cover for his activities."

"I thought it might be that way."

Warming to his subject, Cutler's voice took on a livelier tone. The coldness and formality with which he had greeted her faded, and he spoke as if describing one friend to another. "The Player was a sailor too. He and Drake were great friends."

"How did he manage three careers?"

Becoming aware of the fly's buzzing he turned the lampshade, shooing it out into the room. The creature immediately flew to the window and began a similar attack on the glass, determined to tilt at windmills. Cutler turned to Mercedes with a tiny smile. "He was like a ghost, slipping in and out of character as it suited."

"There's no record of his real name?"

He shook his head a definitive no. "Cecil never wrote down the true names of his spies. There are two aliases mentioned in what remains of Cecil's papers. When the Player left on his last mission, he'd taken the name John Romeo, as you learned from this vicar's notes. As a sailor he usually called himself John Falstaff."

Now it was her turn to take a moment to absorb new information. Reaching down, she touched the caltrop's rough points again, feeling a connection to the past more real than ever before. She knew why John Romeo had wanted so much to find Drake's treasure. It was he who'd been trusted to take the *Madre de Dios* home to Elizabeth. Betrayed and thrown overboard, he'd survived somehow and returned to England. She imagined his humiliation in reporting his failure, his despair at learning Drake would never return from that final voyage. All the Player could do to avenge his mistreatment, he had done. John Romeo had gone to Scotland to set things right.

If John Falstaff and John Romeo were one person, that also explained why he began his search at Kirkfort. He'd known the mutineers and could guess where they planned to hide the gold.

He'd known better than anyone else how to locate it.

"Falstaff didn't drown when the mutineers threw him overboard?"

He was surprised, and she felt his respect for her rise a notch. He shifted in his chair, eager now that real information was being exchanged. "No, he managed to make it to a rocky island. There he waited for a passing fishing boat to rescue him. It took some time, of course. Cecil was delighted he'd survived, but he allowed the world to continue to believe Falstaff was dead. It created another blind alley for his enemies, another nameless man to do his bidding."

"So John Falstaff disappeared and John Romeo was born. I wonder how many mourned a death that never occurred."

His expression turned hard. "Cecil wasn't a kind man. For all my interest, I don't think I'd have liked him. Still, he was dedicated, as fanatics often are, and he served his queen, and later his king, well."

That brought another question. "Can you picture Cecil or Walsingham erasing the records of a man's birth so the spy had no identity at all?"

The old gentleman almost chuckled, but the action was so unusual that it came out a cough. "Cecil is known to have 'edited' documents when it pleased him. I would never doubt that either man did whatever made his way easier."

Tea was brought, the old woman looking askance at Mercedes as if amazed at this break in her employer's habit. Calling up long-neglected training he said, "Thank you Mrs. Peterson," which shifted her glance to him distrustfully. As she scuttled nervously from the room he surprised Mercedes by asking politely, "Do you take sugar and cream?"

She didn't usually but knew it was the custom, so she said, "Please," and he poured with a steady hand. She sipped the hot brew carefully, the cup's thinness evident as it touched her lips. It wasn't bad. The tea was excellent and the cream real, making a heartier drink than the plain tea she was used to. There were cookies as well, biscuits, she amended, and he offered her the plate before taking two for himself. They were still warm.

"They've told you I'm a misanthrope," he said, shaking a cookie at her, "because I refuse to blather about the weather or the state of politics in the UK. They see a miserly old man, but I see hypocrites buttering me up so they can beg money or enlist my aid for their inane causes. Easier to send them packing." He bit the cookie as if it were a persistent fund-raiser.

Despite stories where an old grouch is saved from his loneliness by a kind-hearted child or a daffy female, some people are actually happier by themselves, Mercedes believed. They simply have no patience for social conventions. Grinning impishly she asked, "Why haven't you sent me packing?"

He looked down his nose at her for a moment, but in the end answered truthfully. "For one, you stood up for yourself. For another, I believe your vicar."

She nodded. "I did too, almost from the start. He's too forthright to be lying. He never published his work, so he wasn't out for glory. He was genuinely interested in the account, and," Here she set her hands on the arms of her chair, "I think he was successful in solving the mystery of the prisoner's identity."

"So you know who John the Player was?"

She wasn't ready to share that information. "I have no evidence, only the vicar's theory."

"Might I hear it?"

Mercedes shook her head regretfully. She'd won this man over with part of the story, but she feared dragging Shakespeare's name into it would cause those blue eyes to go cold again. "I haven't had much luck telling it. I'm either dismissed or taken advantage of, and I'm sick of both. If you don't mind, I'll keep it to myself."

He did mind, wasn't used to being refused anything he wanted. One long index finger tapped the leather chair arm petulantly for a few seconds, but he merely said, "I hope you'll tell me when you feel ready. John is quite a favorite of mine."

"A man mentioned a few times in obscure notes from centuries ago?" She couldn't help the incredulous tone in her voice.

He smiled tightly. "Some people read novels and fall in love with the characters, but how much more interesting is history!" Setting the bone china cup down with a careless clink, he leaned forward, his manner almost comically earnest, the white brows lowered in an intense gaze. "What was it like to converse with Elizabeth Tudor? Did Robert Dudley murder his wife so he could wed the queen, only to learn she'd marry no man? Was Robert Cecil truly as crooked inside as he was out, was his hunched back a symbol of his evil soul?" He rose and paced the room, kneading hands knotted with age. "These questions are better than any mystery novel, because no neat answer is provided at the end by an omnipotent author. We have only tiny clues that lead one way and then another."

"Yes," she agreed, setting her own cup aside more gently, "there are plenty of mysteries in the past."

Cutler looked out from under bushy white eyebrows. "Like the mystery of the Mary Matter?"

She should have guessed. "You know why John Romeo went

176

to Scotland."

He made an impatient gesture. "That's easy, though why anyone would go there voluntarily is beyond me. The harder question is did he find what he was looking for."

She was honest. "I believe he did. He tried to send a message back to England, but it never got there."

"And your vicar discovered this message?"

Mercedes felt her resolve fading. She longed to trust someone, but everyone she'd told so far had let her down. Should she relate the story once more to this eccentric man who fairly burned for information about John Romeo? Surely he cared, and he didn't seem like the type who'd lust after treasure. But neither had Colm Kennedy, at first.

Cutler watched the struggle on her face as she tried to hold to her intended silence, and he added a final argument in a gentle voice. "Young woman, I'm an old man with no time for delay. My interest, my whole life's interest, has been learning everything I can about the past: why history unfolded as it did, what quirks of personality and fortune caused plans to succeed or go awry, what small fact ignored for years can put a new face on an old story."

Sitting once more, his hands resting on his bony knees, Cutler spoke earnestly. "I have no desire to cheat you. I will disbelieve you if the evidence is weak, but the fact that you've been through some distress is obvious in your manner. If I have all the facts, I might be able to relieve your mind, either confirming what you fear or explaining your fears away. All I ask is the chance to know what you know." His expression turned comic. "If it's of no use to me, I promise to forget it right after showing you my front door."

Well, that was putting things as truthfully as possible. Sighing, she settled her elbows on the arms of her chair. "Maybe you'd better pour us each a second cup of tea," she said, indicating the cozied pot on the small table between them. He complied, and as they sipped the hot brew she told the rest of the prisoner's story: the *Macbeth* script, the marginal note, and the pin pricks under certain letters.

The old man's interest was intense, and his eyes rested unswervingly on her face until she finished. "May I see the letters that were marked?" he asked when she was done.

"I've made a copy." She took the folded sheet from her pocket and handed it to him. The old man looked at the paper for some time, frowning and trying different angles.

"It's some sort of code."

"Yes. I suppose Cecil would have been able to read it, but we have no way of knowing their methods."

He grunted in disgust. "What do you mean, no way of knowing? I've studied the man and how he operated." He tapped the paper confidently. "Given time, I'll decipher it."

"I have very little time. There are others who want the treasure, and they know I have the clue. I'm in danger until this matter is resolved."

He frowned, his face unreadable. Would he send her away, fearing she'd put him in danger as well?

"Does anyone know you've come here?"

"I don't think so."

He thought for a moment. "Move your car into my garage. There's plenty of room."

"But what will that do?"

178

"You will stay here until I've broken the code." As he said it, it seemed to dawn on the old gentleman he'd just asked a woman to sleep over at his house. He flushed slightly, blinking rapidly and looking at some point beyond her on the wall. "I'm sure Mrs. Peterson will stay over and do for you. She is very reasonable, for a woman."

Mercedes didn't bother to tell him that no one much cared if a woman "stayed over" at a man's home these days. It was charming of him to be concerned for her reputation. "If it won't be too much trouble," she told her host, "I appreciate your invitation very much."

CHAPTER TWENTY-TWO

Mercedes spent the night in an upstairs room that smelled faintly musty but boasted an amazing array of Victorian furniture melded with Middle Eastern brass, Italian wall hangings, and even an Edwardian commode, which she was relieved to learn she was not expected to use. She slept soundly, feeling completely safe for the first time in days. Only her host and the dour Mrs. Peterson knew her location, and neither seemed likely to gossip over the back fence. From his reputation, no one would guess David Cutler would become her ally. Mrs. Peterson hardly knew how to act.

Morning shone brightly through the mullioned windows, and she found herself with the early riser's conundrum: what time might her host expect to see his guest? At seven she went softly down the stairs and was glad to encounter the aroma of coffee and bacon. Cutler was almost exactly where she'd left him the night before, though he was clean-shaven and crisply dressed in similar but fresh clothing. He must have rested a little, but Mrs. Peterson looked tight-lipped with disapproval at his determined pose.

"I've failed," he said as he reluctantly moved with her to the breakfast table. "There's no sense to it, no matter what I try." As they ate, he explained the code-breaking methods he'd tried.

"Cryptography is a very old technique with its own rules. For example, when the name of a place or person must be repeated in a message, it would always be misspelled." Cutler had brought his work to the table, and he regarded it as he spoke, unwilling to admit defeat. "Cryptanalysis does not depend upon comparing styles, or vocabulary counts, or literary opinions. The "probable word" attack is most useful in breaking a mono-alphabetic cipher, which I believed this to be. A cryptanalyst, suspecting the word *Scotland* might appear in the text, can use that as a useful tool to solve a cipher."

"I see," she commented. "You find all the words with the same formation and number of letters and you've got eight letters solved."

He nodded, buttering a scone and tucking into a plate of fluffy scrambled eggs. "Of course, misspelling of this word in as many ways as possible is done by the writer in order to attempt to defeat a solution. I tried all the probable words I could imagine, with no success."

"I assume you tried treasure and ship," she began, but a look from Cutler said she shouldn't consider him a fool. He helped himself to a second slice of bacon. Remembering Colm's disgust for Americans' fussiness about diet, Mercedes took a second one herself.

"Some ciphers of the day were steganographic, designed to be concealed. One artifice was to hide the significant letters in the capital letters of a verse or text. This type of cipher is called acrostic, popular with the Tudors. It might be complicated even more by substitution. We have no capitals here, though there might be capitals in the script itself. I hope your vicar was clever enough to transpose them as they appear."

"I'd guess he wrote down exactly what he saw."

"Quite right. I tried several substitution ciphers, very simple devices. Substitute the letter *B* for the letter *A,* substitute *C* for *B, D* for *C* and so on. That may be complicated by a key in which the alphabet is reversed, scrambled, or altered in some other way, or the substitution would be more extreme, such as *G* for *A, H* for *B, I* for *C*, et cetera."

181

"How does one solve something like that?"

"Hard work," he growled, "but even that didn't succeed. I've tried everything and revealed not one word." He'd filled page after page of notes filled with crosses, half-begun gambits, and scribbles of frustration.

Mercedes set her plate aside, satisfied with the food but dejected by the news. She'd hoped he might pull it off, and he'd done as much as anyone could. "What do I do now?"

The old man rose from his chair, helping himself to a second plate of eggs and coffee from the sideboard. "The answer must be something in the original script, something that can only be discerned by seeing what John did to it. The script was all he had to work with, and he wanted to pass his secret only to certain people. I'd say there is something we will see when we look at the script itself."

"We?"

"You know nothing of codes." He gave her a sidelong glance and added, "And I plan to be nearby in case you decide to tell me who John the Player really was."

The next half hour was spent trying to convince David, as he insisted she now call him, that it was too dangerous for him to accompany her to Kirkfort. In the end she told him about the murders, about being wanted by the police, and about escaping Colm Kennedy. "I don't even know if that's his real name," she concluded.

David looked at her in amazement. "Chased by madmen and the police, you've traversed England and even godforsaken Scotland interviewing experts to put together the pieces of a centuries-old puzzle?" He shook his head. "You've done well, but now you need help."

"David —"

He raised a hand, his craggy face a scowl. "I might look like a useless old man, but I know how to conduct myself. You won't be sorry I came along, and if you're going back to that lawless place, you'll need a champion."

Though she feared Cutler held some medieval image of Scotland gleaned from his study of history, something in his demeanor convinced her he wouldn't be put off. She couldn't find it in her heart to argue he'd be a liability, and she thought she was a step ahead of her pursuers at this point. "All right, then," she said with a sigh of defeat. "We should leave as soon as possible. Once they discover I haven't gone to London, there'll be only Kirkfort left."

***

"I cannot believe he let her get away again!" the caller almost shouted into the phone. "Couldn't you hire someone with a touch of competence?"

"I didn't exactly have my choice of private investigators," the other answered. "Did you do any better when you had her right under your nose? She was on foot. Surely you could have done as he did and tracked her to the nearest car rental."

"Where has she gone?"

"She's at Salisbury, for some reason, but my guess is she'll go to London, try to lose herself in the city."

"But if she wants the treasure—"

"She might want it, but there's not much chance of her getting at it alone, is there?"

"Right," the other agreed. "She has no help, she's in a strange country, and she's afraid to go to the police. When she sees a familiar face, she'll fall into your arms despite any suspicions she might have, believe whatever story you tell. But you must find her, while she's still alone and vulnerable."

***

Vincent waited outside the fine house he had discovered was the home of Aletha Ballert. Two people had been inside when he arrived, an older man and a thirty-ish woman of stunning beauty. Vincent waited for a chance to catch her alone. There was no sign of Mercedes or Colm Kennedy, but he was hours behind them now. If they'd been here, they had gone on. He had to know where.

For an hour he watched bits of activity, like disconnected scenes from a play. Aletha and the man breakfasted on the terrace. Afterward, she went upstairs and disappeared from view while the man spoke on the phone, pacing nervously from one window to the next. He hung up just as she returned, her hair wrapped in a pale blue towel. After they spoke briefly, the man gathered up a coat and briefcase. Vincent smiled. Things were working out nicely.

The man got into an elegant sedan and left, his distinguished face concentrated on steering cautiously up the drive to minimize the dirt and gravel raised. When the sound of the car's engine had faded away and the only thing he could hear was the rustle of the breeze in the irises around him, Vincent started for the house.

He was almost to the side door when a noise behind him caused a backward glance up the drive. A delivery van had crested the hill, coming toward him. On the side was lettering: *Glenna's Carpets and Decorating.* One of the van's back doors hung open, and a roll of carpeting with a bright rag attached to the end stuck out a few feet from it. Inside were two strapping young men, sleeves already rolled up in anticipation of heavy physical labor.

The professor was having new carpeting installed. Vincent

184

faded into the bushes again, despondent. There would be no way to get to her today, and he couldn't afford to wait until evening. He'd have to guess where Mercedes Maxwell was going. She'd been bound for London, but if the lovely professor had been able to provide the information she sought, she might be headed north again—to Kirkfort.

***

After a two-hour nap, David insisted he was totally reinvigorated. "Old people are like that, my dear," he assured Mercedes. "Catnaps are much better than the recommended eight hours' sleep of the first five decades." Leaving the rental car in David's garage, they took his vehicle, which was, naturally, not new. It was a Rolls, a 1985 Silver Spirit with elegant styling and a pristine look both inside and out. Only 1152 of them had been made, he told her proudly. Mercedes stroked its immaculate fender admiringly. "It's almost a shame to take it out of the garage," she remarked. That obviously didn't happen often.

The drive to Scotland was uneventful. David was not one for idle conversation, and she was content to simply watch the countryside pass by. He took less-traveled roads, driving with relaxed confidence, not fast but efficiently. England ended and Scotland began, but castles, churches, fields of cattle, and stone fences repeated over and over. Countless sheep, their wool spray-painted with bright fluorescent colors to identify their owners, rested on the hills, in the valleys, and sometimes on the verge of the roadway itself. It was peaceful, and though she didn't sleep, Mercedes felt relaxed, in a sort of limbo that couldn't last but served to prepare her for events to come.

Only as they passed a particular landmark did he break silence. "Castle Caerlaverock is down that way." He indicated a south road. "Built in the 13th century by the Maxwells."

She'd told him her real name along with the rest of it, and she grinned at his reference. "Perhaps they'll give me a free night's stay on the way back."

David grunted negatively. "They are Scots, after all."

Kirkfort looked like a movie set. After they turned off the main highway, a rope of a road wound for some distance down a forested slope to the Firth, the last curve revealing the town nestled on its banks. The land formed a small bay that sheltered the village from rough seas, and the harbor was crowded with private sailing vessels of all sizes. The town itself was small but attractive. Quaint and immaculately kept, several tastefully designed public structures signified refined prosperity.

"The place is a jewel," Mercedes said in surprise as they parked the car and strolled around to get a feel for the place. The air had a dichotomous tang of both cleanness and fishiness common to seashores. A large building set against the hillside loomed over the bay at the end of the village. "That must be the hospital they built on the site of Willie's fortress."

David nodded. "The location is perfect for defense." Two modern wings had been added to the hospital's older central structure, but the architect had artfully blended the old with the new. "The town must get tourist trade from pleasure sailors," he observed, nodding toward the snug little harbor. "It's too far off the beaten track to be visited much by car or coach."

They had little trouble locating the Kirkfort Historical Museum, housed in a small stone building that was the former church. Standing next to it was the larger present church, also of stone. As they approached the museum entrance, Mercedes noted the cornerstone of the newer church, dated 1885, and smiled to herself. The town's "new" church was older than most buildings in America.

Inside the museum, everything seemed a size smaller than reality. An ancient lady barely five feet tall cheerfully explained the place's points of pride, ending with a request for a donation if, at the conclusion of their visit, they felt it was warranted. Tiny display tables around the outside of the room offered views of Kirkfort's past: artifacts, documents, and photos of what used to be. Their footsteps echoed on the stone floor as they made a cursory circle of the place, taking stock.

Since the museum was one open room, they easily located what they'd come for. As they'd hoped, the script was laid out page by page in a long, glass-topped display case. The enclosure had been conceived by experts, the rules of preservation meticulously followed.

David stood beside her as they read the display note. *An early handwritten copy of Shakespeare's* Macbeth, *probably an actor's script, found in Kirkfort. It is unknown how this interesting piece arrived in Scotland. The most plausible explanation is that it was left behind by a traveling troupe and preserved by a local chieftain who admired the work.*

The two slowly made their way along the entire layout in an initial scan, noting surface features. A series of clicks behind them signaled the lady at the entrance had taken up her knitting and was busily at work on the baby afghan Mercedes had noticed in a tote bag behind the desk.

A second placard at the end of the case stated the script had been donated in 1870 by Malcolm Seylor, vicar at the time. "Two years after he began his notebook," she murmured to David, who nodded thoughtfully.

"Wanted time to study it before giving it up."

The script had been well cared-for in the last century or so, but earlier abuses were obvious. The pages had been rolled at some times and folded flat at others. They were a dull brown, edges brittle and broken. Water spots here and there had faded the writing, and other areas were greased-stained and finger-marked. Willie Reid's personal habits had not been stellar.

Still, it was exciting. Most of the writing was readable if they used the magnifiers they'd brought along. Mercedes was thrilled at the tiny pinpricks under certain letters. This was what had been missing: John Romeo's original document.

After a few minutes, David spoke to the woman at the door briefly and returned to his car. He came back with two yellow legal pads and two ballpoint pens. "I've told her we want to study the script for variations from other published versions, so we'll be here for a while," he murmured in Mercedes' ear. "Oddly enough, she says another gentleman was here only a week or so ago, doing the same thing. They don't have that many outside visitors, so she remembers him."

Mercedes shuddered, but she consoled herself with the hope that if he'd been here once, the killer would not return. Shaking off her dread, she turned to the task at hand, taking one of the pads and a pen from David. They began at opposite ends, searching slowly and carefully for something. They didn't know what.

An hour later she straightened and broke her concentrated focus on the script, her spine stiff from bending at such an odd angle. The woman at the doorway looked up and smiled, her needles flashing as if by themselves. Mercedes could see nothing in the manuscript that the vicar had missed. Each marked letter had been carefully recorded in his little book.

Laying the pad on the counter, she walked around the room to give herself a break. David appeared not to notice, and he seemed unfazed by physical discomfort. Rubbing her back, Mercedes tiptoed to the other side of the room, careful to make no noise that would break his concentration.

On the walls documents chronicled Kirkfort's history. The story of Kirkfort Willie was there, romanticized somewhat but with the same factual information Professor Rankin had found. There was no indication of Willie having written a journal. The vicar must have kept that part to himself. There was no mention of his starving Shakespeare's twin brother to death either.

The other item of interest was a pamphlet on Kirkfort in the 1800s. The area had been economically depressed, like much of Scotland in those days, and many young people left for better lives in America. Toward the latter part of the century things turned around, mostly due to a Kirkfort emigrant who'd made good.

In 1872, after becoming a millionaire in Ontario, Canada, Lanford Maxwell endowed his home town of Kirkfort with funds to improve the welfare of its citizens. As a result, the harbor was dredged and improved, a hospital was erected, and the shipyard was greatly expanded, creating desirable jobs.

From that point onward, things improved for Kirkfort. Maxwell left further monies in his will which were to be invested and the interest drawn upon as needed. The management of the Maxwell Trust fell to the vicar of the local Presbyterian Church and continues to the present day.

It was good to see that a local man (and a possible ancestor of hers as well) had done so much for his birthplace. The fact the vicar had been trusted to administer the money said something for his honesty, if he was in fact the same vicar who'd written the notebook. His increased responsibilities might explain, too, why he'd been unable to keep up his search for Drake's treasure.

Mercedes approached the attendant, who politely put down her knitting to give her full attention. She evoked an image of one of the aunts from Disney's *Sleeping Beauty*, all goodness and pumpkin muffins. "Kirkfort's history is very interesting," she began. "Do I understand that the vicar still manages the Maxwell Trust?"

"I suppose it's odd," the woman replied, "but we're used to it here. We're small, and there's no room for expansion with the hills all around us, so we operate rather as a large family. The vicar has the final say, but he listens to the wishes of the rest of us."

"Could I meet the vicar, do you think?"

"I don't see why not. He's probably across the way, at the church." She gave Mercedes a knowing look. "But I must warn that if you're looking for financial support, the Maxwell funds cannot be spent outside Kirkfort. That's the way the trust is written."

CHAPTER TWENTY-THREE

When Mercedes told David she was leaving for a few minutes, he merely grunted assent. She walked across the green lawn, taking in the simple beauty of the "new" Kirkfort Church. Neither overly large nor very dramatic, it was instead simple and beautiful.

Inside she found the hushed atmosphere common to old churches. The sanctuary was cool and deep, its sides fitted with tall stained-glass panels that Mercedes believed should be the only type of windows in a church. The pulpit was raised and bannistered, the altar behind it dark, solid wood, reverent enough to please even dour John Knox.

Finding a hallway off the side of the sanctuary, she followed it to several practical rooms that evinced the work of children at Sunday school, the storage of ceremonial items necessary for services, and finally a small office where a man sat working at a computer.

The vicar, dressed in jeans and a sweatshirt, looked up in surprise as she peeped in the doorway. "Hello," he said with a tentative smile. He was probably forty but had the youthful demeanor many clergymen have until they suddenly acquire the look of Biblical prophets. Dark brown hair lay straight across his forehead and soft brown eyes looked out from gold-rimmed glasses. It was a face to trust, to assure the dying, and later those they'd left behind, that life and death are parts of a whole not to be understood, merely to be accepted.

"Are you the vicar?"

"Alfred Soames." He rose and offered a hand. A firm grip,

again inspiring trust.

She didn't know how to begin. "I'm an American." He'd probably figured that out already, so she tried again. "I'm interested in the history of your village."

He frowned quizzically. "We have a very nice museum next door. You might have passed it coming in."

"I've been there. That's why I wanted to see you."

The man took off his glasses and said politely, "Perhaps you'd like to sit down."

She did, and when she was comfortable (he had to move some books on religion to provide a chair), he waited.

"I recently saw a notebook supposedly kept by the vicar at Kirkfort. It was from the 1860s. I'd like to know who he was, and if what he wrote in the book is factual. It has—I think it has—historical significance."

The vicar smiled. Behind him a picture of the church taken from the air hung just a hair crooked. She forced herself to ignore the urge to straighten it and listen to what he said. "I can guess who might have written something like that: Malcolm Seylor, my great-great-great-uncle." Soames stopped and counted good-humoredly on his fingers. "There may be one more great in there somewhere. Anyway, he's one of the family."

"You're a family of vicars?"

"Things here aren't like in America," Seylor told her. "Many people still follow family professions, and they often stay where they were born, or in my case, return there. I was educated at university, but I always knew I'd come back here and become vicar." He grinned. "The church hierarchy doesn't approve, but that's how the people want things. The Kirkfort Trust money is controlled by the vicar, and they insist he be one of their own."

Glad he'd brought up the subject of money, she said, "I understand there was a bequest to the town?"

"Yes. One of the local lads became wealthy and wanted his village to benefit. The money is available for public works, provided the vicar and the town council agree."

"And the vicar I'm thinking of was your ancestor?"

"Technically, almost all of them are," Soames said with a grin. "But old Malcolm was a bit of a standout. Quite the scholar, I've been told, and very civic minded. It was he who built this church, at least he planned and oversaw the project. When the money was offered, he saw a chance to make this tiny area special. Before he died, plans were in the works for all kinds of projects. We're luckier than most, of course. Vicars don't usually have a benefactor as generous as Lanford Maxwell."

"I'd say not," she agreed. "What do you know about him?"

The vicar idly twirled an ink pen through thin fingers. "Made his fortune in railways, I think. A rags-to-riches story: he left Kirkfort with hardly a penny and twenty years later was the richest man in Ontario."

"And Malcolm Seylor knew him?"

"Yes. During his lifetime, Maxwell insisted he remain anonymous, working through the church. It was only when Malcolm died that the benefactor's name was revealed. Of course the Maxwells are well known in this area." The vicar smiled ruefully. "Lanford's bequest was a great boon, but it also requires a great deal from the vicar in addition to his expected duties."

So the bequest did explain Seylor's failure to keep up his

notebook. He'd come into a responsibility far greater than treasure-hunting, and he'd had to put the quest aside for the good of his community. Had he longed at times to return to his pursuit of John the Player and the message he'd left behind?

She rose to leave. "I won't take more of your time. I only wanted to satisfy myself that Malcolm Seylor oversaw the demolition of the original Kirkfort."

The vicar rose politely and saw her to the door. "Oh, yes. That was his other coup, rescuing the *Macbeth* script from destruction. Evidently the workmen were going to burn it."

"That would have been a great loss." Thanking Soames for his time, she retraced her steps, noting the coolness of the church's interior, the lingering odor of floor wax, and a faint smell of magic markers emanating from the children's room.

When she returned to the museum, David still pored over the script. Mercedes had yet another idea. Indicating two computers in a corner of the museum she asked the patient woman at the entry, "Are those internet-connected?"

"Oh, yes. People come here wanting to trace their ancestry, and we connect them with a databank that can help. Would you like to try it?"

Mercedes was soon seated at a terminal where she was given simple instructions and left alone. She typed in *Maxwell* and got a huge list of names and related information. Under "New Search" she typed in *Lanford Maxwell*. In seconds the screen informed her there was no listing for that name. Reading further, she found that for a small fee she could have an exhaustive search performed of all records extant for Lanford Maxwell in Scotland. She approached David.

"Do you have a credit card?"

"What?" He was grumpy at another interruption.

"A credit card. I need to pay for something online and I don't want to use mine."

Without argument he handed her his card and returned to the pages of script. *Trusting man for a misanthrope,* she thought with a smile.

Returning to the computer, she gave the required information and received the message: "Your request will be processed as soon as possible and emailed to the address you provide below within twenty-four hours."

Twenty-four hours! Approaching the entry once more, she explained her problem. The obliging woman provided an email address and promised to print the message off when it arrived. Mercedes made a generous contribution to the small wooden box in gratitude.

She'd begun to wonder how much David would suffer for his persistent attempts to decode the script's clues. After all, he'd spent all last night poring over the list of letters, and now he'd spent hours bent over the glass case. Tapping him gently on the shoulder, she said, "Let's stop for today. We can come back later if you think it's warranted—"

She paused at the look he gave her: half-triumph, half-awe. "I've got it." All thought of leaving flew from her mind. "The clue is in the line written along the edge." He kept his voice low but couldn't conceal his excitement.

"'Something wicked this way comes?'"

"No, the first part. 'By the pricking of my thumbs.' Look here." He indicated the script. "Look at the second page, about three lines down." It was frustrating not to be able to touch the pages themselves. "See the letter *s* in the third line? It has a pinhole under it."

"Yes, so does an *f* before it and a *p* and an *r* after."

"But look at the pinhole under the *s*. How is it different from the others?"

"It's browner than the rest of the page, like the pin was stained when it went through." She stopped in amazement. "You've got to be joking."

David grinned like a ten-year-old. "'The pricking of my thumbs.'"

"John pricked out a message with holes, and he marked them with his own blood. Afterward he pricked lots more holes to hide the message. Only the bloody ones matter!" David put his hands on her shoulders, indicating the woman busily knitting at the entry.

"I'll start at the center. You start at the beginning," he ordered. "Write down only the letters that clearly show stains. We may have some accidental ones and we may miss a few, but I'm guessing we'll have something to work with when we leave here."

It took a long time. She tried not to let herself think about the words that formed under her pen: *south, thane,* and so on. She simply wrote what was there, putting parentheses around letters that seemed doubtful so they could discuss the results together later. David did the same. In the end they added his first three letters to her last two to form the final word, *blood.* She shivered. There had certainly been blood spilled over this puzzle. She hoped it wasn't an omen.

CHAPTER TWENTY-FOUR

Along Kirkfort Bay Mercedes and David found several attractive B&B's. They chose a cottage tucked almost into the hillside and so overgrown with plants and gnarled tree roots that it called to mind Middle Earth. The owner, Mr. MacPhearson, was rather Hobbit-like as well, fussy and kind at once. Like Bilbo Baggins, he showed no sign of wife or other female companionship, doing for himself and his guests with efficient politeness.

After settling in rooms clean and comfortably furnished, they walked to a nearby pub with a lovely side garden and ordered a meal that served as both lunch and dinner. With the cry of sea birds above and the sweet fragrance of feverfew all around, they studied their findings.

David placed the completed sheets between them so they both could see. His printing was bold, the letters leaning neither right nor left. Her own was almost scrawled, as was her tendency when she concentrated on the message and not the means. Mercedes read: *south from the lest of duncan(s) thanes wit(c)h three batt(l)e (m)ending the primros way the(n)fo(e)ol's way a(n) painted dev(v)il the secrets(t) man of blood(d)*

"At least we have words." She tried to sound hopeful.

David scowled at the paper. "I'll have to start over with code-breaking. It's a cipher within a cipher."

Taking a fresh sheet, she transferred the two halves of the message onto it, making a neat copy with several blank lines between each line of letters. Then she methodically tore the originals into tiny pieces and sifted them into a trash bin concealed behind a lattice frame at the corner of the building. While she did, David stared at the newly copied sheet.

"The mistakes could be his spelling, our transcription, or both," he observed when she was seated again. A particularly bold gull landed near his feet and bob-walked toward a crumb of food dropped in the grass, its tiny eyes shiny-black. David shooed the bird away with an irritable gesture. "Cheeky devils." The comment returned his attention to the page before him. "Devil doesn't need two *v*'s. The doubtful *c* makes the word witch, but it makes little sense either way."

Mercedes sat very still for a moment, teetering on the brink of a decision. "What if the words were meant for someone familiar with the play," she said finally, meeting his eyes directly, "not necessarily a code breaker?"

"What do you mean?"

It was time to tell her new friend the last part of her secret. With a nervous glance at the empty chairs in the tiny garden, she went on, "I believe John Romeo, the Player, was William Shakespeare's twin brother John."

The rugged face froze, and she hurried to explain before David dismissed her as a lunatic. "My theory is the two of them were close all their lives, even though one was a writer and the other a spy. The message might be intended for Will, not Robert Cecil, to decipher. John couldn't send a message to the Crown, but he hoped Kirkfort Willie might grant his last wish and return the script to a supposed friend. It was the best chance he had to relay his information and lead the English to the treasure."

David said nothing, but he listened with an intensity that was encouraging. She ran her fingers lightly over the sheet of yellow paper lying between them. "If all that is true, he would have used Will's knowledge of the play to create the clues, things that would mean something to his brother. That's what this looks like to me, with words like *witch* and *thane* included."

David continued to stare at her for some time after she lapsed into silence, and a now-familiar dread formed. Would he inform her about tourist hoaxes, as Callard had, or explain away her conclusions, as had Professor Rankin? She waited as the information penetrated, saw faint changes in David's patrician features as he absorbed the information. She heard voices inside the pub, friends greeting friends on a family evening out. He was quiet for a long time. Finally he croaked, "John Shakespeare?"

She took it as belief and rushed to cement his agreement. "I can't prove it. Still, it makes sense to me that Shakespeare, a genius who wrote wonderful plays, had a close acquaintance with someone who longed for adventure and couldn't abide the day-to-day life most people led. John was the inspiration, but Will had dedication, and that's what brought fame in the end. Poor John died in Scotland, and Will probably never knew where or why."

"No, he didn't," David said thoughtfully, and she looked at him quizzically. "I mean, he wouldn't have, would he?" He rose, scaring off the gull that had surreptitiously returned to get the bit of bread denied it earlier. It took off with the bit in its beak, victorious despite the human. He looked down the shore at the town arced around the peaceful bay. "This is rather a lot to take in at once. Shall we walk on the strand and allow it to percolate for a while?"

Just then the woman from the museum appeared in the pub's rear entrance. She'd put on a colorful silk scarf to protect her tightly curled hair from any possible breeze, and she carried her tote bag with yellow plastic flowers woven into the side. An umbrella rested in a specially designed quiver at one end of the bag.

"There you are," she called. "Your information came just at closing, and I thought I might catch you here."

"Thank you so much." Mercedes rose to meet her. "It was good of you to bring it."

"There isn't much," the woman said apologetically, her face pink with pleasure at providing assistance. She handed over a folded sheet of paper and left by a low gate at the far end of the garden, clicking it shut behind her with a cheery wave.

David watched her expression as she scanned the sheet. "What is it?"

"They couldn't find a Lanford Maxwell on any list of emigrants to Canada. It says that's not unusual for the time. However, older records show a sailor by that name left with Drake on his last voyage to the New World. He isn't listed as ever having returned."

David raised a bushy eyebrow. "Let me guess. Lanford Maxwell was from Kirkfort."

"County Galloway is as definite as it gets."

Shaking his head, he marveled, "It's coming together, my dear. Your spy is real, and we know how he knew where to look. John heard Maxwell and his mates plotting where they'd hide the treasure."

"If Lanford Maxwell was one of the mutineers, and if he was from Kirkfort, John might have tracked down someone who knew about the treasure."

He frowned. "But if someone here knew where the treasure was, why didn't he or she take it?"

"Maybe he did, and all the searching over four hundred years has been for nothing."

David's lips twitched with humor. "Do we give up and go home, then?"

With an answering grin Mercedes said, "No. We take that walk you proposed a few moments ago, and then we go back to work."

Folding the sheet of clues carefully, David put it into his jacket pocket. Going inside, he paid their tab then returned to meet her at the side gate, which opened onto a beach pathway. Somewhat rocky, the path paralleled the water, offering a breathtaking view. Cliffs rose on both sides of the village, cradling it against the sea and smoothing the rough waves of the Firth to gentle slaps as they hit the beach. The pub was the last structure on the western end of the bay, its back resting against the steep hill. The short expanse of sand that stretched before them was protected from the breeze, warm from the afternoon sun. The entire village lay to their right, and their vantage point was slightly above it, so they could pick out the museum at some distance as well as their inn, much closer.

Taking in the panorama, Mercedes was struck again by the town's post-card perfection. The marina below them was almost full with every kind of ship from single-masted twenty-footers to larger ones that fairly bristled with a perplexing array of masts and antennae. The water was a cool green close in, growing darker as distance and depth changed its aspect. She remembered from her reading at the museum that the harbor had been dredged, an improvement provided by wise consensus among the villagers.

Along the shore neat buildings and houses clustered in the small space available for habitation while a few structures farther out clung to tiny plateaus in the craggy hillside. The lack of room for expansion had probably been Kirkfort's good luck. Ships could visit, and tourists could pour money into the economy, but there could be no multi-family dwellings erected here and no sprawl of development. Kirkfort provided no place for visitors to stay beyond their welcome.

By tacit consent Mercedes and David turned away from the village and took the path eastward, along the beach and up the slope still further. David was silent, but she'd become used to that. She enjoyed his company despite his stiff manner and outward gruffness. There was a stalwartness to him that inspired confidence. Mercedes felt more and more confident they'd solve John Shakespeare's last riddle together.

The coastline rose before them, a rounded outcropping of rock screening their view. Mercedes hurried ahead, anxious to see what lay beyond, but David noticed a comfortable niche just under the crest. Facing the village, it looked like it had been carved in the rock to provide a perfect place for rumination. He ran a hand over the smooth rock, dusting it lightly, and sat down. "Go on, explore," he told her gruffly. "I'll wait here and look at the same water you'll see on the other side."

The jutting rock before her was a bit of a climb but not dangerous, and she only used her hands twice to accomplish the steep ascent. The rock dipped then rose again, so that she had to climb a second slope to actually see the view to the east.

Of course it was much the same: the Firth with rays of sunlight bouncing in all directions off its waters, a grove of dense bush— was that gorse? —that looked too thick to navigate in street clothes, and a track that led north, up the hill and into scrubby pines clinging stubbornly to the nearly vertical grade. The place smelled of pitch and salty earth. The only sound was the waves, much more fierce as they ended their journey on adamant stone.

Slowly surveying the panoramic view, Mercedes ending up facing the spot where David sat, out of sight. A sudden feeling of isolation caused a shudder, but she shook it off, knowing she was only steps away from him and the path to the village. He'd seemed lost in thought, more so than usual, and she knew he was wrestling with the idea of Shakespeare's twin. It was difficult to accept, and she was willing to give him time to get used to it.

Out of curiosity she went a short way up the northward slope, but there wasn't much to see except pine trees and rocks. In the end she turned back and headed toward the main path, intending to return to where she'd left David. As she passed a large pine, something struck the side of her head, making the world spin wildly. Mercedes fell to the ground, darkness closing in on her like curtains on a stage. The last thing she saw was several blades of coarse grass, standing close to her eyes and blocking everything else out like a dense rainforest.

***

She awoke in a panic, unable to breathe normally. Something covered her mouth. She opened her eyes to darkness, complete except for a slit of light near eye level. She lay on a packed-dirt floor and felt its cold roughness with her hands. Her head hurt when she rolled over, but she couldn't touch the knot because her hands were taped to her sides. Her feet were taped together as well, she discovered as she tried to move them. At first she could make no sense of it, but after a few seconds her mind cleared somewhat, allowing rational thought. The blow that knocked her unconscious, perhaps cushioned by her hair, had caused no serious damage.

She recalled taking a path up the slope and remembered turning back to rejoin David. Could it have been he who hit her? The thought came and went quickly. If he'd wanted to hurt her, David could have done so at any time in the last day or so. More likely he was looking for her right now. Mercedes said a prayer that he was safe.

There was little doubt the man who'd murdered Mrs. Flowers

and the others had captured her. The only reason she wasn't dead was because he wanted to know what she knew. The page was safely hidden at the B&B. David had their notes, but she didn't dare let the madman know that or he'd surely kill the old man. What would he do to make her tell? The darkness of her earthen prison seemed to grow even darker, and the odor of dank earth smelled like death. Remembering the victims before her, Mercedes had never been so afraid in her life.

She tried to find some small ray of hope. Surely they were looking for her by now. David would have gotten help. If she could make noise, they might find her before her captor returned. A sound nearby interrupted her thought. It was the scrape of branches being pushed aside. A slight rumble followed, and suddenly a rectangle of dim light opened above her, a figure blocking out its center. "Hello, Mercedes. I'm so glad we have finally met."

The man who stood over her was tall, with a muscular frame that called to mind the alley outside Glasgow where she'd been attacked. He was strong, she remembered, with a grip like steel. Stepping toward her, he lowered himself into the shallow pit and closed the opening carefully, shutting the two of them inside. Kneeling beside her, he switched on a flashlight, illuminating his features in an eerie glow that made him seem otherworldly.

He was dressed for hiking in sturdy boots and khaki pants with a greenish windbreaker that would easily blend into the trees. He looked at her over a nose that precisely defined *aquiline*. The eyes under dark brows were equally dark, fitting well the rest of the strong facial structure: square jaw, broad forehead, and well-defined cheekbones. His hair was almost black, and a squared patch of beard extended from the very end of his chin as if it had been pasted on as an afterthought. Despite his imposing presence, the man's expression was friendly, as if they'd met on the beach by chance.

He reached toward her and she winced, but he merely tore the duct tape away from her mouth with a quick scrape, causing a brief but welcome sting. Breathing was easier now, and the claustrophobic feeling of helplessness faded a trifle.

"Now we can talk," he said calmly. She didn't bother to ask what he wanted. Waiting in silence, she tried to meet his eyes, tried not to show fear, but all the time her mind replayed what she knew of past victims: eyes gouged out, throat slit, hands missing. What fate had he decreed for her?

"I'm Vincent," he said conversationally. "You know what I want from you."

"You want to know if I've discovered the hiding place," she responded, voice shaking. "The answer is no."

"But you know something."

"Where am I?"

"In an old root cellar. I lived near here as a boy, and the location came back to me when I returned. It's a perfect place to hide, and I made some adjustments so it's no longer easy to locate. We have to wait here for darkness, so we might as well discuss items of mutual interest."

The only way to stay alive was to give him something. She said in a tightly controlled voice, "We have words."

"From the script?"

"Yes. He pricked holes in it."

"I knew that."

"Well, some of the letters he marked were important, others

not. Once you know which ones matter you get words, but it's still in a sort of code."

"Clever fellow, John Romeo."

Her mind raced. This man couldn't have carried her far through the dense wood and steep terrain. There must be searchers who might hear them talking. She wondered how much time had elapsed. Minutes? Hours?

"How do you know about John Romeo?" She spoke loudly, but Vincent didn't seem worried about discovery.

He settled into a storyteller's pose, hands together in front of his chest, eyes slanted upward and to the side. "Some years ago, four young people who lived near here found an old book in the attic of a rented house. It was the book you recently stole from me." His eye lit briefly on Mercedes, a glow of anger in it, but when she didn't respond, he went back to the story. "The cleverest of them knew the book was valuable, and he arranged to keep it for later study. Circumstances, however, caused him to leave the book behind when he left what passed for his home and the people who were, in biological terms, his parents.

"The young man, Vincent by name, went back for the book when he was able, but it was lost." His voice took on a hard edge. "She paid for that."

Vincent's mind had gone into the past, and his expression in the dim light frightened Mercedes even more than before. "But you recently learned the book had been found," she prompted.

"Yes. The book had been tossed in among others, and it turned up in the hands of someone unworthy of its value."

"Sylvia."

"I'd forgotten you and she met." An odd phrasing—finding the poor woman dead was hardly acquaintance. "She was my Juliet, of course."

"Yes. I recognized the pattern in your actions."

"A tribute to the Bard, without whom I might have come to a bad end. You see, those first boyhood dreams of wealth sparked my interest, and I discovered in myself a passion for the works of Shakespeare." Vincent's expression became prideful. "The plays became my focus. I've even published on the subject."

"You write about Shakespeare?" It was hard to imagine him as anything but a monster.

"If you were a Shakespearean scholar, you would know the name Vincent I. Parks. I like the acronym, because my work has made me a Very Important Person."

Her eyes widened. This was the man whose book she'd studied at the library, the one who claimed Shakespeare's plays taught moral lessons. "I read some of your book."

His voice reflected pleasure. "It's good, isn't it? All the righteous citizens who pitied me when my parents drank themselves senseless every night, the teachers who pursed their lips and said I was no student, I've shown them. 'There is a tide in the affairs of men,' he says in *Julius Caesar*. I took advantage of that tide."

Attempting to establish camaraderie she said, "You made something of yourself without anyone's help."

"There was someone." Vincent's voice softened. "When I was seventeen, I met a man. I was living on the streets of Edinburgh, and this man...took me in." Something in his tone gave Mercedes a glimpse at the reality beneath the casual phrase. Surely the man had had a motive for taking up with a homeless, recalcitrant teenager, but Vincent didn't seem to mind.

"When he discerned my appreciation of Shakespeare's work, he began to treat me as more than a casual friend. He taught me how to act, speak, and dress." His voice took on an edge. "How to hide my past, how to fit in with the best people, as he had learned to do. When I was ready, he introduced me into certain circles, and I managed to make an impact." Vincent's voice faded almost to a whisper. "He became my first tribute."

"You killed him?" The unwise words burst out before she could stop them.

He blinked uncomprehendingly at her for a moment but then recovered. "Of course not. He couldn't face getting old." There was real pain in his expression. "He feared he'd lose my affection, since my star rose as his fell."

Had losing his protector unsettled Vincent's mind, or had he always been insane?

His tone turned back to pride. "I dressed him as Othello, who died of grief over the loss of his love. To my surprise, the gesture added to my renown."

And that was what he wanted more than anything. The boy who'd been nobody, been pitied and rejected, wanted people to speak his name with respect. Finding Drake's treasure wasn't about the wealth it would bring, at least not totally. It was about putting Vincent I. Parks, V.I.P., in the history books.

This terrifying man knew his victims were dead, knew he'd killed them, but he no longer recognized the difference between fame and infamy. The murders added to his enjoyment of the chase, like trophies picked up on the way in a scavenger hunt.

Mercedes left her thought too long in silence, and Vincent heard movement outside their hiding place. Before she could react he switched off the flashlight and placed the knife against her throat in tacit threat. As the searchers moved around them, she heard the rumbles of low male voices asking and replying in the negative. Two men neared to the point of almost stepping on the wooden cover over their heads and then moved off, unaware they'd been so close to the object of their search. She almost sobbed aloud as their footsteps retreated, but the knife point cold against her neck reminded her not to make a sound.

They were silent a long time after the searchers could no longer be heard. The pit was silent as the minutes crawled by, and Mercedes wondered what Vincent would do next. Finally he moved purposefully into a crouch.

"I believe we're safe," he said, apparently unaware of the irony of the statement. "You were going to tell me what you've deciphered of John's message."

She was again cooperative. David had the police out looking for her, and she had to extend her life as best she could until the search found success. "As I said, we found words, but they're ambiguous." Frowning, she tried to remember them. "'South from the lest of duncans thanes witch three battle mending the primrose way the foeole's way a bloody man.' That might not be completely correct."

"Write it down." He produced a notepad and pencil then provided light so she could comply. Once she'd written it as best she could remember, he folded the sheet and put it into the pocket of his windbreaker.

"And have you decided on the other question?" he asked.

"The other?"

"You know!" His voice was excited. "Was the spy

Shakespeare's brother or not?"

She felt an emotion akin to what John Romeo must have experienced: unwillingness to give up anything that would satisfy her captor. Like John, she knew she was likely to die, and like him, she chose to withhold what her adversary wanted. "I doubt it," she said coolly. "I think he used the name somewhere as an alias, and the vicar misunderstood and drew the wrong conclusion."

Vincent was silent for a moment. Finally he moved toward her, light bobbing, and she pulled away, but he only sliced through the duct tape on her ankles. "Let's go."

CHAPTER TWENTY-FIVE

David Cutler raised the alarm within minutes of losing sight of Mercedes. When she didn't return, he clambered up and over the jutting rock and, calling and finding no sign of her, hurried to the pub for help. Impatiently he answered the deputy constable's questions: No, the young lady wasn't his daughter. Certainly not his lover. No, they hadn't quarreled, and she was not the type for practical jokes. Finally he exploded at the man's patronizing approach. "Look, you ninny, someone's taken Mercedes. Now send out searchers or I'll call whoever it takes to have you replaced!"

Within a half hour, the village functionaries were convinced Mercedes hadn't wandered off to pick berries. They became briskly efficient, branching out in all directions from the spot where David had last seen her. He insisted on going with them, though the gathering dark had cooled the air and mist from the sea made the path slippery and perilous. One searcher found parallel lines on the pathway, as if heels had dragged, but they disappeared. There were no other tracks nearby.

"Too rocky," the constable reported, "and the dark isn't helping. We'll keep searching in the morning. Finding tracks will be easier in daylight."

An abandoned lighthouse on the strand was the subject of a thorough search, but it revealed nothing. The living quarters on the ground floor were heavy with dust, the upper part in ruins, the roof gone. No place to hide a prisoner—or a body.

No one thought of the lighthouse's root cellar, a six-by-six hole in the ground a few dozen meters feet up the slope where a long-ago keeper had stored vegetables to keep them cool. If anyone had remembered, they wouldn't have found it easily, for the old wooden cover had been draped in camouflage fabric and covered with brush so it blended into the landscape.

With a borrowed flashlight David tramped the beach, hoping to find something the police had missed, but there was nothing. He agonized over how much to tell them of the situation. Mercedes was in danger, but would it help or hurt matters if the police knew from whom? David saw no advantage in saying more than he had, since all that could be done was underway.

He returned to the inn on the chance that someone had called with news, but the host shook his gnomish head sadly. Wandering outside to the flowery porch, he was unable to sit but equally unable to decide what he should do. The air smelled like a funeral home, an unpleasant association in the circumstances. His eyes raked the darkness in frustration. He liked and admired Mercedes, with her passion for order and her insistence on closure. If only he could help her now.

The whine of an engine climbing the hill interrupted his thought. As he turned to the impossibly steep, uncomfortably tiny parking area, a dust-covered Aston-Martin raced to a stop, its wheels throwing dirt as they skidded. A man jumped from the car and hurried toward him. He was medium height, every inch Scots in appearance, and agitated. "Are you Cutler?" Without waiting for an answer he said, "I've come to find Mercedes. Show me where you saw her last."

***

When Mercedes and Vincent emerged from the pit, a partial moon provided pale light by which they could dimly see the way. The root cellar was slightly uphill from an old lighthouse on the shore, now silhouetted against the starlit sky. Vincent release her hands due to the steep climb before them and pushed her onto a path away from the village. He followed with the slim-bladed knife in one hand and the light in the other. "I can kill you quickly," he said matter-of-factly, "but the longer you're helpful, the longer you'll live."

The path quickly joined the one she'd taken earlier, climbing upward to meet it near the place she'd left David. The main path was wider, going down the beach for a long way with occasionally turnings inland that scaled the hillside. Past the cliff over which she'd lost sight of David there was another one, sharper yet. Vincent watched carefully for a few moments. There was no sign of movement, no flash of light.

"That way," he ordered, and she began a reluctant climb up the second cliff. Each step took her farther from David and from help.

The way grew steep, and they had to use their hands for balance. Beyond Kirkfort's protective bay, beyond the inhabited area, lay a rocky section of coast that scowled over crashing waves The path slanted inward as it rose, skirting the cliff for a way, the steep drop invisible in the darkness except for flashes of white as the water foamed below.

Mercedes slowed, half-pretending she was winded, half really so. If Vincent came close, she might push him over the edge and escape.

He didn't. He stopped some feet from her, his expression unreadable in the dark, his voice mocking. "Tired, my dear?" He'd guessed her thought.

Suddenly something moved past her. She heard a grunt from Vincent followed quickly by a second grunt from someone else. There was a metallic clunk as the light went bouncing away, spinning to the side and shining uselessly at the sea. Two men fell heavily to the ground, and a confused, desperate struggle followed.

In a silence broken only by the crunch of feet scraping on rock, each sought traction and advantage. Exhalations sounded as effort was exerted against each other's strength. Several times Vincent knocked his adversary to the ground. Each time the other rose like a wave from the sea, slowed but never stopped. He launched himself at Vincent, and they rolled dizzyingly near the edge of the cliff, knotted in combat that admitted no quarter.

Mercedes stepped toward them, desperate to help her rescuer but unable to see who was who. The flashlight lay on the edge of the cliff, and the men's struggle blocked her from reaching it. There was no sign of the knife. Vincent must have dropped it along with the light.

Finally one man struck the other a heavy blow, and she heard the wind leave him. He rolled away, and she heard him gasp in air. Weakness now was defeat, possibly death.

The other man crouched and fumbled on the ground, and Mercedes knew why. Vincent was searching for the knife. If he found it, he'd kill the other man, and her hope for rescue would be over. Thoughts of flight entered her head as Vincent's hands brushed the ground, sending small pebbles bumping away as he muttered low curses. If she ran, she might get away. She might live.

But what about her rescuer? He lay flat on his back, struggling for breath. She couldn't leave him there. Vincent was still searching, and she saw his silhouette against the sky. Taking the only chance she saw, Mercedes ran forward in a crouch and hit him from the side, pushing up from her knees the way football players are taught to do. The jar of impact with the much larger man knocked her backward onto her rear, but the impact was enough to unbalance Vincent.

He staggered backward, teetering, and one foot slid over the cliff's edge and scraped down the surface. His weight carried him on, and the other foot slid over as well. With a Herculean effort, he threw his upper body forward. Mercedes heard a grunt as his chest slammed against the rocky face. He reached out desperately, clutching at anything that would save him, clawing at the rock itself for a hold. At the last instant he pulled himself up enough to grasp Mercedes' outstretched foot. The weight of his body began to pull her toward him, toward the cliff edge. Desperately she fought to free her ankle, but Vincent, his lower body hanging over the edge, held on. She couldn't counter the pull of the much heavier man, but neither could her weight save him. If he didn't release her, they would both go over the edge.

Mercedes scrabbled frantically to brace herself with the other foot. Vincent's head dropped below the cliff face, but his hands kept their desperate grip, one on the ledge and the other on his victim. As she slid closer and closer to the edge, Mercedes scratched for a hold on the rocky ground. The skin of her palms scraped away, but she succeeded only slightly in slowing her imminent approach to the sheer drop.

Suddenly the other man was beside her. Having gained his feet again, he stomped Vincent's wrist sharply. The iron grip released, and the newcomer rolled away from the edge, pulling Mercedes with him. Vincent's other hand wasn't strong enough to hold his weight, and he disappeared into the darkness below without a sound.

Winded, with the body of her rescuer pressing her into the rocky ground, Mercedes felt a shiver down her spine. They both lay panting, spent with the effort of the last few minutes. Except for their breathing, there was no sound, and the silence was eerie. A man dies with no cry to heaven, no appeal to earth? She wondered if any part of Vincent Parks had been human.

CHAPTER TWENTY-SIX

Colm regarded his bleeding knuckles. "It seems whenever you go walking, Miss Maxwell, I end up half skinned alive. Are you all right?"

"I think so." Delayed panic rose like icy water in her veins, but Colm rolled aside and helped her sit up. Gingerly she felt the back of her head where it had hit the rough ground when he landed on top of her. Rising to his feet, Colm stepped to the cliff edge and peered cautiously into the blackness below. Then he stooped to pick up the still-lit flashlight.

After he assured himself she'd sustained no serious damage from the ordeal, Colm gently helped her to her feet. "Did he—?" Colm didn't finish the thought as he felt the tremble in her cold hands. Instead he pulled her close, enfolding her in arms like iron bands enclosed in warm quilting. Her face rested on the flannel of his jacket, its tears absorbed by the soft fabric, and her arms went around him. Colm's warmth flowed into her and her fears and doubts ebbed.

"Is he dead?"

"I certainly hope so," he said into her ear. "They'll have to search in the morning." He went on holding her, apparently unwilling to let go. That was fine with Mercedes.

"How did you find me?" she asked when logic began to re-assert itself. "Did David call you?"

He handed her a handkerchief and she made facial repairs as he answered. "He apparently called everyone in Scotland except me. I'd just entered the village when the hue and cry went up. I figured you'd had another meeting with our old acquaintance."

"His name is Vincent. Vincent Parks."

"Vincent then. I figured, at least I hoped, he'd keep you alive until he discovered what you know. He couldn't have taken you very far, but the police search uncovered no sign. Then I saw the abandoned lighthouse. It was only a hunch, but I decided to hide there for an hour or so after dark and see if anything happened once he was convinced the search had ended for the day. About the time I concluded I'd made a wrong choice, the two of you passed by." His arms tightened about her supportively. "And here I am."

"You're very clever." Mercedes leaned back to peer at him in the dimness, "and I'm very grateful. But how did you come to Kirkfort? We were headed to London."

"What made you take off like that, anyway?" Colm sounded aggrieved. "I felt a perfect fool."

She wrapped her arms around herself, still in need of something to hold onto. "I heard you talking about me," she replied, her voice taking on a note of anger. "Twice. You knew who I was before we met, and you told Aletha you were watching me."

"Watching over you," he corrected, turning back toward her. His manner softened and he brushed a section of leaf from her tangled hair. "There's a difference."

"Yes, well, could we get back to civilization now?" Mercedes told herself to tread carefully. He hadn't answered her questions, merely put them off. "I'm sure David is frantic."

She sensed rather than saw the grin that accompanied Colm's answer. "He is, actually." He left it at that for the moment and acceded to her request. "Here. I have a torch in my pocket, so you can have Vincent's."

They began the laborious retracing of the path, which was as treacherous traveling downward as it had been moving up. She tried to concentrate on her steps, but questions kept popping up concerning Colm. He seemed to follow her thought, because when they reached a fairly smooth section of the trail he volunteered, "I told Aletha very little about you, but I owed her an explanation. She's been good to me."

"I'll bet she has."

He emitted a sigh of frustration. "I never denied our past association, but as I told you, it was over long ago. She's good company, intelligent and fun, but that's it." She began to believe that was the truth, at least as Colm saw it. She sensed a grin in the darkness. "You can't hold it against me. I hadn't met you yet, didn't know you'd banish all thought of other women."

Mercedes wanted to hear more, but a section of rough terrain prevented prolonged conversation. They reached the last steep slope, and Colm directed the flashlight beam downward, studying how best to navigate it. Once he'd done it, he reached back to steady her descent. The touch of his hand reminded her how attracted she was to Colm, but, steeling her resolve, she removed her hand from his as soon as she'd reached level ground.

Colm stopped and faced her, raising her chin until she looked him in the eye, even though his face was barely discernible in the darkness. "Here it is, then. You want to know what made me come with you, why I've chased you across the United Kingdom and taken on a crazed killer—" He held up two fingers "—twice. For you." He paused, and the roar of the sea behind him seemed to fade as Mercedes concentrated on what he'd say next. It was important for her and for him; she could feel it. Colm's face came close to hers, and he turned aside so his lips were next to her ear. "The first time I saw you I was enchanted. When you told my uncle your crazy story, I decided it was my duty to talk you out of this

218

crazy quest. But that night in Larkhall, after I'd spent one hour with you, Mary-Mercedes Martin-Maxwell, I became convinced that first, you were not crazy, and second, nothing mattered to me except remaining with you. Not gold, not danger, nothing."

Colm had saved her twice from death. The brief touch he gave her face now was warm despite the damp air and the cool night, and it was with great determination that she fought back the emotions clouding her judgment. "How could I not be suspicious? How did you find me in Larkhall, and again here in Kirkfort?"

To her surprise, he chuckled in response. "John Romeo isn't the only spy of your acquaintance, my dear. Now let's get you back safely to your elderly guardian. You must let it be known you're alive, and then you must get some rest. Everything else is secondary."

She allowed him to pilot her back to the inn, his arm around her for warmth and support. She felt safe, protected from the evil she'd faced, and she wondered why she had let her mind doubt Colm when her heart never had.

***

Upon entering work the next morning, the policeman asked the night duty officer for news. "Not much on except a report from Kirkfort, down on the coast. An American woman disappeared while walking along the Firth."

"Disappeared?"

"Right. She was walking with a friend who apparently has money or influence or both. They got separated, and he claims she was abducted." He slammed a drawer shut and gave a derisive snort. "More likely she had one whiskey too many and fell into the water."

219

"American, eh? Do you recall the name?"

"Something generic, I think." The officer shuffled through the papers on his desk. "Here. It's Martin, Mary Martin." He handed over the report and departed.

The policeman read the report through twice, glanced around the office to assure that no one was paying particular attention to him, and then placed two phone calls. The first confirmed what he'd read, the second was a call to his partner. "She's at Kirkfort."

"Good, let's not lose her again," the other replied.

The sarcastic tone irritated him. Already he'd formed a personal dislike for the fastidious snobbishness his new partner evinced, like a film star breathing better air than mere mortals. He couldn't resist a retort. "You had a golden opportunity to keep track of her yourself."

"But I didn't know then what I know now." A lighter's flint grated and there was a pause as cigarette smoke was inhaled. "Can you go there and see what she's up to?"

"There's a problem. She's gone missing."

"Vincent?

"Very possibly."

"In that case you needn't worry about her at all."

The policeman smiled grimly. "True. But Vincent will be there. It's where he's been headed all along, only now he has the information he's wanted for twenty years."

"Then we both should go."

"I agree. I don't trust what Vincent might do if he saw me, but he won't know you."

"You can trust me, at least where money is concerned. Where shall I find you?"

After plans had been made, the policeman went down the hallway to his superior's office. The fact that his boss was working on reports was obvious from the sound of muttered curse words and the un-rhythmic clicking of computer keys as he plied his two-finger typing method.

"I'd like a closer look at the possible kidnapping in Kirkfort," he suggested when one eyebrow raised toward him in question. "It may relate to the murders."

The chief inspector stopped, rested his wrists on the gel pad along the keyboard front, and regarded him for a few seconds thoughtfully. "We've just had word the woman was found safe. She was indeed abducted and held for some time, but the man who attacked her is dead, went off a cliff into the Firth."

A shudder of relief passed through him at this news, but his face betrayed nothing more than professional interest. He hadn't realized how reluctant he was to face his one-time companion until the threat was removed.

"I'd still like to go down there myself and see what I can learn. I'll speak with the woman and try to put what she knows together with our information. Maybe we've got lucky and our killer has been stopped."

"Shall I send someone with you?"

"No, thanks. It might be nothing, a lover's quarrel or some such nonsense. If I need an officer I can always get someone locally."

"If you think there'll be something helpful toward ending this mess, I can make do without you for an afternoon." He checked his watch. "Drive down after lunch, once you've finished court duty. That will give the locals a chance to find the body and get the details straight. See what's what, and keep me informed." He frowned at the dusty screen before him, head and shoulders pushed forward in a decidedly non-ergonomic position. "Don't waste time if it's nothing. We have plenty to keep us busy here with our own grisly affairs."

He was tempted to argue he should skip his appointment to testify, but he couldn't afford to raise suspicion at this point. He hoped Mercedes would keep quiet until he could reach her and accomplish what he had in mind. "Thank you, sir. I'll try to wrap things up quickly."

***

Upon her return, Mr. MacPhearson metamorphosed from a timid, kindly host to an almost bellicose guardian of Mercedes' health. When Colm brought her shivering to the inn, MacPhearson called the police station and informed them of her safe return. He allowed the local constable only the briefest of interviews before announcing that since she was safe and the threat from the evil abductor was ended, Miss Martin, who had refused medical care, would be resting in her room until she recuperated from her ordeal. He assured the deputy constable he'd be contacted as soon as the lady was rested enough to complete the interview. Oddly, that was all it took for them to be left alone for most of the next morning.

"Of course you won't be left alone once it's known who your abductor was." David muttered as they stopped briefly before retiring to their separate rooms at the back of the labyrinthine guest home.

"I'll have to tell them everything."

"They can no longer accuse you of collusion, I would think."

He rubbed his eyes tiredly. "We have information that may solve several murders."

"I'm ready to be done with all of this." She stifled a yawn. Her backside hurt where it had connected with the rocky ground, and her head still ached where Vincent had hit her. Shaky and colder than the warm night warranted, she had the feeling she might burst into tears at any moment. She was grateful to Mr. MacPhearson for demanding time for her to rest, time to decide how to end the nightmare that had surrounded her for days. She would tell the truth, assure that someone in authority besides Callard knew about the journal, and depend on the influence of her friends, Colm Kennedy and David Cutler, to support her claims. She was no longer a lone tourist with no connections.

"Too bad we didn't solve the cipher," Colm said, "but you've been through enough." He touched her shoulder lightly, and she felt both tenderness and encouragement in it. They hadn't found the treasure, but they'd ended Vincent's reign of terror. That in itself was a relief.

CHAPTER TWENTY-SEVEN

Mercedes awoke after a few hours, not really rested but unable to sleep any longer. The smell of food hinted that David, Colm, or both had left their rooms. She joined the two men, who were digging into a heavy Scottish breakfast as if there was no such thing as cholesterol. The aromas of bacon, toast, and coffee mingled invitingly, and Mr. MacPhearson stood in the doorway, anxious to see that no detail was overlooked. She noticed that as soon as the host left to get her breakfast David pushed the small, round chunk of black pudding off to one side of the plate. Otherwise he ate as heartily as Colm, who explained his presence in her life between forkfuls of fried egg and grilled tomato.

"I am not a spy, but my uncle served in Her Majesty's government for twenty years before retiring to take up his true love, the study of Scottish history."

"Professor Rankin? That cherub is a retired spy?"

He grinned. "The best ones are those you'd never suspect, right?"

"So your uncle sent you to watch over me?"

"In a way. He called me when he heard on the news about the death of the librarian in Dumfries. It gave him second thoughts about the importance of the vicar's book, and he decided he might have been premature in dismissing your theory. Since the murderer seemed to be following you, Uncle Allan worried for your safety."

Of course someone with Rankin's background would doubt a romantic tale and discount an amateur's assessment of danger.

"By the time he learned the threat was real, I was gone."

Colm spooned sugar into his coffee cup and stirred noisily. "We discussed calling the police, simply for your safety. Then he mentioned seeing your hotel receipt. I volunteered to drive out to Larkhall and talk some sense into you." He tasted the coffee, grimaced, and added more sugar.

Mercedes sipped her own coffee, black and strong, the way she liked it. "But then you decided to throw in your lot with mine. Did you tell him that?"

"Not at first. I didn't think he'd approve. When I did phone, that night from the inn when you apparently were eavesdropping —"

"Quite by accident."

He nodded. "—Uncle Allan called me all kinds of a fool, but he agreed to provide expert backup through the wonders of technology."

She met his gaze for a moment. "I'm glad you came along, Colm."

He grinned. "It was kismet. Our future together was in the stars."

A small sigh escaped Mr. MacPhearson, as if the principals of the movie had finally kissed for the first time. Colm's eyes lightened with humor and his lips twitched slightly. He brushed back the ever-unruly lock of hair and shrugged. "A knight doesn't desert a lady until the quest is completed. It's part of the code. Section B, Paragraph 9, I think."

Mercedes finished her breakfast, assuring their host she had everything she needed at the moment. "Do you think the guy with the blue hair told Vincent where I was?"

"Maybe." Colm took a slice of toast from the rack at the center of the table and buttered it lavishly. MacPhearson hovered nearby, ostensibly warming their coffees but also eavesdropping on the most excitement Kirkfort had had in decades as he continued. "Vincent doesn't strike me as the type to work well with others. Is there another way he could have known where you were staying?"

She considered for some seconds before replying. "There was a brochure with a map lying on the car seat. I was nervous about driving in city traffic on the opposite side of the road, so I highlighted the route from Larkhall to the university."

"Right." David outlined the scenario. "Vincent finds out what sort of car you're driving. He discovers you're on your way to see Rankin." She shuddered at the memory of how Vincent got that information, but Colm picked up the thought.

"If your bag wasn't in the car, he'd conclude you planned to return to Larkhall. He'd have had enough time to sneak into Uncle Allan's office, peek at his files, then drive down in time to intercept you."

"But you were there by then."

"Yes. I asked at the inn, and the clerk said you'd asked the way to the library."

"You were nearby when Vincent attacked."

"I was studying my lines and waiting with a vague idea of managing to meet you when you left the library. When Vincent pulled you into that alley, there was no question you were in danger." He glanced at the two other men but then said it anyway. "I had to protect you from it, whatever it was."

Both listeners beamed like proud parents on Prom Night,

David without slowing his dignified but complete enjoyment of his meal.

"Anyway," Colm continued, "the rest is true. I'm missing rehearsals as of now, but I called my director and told him that's the way it must be."

She smiled ruefully. "And I rewarded your efforts on my behalf by running away in the night."

His expression turned sober. "When you left Aletha's I didn't know what to think."

"I heard you talking about watching me and I thought—"

"You thought I wanted the treasure." He shrugged. "I guess that doesn't say much for my honest face."

"I was scared. I didn't know who to trust."

"Whom." Setting his knife and fork aside with metallic finality, David signaled he was finished. With no further excuse to stay, MacPhearson removed their plates, poured one more half cup for each of them, and left them to themselves. Peering through the doorway to assure that their host was well away, David asked, "Now that we're all willing to trust each other, might we put our separate talents to use?"

"What do you mean?" Colm asked.

"You're an actor. Have you done *Macbeth*?"

Colm winced. "You mean the Scottish play? Of course. I do a passable Malcolm and I bring down the house as the drunken porter."

"We have need of your experience, then." Briefly David explained the clues they'd gleaned from the script. Digging in his pocket, he pulled out the yellow notebook paper and laid it before him.

Colm studied it for some time. "I don't get it."

"Mercedes here thinks that the author —" David looked to her to see if she'd given Colm the whole story.

"He knows everything," she told him, "except that I have the last page of the vicar's book." She turned to Colm. "That's why Vincent was after me."

"It had to be something like that."

David brought them back to the clues by tapping an impatient finger on the sheet. "Mercedes believes John was giving clues to his brother, not to Cecil. If the script found its way anywhere, it would have been to the theater rather than the King's spymaster."

"John probably intended to bribe someone to take it to William."

"If he did, Reid intercepted it," Colm said grimly. "In all likelihood, Shakespeare the playwright never learned what became of his multi-faceted twin."

Mercedes recalled an item she'd read somewhere in the past few days. "Someone broke into Joanna Shakespeare's home after her father died and searched his papers. Maybe Cecil wanted to know if Will ever heard from John."

"Just the sort of thing he'd do," David affirmed. Sliding the heavy wooden chair closer to the table with a hollow scrape, he turned the page so they all could see it and ordered, "Now let's get to work on the clues."

They bent over the paper, but sharing one copy was awkward. After a time he pushed his chair back again and ordered brusquely, "You two go for a walk or something while I arrange more copies.

I'll also call home and say I'll be away a while longer." He chuckled. "Mrs. Peterson will have apoplexy. I' haven't been absent more than one night at a time in the ten years she's been with me."

CHAPTER TWENTY-EIGHT

Colm seemed pleased at the chance to get Mercedes alone for a while. They stayed out of sight of the street in order to preserve the fiction she was unable as yet to have visitors. She reported the details of their discovery in the museum, explaining how David had seen the slight difference between letters with and without bloodstains.

"Not something most people would notice."

"That's why John added a hint, a handwritten note on the cover: 'By the pricking of my thumbs/Something wicked this way comes.' John was telling his brother to look for the blood."

"Small good it did the poor devil." He leaned against a post, staring at the sea before them, calm today and almost green. "I wonder why he didn't tell what they wanted to know."

"I think he knew he'd die anyway. I felt the same way when Vincent had a knife to my throat. All I could do to stay alive was not tell him everything I knew, at least not before I had to." They left the porch and made their way through the garden. "Maybe John let Reid know he was concocting the code, as a way to prolong his life. If it reached his brother, that was all the better." Colm mused. "Unfortunately, Reid misjudged his prisoner's condition and withheld sustenance for too long."

"What a monster he must have been." They had all come to think of John Shakespeare as a friend, and his death at Willie Reid's hands was an injury, even so long after the fact.

From a corner of MacPhearson's garden, Mercedes looked down on the narrow streets of Kirkfort. "Odd that such a lovely little town grew out of the hideout of Willie and his cohorts." They regarded the scene of the long-ago crimes, much changed now. The village's central buildings were made of stone, giving a sense of permanence and stability. In the harbor sailing vessels came and went with graceful efficiency or sat idle like proud swans riding the gentle waves. "A tourist trap," she murmured, "but a very classy one."

"Right. Somebody in Kirkfort had an eye to the future and managed to capitalize on that protected harbor. The bay is small, but it's perfect for sailboats."

"And mutineers with treasure." The breeze from the bay was fresh and cool, bringing to mind images of a creaking wooden vessel manned by a few desperate men, sliding silently along the shoreline seeking a place to debark unseen. How far away was the spot they'd chosen, and in which direction? Where had they hidden the treasure for which they would never return? Only a few yet alive had read the clues left by a man dying slowly, painfully, only a short distance from here.

Turning from the postcard view, Mercedes said, "Vincent came from near here, and so did his first victim, Sylvia. She found the book, and he killed her to get it, hoping to solve the riddles he hadn't solved as a boy."

The breeze played with her dark hair as she spoke, and the sun picked out its highlights and turned them to gold. A pot of bright yellow begonias hung from the gatepost, and Colm touched a velvet petal, apparently unresponsive. "I was frantic when I learned you were missing," he said finally. "I thought of how those people died."

She kept it light. "I was pretty frantic myself."

"I don't know what I'd have done." His eyes met hers now,

serious.

She looked away, unnerved by the intensity of his gaze. Emotions were running high. They were in the middle of a crisis that might make their relationship seem more than it was. Did she simply need someone to lean on right now? Was Colm mistaking the need to protect her with another sort of need? Suddenly her gaze focused on what she was looking at and her eyes widened. "Look!"

Turning, Colm caught a quick glimpse of Blue Hair disappearing around the corner of the house. He was off like a shot, leaving Mercedes behind. She heard the sounds of scuffling feet and shaking branches before she rounded the house, and then, "Oy, leave me alone, you great bully!"

"Calmly, calmly, lad. I'm not going to hurt you if you cooperate." Colm sounded pleased with himself, and she found him only slightly out of breath, holding Blue Hair against the wall with a muscular forearm. The young man's face showed obvious pain, which Mercedes didn't understand until she noticed Colm's other hand. He firmly grasped the youth's right wrist, two fingers on the back of the hand and the thumb against the arm bone. Evidently it hurt enough to incapacitate a person, for his prisoner cooperated, reluctantly but completely.

"Goose-neck come-along," Colm said happily. "Part of military training. Very effective with drunks, aggressive types, and, it seems, Peeping Toms."

Mercedes regarded the unique figure seen several times before, at the university, at the roadside comfort station, at Salisbury, and at Aletha's, where he'd climbed the fence and spied on them. Now here he was in Kirkfort.

Up close, he wasn't impressive, pale as a mushroom and skinny to the point of emaciation. The unconventional outfit he wore had been a long time without laundering if smell was any indication, and he had studs in places that made her wince just to look at them.

Keeping the wrist bent and taut Colm asked, "Why are you following this lady?"

Blue Hair was no hero. He told his story in a disjointed style that indicated either terrible allergies or chemical alteration to what brains he had. "Bloke hired me to watch her. Said he was 'er husband, an' she's stepping out on 'im. I get a hundred quid a day to keep track and call 'im."

"And when did you call him last?" He paused and Colm tightened his grip. "It takes very slight pressure to break a wrist."

"Ow! I left him a message this morning after the to-do was over and the three of you was in the B & B." He managed to leer through his pain.

"News, Friend. This lady is not married and never has been." He stopped and looked at Mercedes uncertainly. "I'm right, aren't I?"

"I've never been married."

Satisfied, Colm returned his attention to the captive, whose gaze traveled from one to the other as if trying to decide who was more likely to take pity on him.

"The man who hired you is not one of the good guys. He wants to hurt this lady, and I'm trying to stop him. Now that you've called and told him where we are, whatever happens to her will be on your head. How do you feel about that?"

Blue Hair turned to Mercedes and sniffed like a child with a cold and no tissue. "No lie?"

"No lie. We haven't broken any laws or any commandments."

"So what now?" Colm released the pressure on the man's wrist, and he rubbed it with the other hand, wincing.

The thought process was almost comical to watch. Blue Hair ran his tongue stud around his mouth several times, clicking it audibly against his teeth. "Bloody hell!" he finally managed. "The blighter lied to me."

He turned to Mercedes and sniffed, apparently a prelude to any communication. "Look, Miss, I'm sorry. I need the money, but I don't want anyone hurt. I thought he was all right, cuz he said he needed dates and places, things like that, so he could know for sure. I figured you was doin' wrong, 'specially after I saw you with three different blokes. I meant no harm."

Looking past the odd clothing and various metallic additions to his flesh, Blue Hair seemed just an ordinary sort of loser, the kind who are neither criminals nor good citizens but somewhere on the fringe. "What's your name?"

He sniffed once, deeply, and swallowed heavily. "I go by Lonnie."

"And who hired you, Lonnie?"

Another sniff, this time accompanied by a facial twitch worthy of a silent movie actor. "I don't know his name. He come up to me in the parking lot and said did I have a car and would I like to earn some decent money. I had a job at the university cafeteria but this sounded like more fun." His face drooped. "I suppose the cafeteria job's gone now, too."

"So you call him every day?"

Sniff. "Yeah." Sniff. "He was real mad when I lost you, but I always managed to pick up your trail again somehow." Sniff accompanied by a grin. "First I saw you with this bloke and then you went traveling with the old gent. I figured you really was having a bit on the side." Sniff with a knuckle rubbed hard enough under the nose to turn it red, a secondary sniff afterward. "Then there was another one following you. I figured you had men all over the place."

"Another man following?"

"Yeah, a dark-haired sort. Once I noticed him, I made sure to stay out of his way. Didn't want to get in the middle of anything, y'know?" The sniff was accompanied by a twitch, as if a blow was aimed at him and he ducked it.

"And when he attacked Mercedes you thought nothing of it?" Colm sounded threatening, and Lonnie winced again.

"He attacked her? I never saw that."

"In Larkhall, outside the library."

Lonnie looked confused. "Larkhall." His face cleared. "I must have missed it. Once you went into the hotel that afternoon, I went to sleep in my van. I missed it when you went out again, but I saw you come back later in the evening. I was waiting when you left in the morning with this fellow." He rolled his eyes at Colm, signaling something that might have been approval at Mercedes' ultimate choice of escorts.

Colm ignored the body language and stuck to his goal. "How will you be paid?"

"When he decides he's got enough info, he'll pay me the rest of what he owes."

"And how did you find me in Kirkfort, Lonnie? I know I lost you in Salisbury."

"The bloke said you'd end up here. In a town this size, it wasn't hard to find you." He seemed satisfied with himself, and it was clear he'd enjoyed playing detective these last days.

Leveling a meaningful gaze at Lonnie, Colm asked, "If I were to let you go, not call the police and charge you with all sorts of minor crimes, what would you do?"

"Go back to Glasgow and forget the whole thing." He said it with no sniffing whatsoever.

"Good then. You aren't much of a private eye, Lad. You stand out in any crowd."

"If I really was goin' for detective stuff, I'd get a wig," Lonnie declared matter-of-factly.

"Best find the other two pieces of that suit as well."

"Givin' it up anyway," he grumbled, returning to form with a twitchy sniff. "Can't trust people to tell the truth, and then you got to run all over the countryside, day and night." Sniff. "There's no time to eat or sleep or noffing." Sniff. "It probably ain't good for a bloke's health, and it's nothing like they show in films."

"I tell you what would be good for your health," Colm said pleasantly. "If we never see you near us again. How would that be?"

"I could manage," Lonnie said, doubtful as to his intent. He rubbed once more and gave a final, tentative sniff. "I can go then?"

"As far as you like." With a look at Colm, a glance at Mercedes, and a second look at Colm for reassurance, Lonnie backed away a few steps then turned and loped off, his back stiff as if expecting at any moment he'd change his mind.

"Really nothing the police could charge him with." They watched him disappear. "Aside from trespassing, he did nothing illegal."

"It doesn't seem likely we'll see him again. Up close he doesn't seem dangerous at all."

"Maybe not, but whoever sent him is, and it wasn't Vincent. Someone else is keeping track of you."

"Not hard to guess who," she muttered. "Who knows about the book, wanted me to keep in touch, and insisted I should tell him what I remembered of the clues?"

"The policeman in Dumfries," Colm answered promptly. "What was his name?"

"Callard, Inspector Callard."

He frowned. "You're not out of this yet. When you are—" He seemed about to say something serious, but he didn't finish. "We'll talk then."

Mercedes' mood became optimistic. Vincent was dead, Blue Hair seemed to be no threat, and, most pleasing of all, Colm was no longer a suspect. Callard might attempt to tie her to Vincent, but the truth would come out now. Vincent's attack on her the night before supported her innocence. David and Colm would stand with her, and they were close to solving the clues. They could hand the whole thing over to the authorities, and Callard would have to give up any idea of getting the treasure for himself.

"We should go back inside."

Colm took her cue and lightened the mood, checking his watch and tapping it with a fingernail. "Right. We'll miss lunch."

She swatted him playfully. "With the breakfast you two consumed, I'd have guessed there wasn't another meal coming till the end of the month."

David had found a copier at the village post office and made a dozen copies of the clues. "That way we can write on them as ideas occur." They went outside to a table in the garden warmed by the afternoon sun's rays and watched the Firth change colors in its light. Each studied his sheet of clues, pondering their meaning: *south from the lest of duncan(s) thanes wit(c)h three batt(l)e (m)ending the primros way the(n) fo(e)ol's way a(n) painted dev(v)il the secrets(t) man of blood(d).*

With many pauses between, theories were tossed back and forth. David was fairly sure the words didn't form a code. "It has to be simple clues, I think. John wouldn't expect his brother to break a cipher."

"So the phrases hint at actual landmarks." Colm beat a soft rhythm on the table with his pencil eraser.

David leaned toward his companions, spreading a hand over the clues. "Since they're hidden in *Macbeth*, my guess is we should consider the words in that context. What would the playwright know that no outsider would guess?"

"What if lest is least?" Colm mused, circling the word as he spoke. "The least of Duncan's lords could be Menteith, the role in the play with the fewest lines."

"Exactly!" David exclaimed. "Shakespeare would know that, but Willie Reid would not."

"So 'south of Menteith.' Where's that?"

"Due north of here." Colm was exultant. "John's first clue points to Kirkfort, revealing where he was held captive."

"He couldn't know if his handlers would ever learn where he'd been taken prisoner," David agreed. "He had to start with the general location."

"The 'secrets man' sounds familiar," Mercedes said doubtfully, "but that doesn't seem quite right."

"'The secret'st man,'" Colm corrected. "Macbeth speaks of 'the secret'st man of blood.'"

MacPhearson appeared in the doorway. "The police have called twice," he announced. "They're quite impatient to interview Miss Martin, but I've told them you haven't left your room yet. Still, they'll need to be seen, so I told them to come in an hour. Is that all right?"

Mercedes was grateful for the time MacPhearson had arranged for her. Her old desire to fix things, to make them come out right, wasn't satisfied by simply handing the facts over to people who had no stake in the matter. Would they take the time to ferret out John's clues, or would they be satisfied that Vincent was dead and his crimes ended? That question brought another to mind. "Did they—I mean, has the body been found?"

"No. They searched the shoreline for some distance, no sign of him."

Mercedes felt a chill. They'd seen Vincent go over the cliff, but she'd feel safer with proof of his death.

MacPhearson insisted on serving them lunch. "You'll have to deal with the police and all, and you won't get a decent thing to eat for some time." He'd gone to the pub for fragrant pasties and a tin of warm gravy to pour over them. Smiling shyly at their thanks, the little man left them to themselves. One hour to find what they could in the prisoner's message.

Colm assumed the duties of serving the meal, dishing out three portions and pouring on liberal amounts of gravy. Reaching into a large brown paper bag, he passed out forks and bottles of cold beer to wash their dinner down. Without once glancing away from the sheet before him, David managed to do justice to their host's providence.

"It's exciting to know the words make sense," he said between bites, "but the first tells us only what we already knew. Now what?"

"Witch three is a character, of course," Mercedes offered. "But I don't know about mending battles."

"Have you ever played the role?"

"I've seen the witches played by men as sort of a politically correct, non-sexist approach, but no. I do recognize 'the primrose way', though. I'd say that's separate from what comes before it."

"Yes, we figured it was *primrose* and we missed a letter somehow." Mercedes licked the rich, salty gravy from her fork with a murmur of appreciation.

"And what is the primrose way?" David asked.

"The porter speaks of it as he goes to answer the door." Colm waved his fork like a director with a baton. "The scene with the drunken porter bridges the time between Macbeth's murder of Duncan and the crime's discovery. Shakespeare knew the audience needed a bit of release from the 'dreadful deed.' When someone knocks at the gate, the porter pretends he's greeting businessmen who cheated the public, as if he's doorman at the gates of hell. They have come, he says, by the primrose path."

"The gates of Hell?" Mercedes asked. "In Scotland?"

"Plenty of English politicians, living and dead, would entertain that possibility," David declared. Intent on the clues, he dripped gravy onto the paper before him as he carried a forkful of food to his mouth.

"It's a good thing you made lots of copies if you're going to eat over them," Mercedes scolded.

Looking down at the spot David smiled, pushing away the napkin she took up to wipe away the stain. "Witch Three says something about the battle ending in the first scene, does she not?"

"'When the hurly-burly's done' says One; 'when the battle's lost and won' says Two; and Three says, 'That will be ere the set o' the sun.' Why?"

"My gravy spot, which so upsets the irrepressibly neat Mercedes, has blotted out the m in mended. If he meant 'ended', not 'mended', that fits the witch's line."

"To mean what?" Colm asked.

"The setting sun. The west," Mercedes exclaimed.

"So the site is west of Kirkfort?"

"Willie's journal said John explored several local rivers, following them upstream for a mile or so."

"There are plenty about," Colm said. "From the Uplands there are dozens of streams flowing to the Firth."

They were interrupted by their host, whose face was grave. "There's a policeman here," he said apologetically. "He says he's come to arrest the lady."

CHAPTER TWENTY-NINE

Jared Graham stood stiffly in the sitting room, demeanor solemn but concerned. He shuffled his feet when he saw Mercedes, making him appear even more boyish than usual.

"Miss Maxwell, are you all right?"

"I am, Jared, thanks to Colm here."

"Then I am grateful to you." Graham spoke in Colm's direction but his eyes never left hers. "When we heard you were missing, I—we—were very worried."

"David Cutler, Colm Kennedy, this is Jared Graham, the police sergeant I told you about." Colm shook hands stiffly. David nodded curtly, apparently pegging Jared as a rival for Colm. "Have the police located Vincent's yet?"

"No. With all the pools and eddies near here, he might never be found."

"But you'll look for him, in case he escaped death somehow." David made it a statement, not a question.

"Of course. Mr. Parks may in fact be one Vincent Pemborough, a disturbed young man who disappeared from Kirkfort some years back. Apparently he believed there was treasure to be found near here." This time when his gaze sought Mercedes', she looked away. If she'd been honest with Jared that day in Glasgow, she might have prevented several deaths.

"He was disturbed all right," David commented.

"Young Pemborough ran away from home at fifteen, after a

row with his father. A year or so later the father died in a rather bizarre way. At the time it was believed thieves broke into the factory where he was a security guard, intending to rob the place, and killed him."

It sounded like there was more to hear. "But?"

"He had been stabbed, his body covered with a rug, and then stabbed again."

"Polonius," Colm said instantly.

Clearing his throat Graham said defensively, "Knowing what we know now, that is apparent. At the time, the method was deemed simply an oddity. *Hamlet* was never considered."

"But Polonius was an old windbag, full of meaningless advice and pretty much without any morals of his own. Vincent saw his father the same way."

"How did Vincent's mother die?" Mercedes asked, and Jared looked at her questioningly. "His book claims things about Shakespeare that struck me as wrong, like the idea that parents who fail their children should pay. That was Vincent's opinion, not Shakespeare's."

Jared twitched his shoulders, settling the tense muscles more comfortably. "The mother apparently committed suicide."

"By what method?"

"A rather awful choice." A grimace passed over his face. "An alcoholic will sometimes do anything for liquor. She apparently drank antifreeze."

Colm and Mercedes locked gazes. "Swallowed fire." Colm explained for Graham's benefit. "Brutus' wife Portia died that way in Julius Caesar."

"So the man was a monster with a Shakespearean education. What the Bard used for drama, he made into reality." David was angry. "It's a mercy he no longer walks the earth."

Jared's face showed regret. "I'm sorry, Mercedes, but I'm sent to take you into custody."

Colm stepped between her and Graham aggressively. "You can't believe she's guilty of anything. Why, Parks tried to kill her last night."

"And would have except for Colm here." David put in a plug for his choice for Mercedes' knight.

Jared flushed, his gaze avoiding all of them as he explained. "Certain of my superiors believe you were in league with Vincent in a scheme to find hidden treasure. You did avoid the authorities for several days."

"Which you advised me to do," she reminded him.

He flushed even deeper as his voice took on a hint of defensiveness. "I asked you to keep in contact with me, but instead you went off with these men, who'll be lucky if they aren't charged as accessories."

"That's ridiculous," David growled.

"No, it's true," she admitted. "I should have given Callard the last page of the vicar's notebook as soon as I found it. Even if he'd kept the clues for himself, it would have prevented three needless deaths."

"Those people were killed by a madman who tried to kill you," Colm argued. "You aren't responsible for Vincent's actions."

"I agree," Jared assured them. "I've been trying to convince my inspector Miss Maxwell is innocent." His chest deflated slightly. "It hasn't worked. Your pursuit of the treasure has led some to conclude you are guilty of crimes, though not murder. This morning I was told to come down here and take you into custody."

"But I—" Mercedes stopped. She really had no explanation of why she'd felt compelled to solve the puzzle of Drake's treasure. To stop the killing? To restore the gold to the crown? To vindicate John, dead for four hundred years? What was she doing, anyway? Certainly her desire for closure had made her unwilling to leave the hunt undone. That and a desire to stop men like Vincent Parks from winning.

"When the report came of your disappearance, I couldn't cover for you anymore." Jared's eyes pleaded for understanding. "Inspector Callard knows who was abducted and why. They've turned it all around, and they thing you went off with Vincent voluntarily."

"He planned to kill her." Colm took a step toward Graham.

"You must give a statement as to what you know." Jared spoke only to Mercedes. "I asked the inspector to let me come alone into the village, since I grew up near here and they know me. Inspector Callard and the others are waiting at the top of the cliffs." He touched her arm briefly, giving tacit assurance he was on her side. "Once you explain everything, this will be resolved."

Mercedes looked to Colm and David for help. "Look," Cutler argued. "She was not in league with that madman."

Jared looked deeply unhappy. "It will be sorted out, but for now I must follow orders."

Callard. She had disliked him at first, then distrusted him, and now she had to face him again. Did he want the truth, or did he want to know the location of Drake's treasure? There wasn't any way to find out except to face him. At least this time she wouldn't be alone.

"I'll go. Jared will make sure I get a fair hearing."

"You can follow along once you've checked out of the inn," Graham said, his relief evident. "We'll be at Dumfries station."

He escorted Mercedes to his car, and she was thankful he didn't make her ride in the back seat like a criminal. David followed, his glower conveying a dislike of mankind in general and police officers in particular. Colm came only to the doorway, an odd distraction in his eyes. As soon as the car started off, he turned and reentered the inn. Probably going to collect their things, she decided. Irrelevantly, she hoped she hadn't left anything embarrassing lying out in her room.

Jared said little as they followed the main street through the village. The road climbed steeply, and the houses became fewer. Finally there were only trees and bushes, their leafy arms reaching out into the road as if to slow their passage. They rounded several steep turns on the climb, and the village disappeared long before they reached the main road. Here she expected to see other police cars, but there were none. When Graham turned west, away from Dumfries, she looked to him questioningly. He held a gun loosely in his right hand.

"What is this?" she began, but several pieces fell into place. Jared had told her the police considered her an accessory. Jared had suggested she stay away from the authorities. Jared had left her on her own, hoping she'd lead him to the treasure. Jared had remained silent about the dangers she'd face, knowing that Vincent would kill her if he could. Jared.

"I really do like you," he said, apparently unaware of the irony of such a statement. "I tried to convince you to go into hiding, to keep out of all this. But you chose to become involved, making yourself a target for Vincent."

"Vincent targeted me!" Her voice was sharper than she intended. "I simply tried to stay alive and to find the evidence you need to stop him."

Graham smiled, his eyes on the road. "But I didn't want to stop him. At first I hoped he'd find the treasure himself. Then you joined the search, and he went after you, which means you somehow got the journal he was looking for. Between you, the scholar, and the actor, I'd guess most of it has been put together by now."

"I know nothing," she said disgustedly. "I thought Callard was crooked because he asked me about the journal."

"Ah, the good inspector." Graham shifted his shoulder muscles again. "He recently had a serious accident."

"He's dead?"

"In a coma, and that's good enough, I think, to see us through this little drama. The librarian's death changed his mind about the value of the journal. He called with questions about Sylvia's background. He said he'd been rethinking your story."

"He believed me."

"And you thought he wanted the treasure." Graham chuckled. "Inspector Callard is a straight arrow if ever there was one. He hoped with the journal we could get ahead of the killer and anticipate where he'd show up. A good idea, but then he had bad luck crossing a street."

Mercedes was appalled at both Graham's cavalier manner and her own gullibility. The boyish policeman had hit all the right chords: his charm, her fears, his dependability, and her need to believe someone on the police force supported her decision to keep the journal page.

"You can't think you'll get away with this."

"When—if—Callard revives to accuse me, I'll be gone with my share of the treasure."

"Your share? Then you and Vincent—?"

"God, no! Vincent was a madman, as you well know."

It came to her. "You followed me to Glasgow."

"Yes, your voice mail was very helpful."

"And you've kept track of my movements ever since."

"Do you recall a seeing chap with blue hair?"

"Lonnie?"

"On a first name basis, eh?" Graham shook his head at the irony. "I followed you to Glasgow, but I couldn't keep that up indefinitely. I hired him the day we had lunch together. He looked the sort who could use a bit of cash and wouldn't ask too many questions."

Her lips tightened in disgust. "I actually saw him as you drove away. I never dreamed you'd sent him after me."

"He's more enterprising than I'd imagined. Even when he lost you, he didn't give up."

"Until he realized you'd lied to him. Even Lonnie has his limits."

"Imagine something like that having a conscience." Graham seemed genuinely surprised.

"He's lucky he didn't run into Vincent. He was there in Glasgow too."

"Vincent?" Graham's hands tightened on the steering wheel.

"Wasn't he a friend of yours once?" Vincent had spoken of a group of friends who found the vicar's notebook. Graham had grown up near here. She guessed the shy Jared had been befriended by the intense Vincent, who'd probably longed for an audience even then.

Graham smiled ironically. "I'll tell you the story, since we have the time. It's a roundabout route we're taking, but it circles the cliffs then heads back toward Kirkfort." He navigated a corner and accelerated to exactly 80 kilometers per hour.

"When I was twelve, my family moved to Aldair, the small town we just passed through. It sits on the cliff, and Kirkfort lies below. I spent a great deal of time wandering the area, much of it down by the Firth. I had two friends—perhaps I should say one friend and a companion. Vincent was nobody's friend, but he was entertaining to be around. There was nothing too rash or too awful for Vincent to attempt."

"Like torturing small animals, I suppose."

"There was a bit of that," he admitted. "But if a person needed humiliating, Vincent could devise a way to do it without getting caught. I took a lot of abuse from other kids, who made fun of my weight. Even my best friend called me Bubble."

Mercedes recalled Graham confiding that weight-lifting had given him confidence. How better to gain self-esteem than to build a new body, to become the person you always wished to be?

"If anyone harassed one of us, Vincent would get back at him, even teachers. He was very useful to have around."

"And the third boy, your friend?"

"An acquaintance of yours, I believe: Paul Prescott."

"Our tour guide?" Mercedes frowned as Paul's friendly face came to mind. "Vincent murdered his childhood friend?"

"As I said, he had no friends. Paul knew about the treasure, you see, so Vincent couldn't let him live. No doubt he'd have killed me too, given the chance. It was good of you to push him off the cliff."

She said nothing. The lack of any sound at all as Vincent fell still seemed odd, and no body had been found in the waters below. She shivered at the memory, but the present was just as dangerous. Graham was not the man he'd first seemed. He would have let a madman kill her if it got him closer to Drake's treasure. Mercedes feared when her usefulness to him was over, Graham might be willing to do the job himself.

CHAPTER THIRTY

Graham watched the way ahead, finally turning onto an unmarked road that was barely there. Branches scrubbed the car's metal shell as they drove down a steep incline not meant for vehicles. The Firth was intermittently visible ahead of them as trees parted then closed around them again.

Holding the wheel firmly against the bucking that resulted from their rough descent, Graham explained. "As boys, the three of us were always hiding from adults, chores, that sort of thing. One summer my cousin came to visit, and that made four of us. One rainy day we were up in Paul's attic. Vincent got to snooping and opened a chest. He found stacks of record books we found boring, some ancient tintype photographs we found slightly amusing, and the journal.

"If not for the dreary day, we might have thrown it back in the trunk and forgotten it. But Vincent started reading aloud in a comical spoof of dramatic acting. He was pretty good at figuring out the old boy's writing. My cousin, who's quite a scholar, joined in and helped decipher the text, so the story emerged.

"Of course we knew who Shakespeare was, and Paul, who had a mind even then for trivial but entertaining historical facts, had heard of Willie Reid. Knowing Willie was real, we began to wonder if the rest might be true as well. The story of Drake's treasure is the sort of thing uncles tell nephews on fishing trips and grannies use as bedtime stories."

"Those things appeal to boys of that age," Mercedes murmured despite herself.

"We were gob-smacked. Clues to a treasure, and we might find it. Vincent insisted on taking the book with him. Paul said it didn't belong to us, but it didn't do to argue with Vincent. He took the book despite Paul's objections." Graham's tone indicated more than his words how reluctant they'd been to cross Vincent.

"For the rest of that summer, under Vincent's direction, we hunted the hills around Kirkfort on sunny days and studied that damned book on rainy ones. It was no good. We explored the shoreline for a mile in either direction, and we asked questions whenever we found someone who'd talk about the place's history, but there was no sign that led to treasure. We studied the list of letters, even went to the museum and peered at the original, but no light dawned on us. We needed the key."

It had been an impossible task, but Mercedes could picture the youthful enthusiasm with which the quartet must have taken on the search.

"In the end we let it go, as kids do," Graham said. "I for one forgot about it."

"And what happened to the four of you after that?"

"My cousin went back to England at the end of summer. A year or so later, Vincent had a terrible row with his father and ran away from home. Paul mentioned the notebook at the time, but we couldn't learn what happened to it. He asked Vincent's mother to look for it, but she wasn't much of a housekeeper." He made a derisive sound as a wheel hit a large rock and Mercedes grabbed the armrest to steady herself. "Truth told, she wasn't much of a mother either."

The road leveled somewhat, though it was still too narrow for the car to pass without scraping branches. Graham shifted his hands slightly downward on the wheel, alert for hazards as he continued. "Years went by, as they do. My cousin became a history

252

professor, in part because of the interest engendered by that journal. Paul ended up working for the tour company, using his gift for trivia and personal charm to entrance ladies like your Mrs. Flowers. We kept in touch intermittently, and he sometimes spoke of the treasure." His expression became faintly sad. "He called just before he died and warned me Vincent had come back for the book. I think it was the last act of his life."

She shuddered, recalling how he'd died. "Vincent killed Paul to keep him quiet?"

"Or to keep him from the treasure. I don't know if Vincent recognized me that day, but he knew Paul had contacted someone, so I've been careful."

"How did the girl at the castle get the book?"

"Mostly luck, which I suppose she thought was good at the time. Sylvia stayed in Aldair after leaving school, living with one man and another, each less promising than the last. She worked, as you know, at Castle Kinready. When Vincent's mother died, she helped to clean out the house and for some reason kept a box of old novels for herself. Recently she found the notebook at the bottom of the box, slid under the cardboard flap. No one had noticed it all these years, but Sylvia recalled how taken Vincent had been with the vicar's story. A national magazine had run an article on theatre critics with a picture, and she'd recognized Vincent. She must have figured her old boyfriend was rich, and she offered to sell him the vicar's journal."

"Not a wise move on her part."

"Our Sylvia was not one to think things through." His face turned grim. "I didn't recognize her at the castle, since it's been years since I even thought of her. The girl was stupid and greedy, and she paid dear for it."

"But you were called to the crime scene."

"Yes. I went into police work, which isn't a bad job for a man with no love for books or business." He rubbed a hand over his hair, making it stand up worse than before. "Paul's call brought it all back. Wealth beyond one's wildest dreams appeals, no matter what the occupation."

"You want the treasure."

"I have no interest in Shakespeare's brother, if he had one. But whoever John was, he knew where Drake's treasure was hidden, and we intend to find it."

"You have a partner."

"I have an associate who will handle the business end of things. When we find the treasure site, he'll handle disposition of the gold."

"Meaning illegal sale?"

"There's more profit that way, and no taxes. Freddy has connections in all sorts of enterprises, and I believe he'll do nicely."

Graham swung the car to the left, turning into a field that had a faint track around its outer edge. He followed this track, jouncing over large bumps and wide dips.

"Now that I've told you the background, it's time for you to open your heart to me," he said without taking his gaze from the treacherous ground before them.

Mercedes clung to the armrest, easing the strain on her bruised backside. "So you can kill me when I've done it?"

He grimaced. "I'm no Vincent. You must stay with me until we've removed the gold, but then you'll be set free."

Mercedes' common sense contradicted that assertion. She doubted she'd get out of this alive. Even if Graham really liked her, as he claimed, his associate wasn't likely to be so trusting. They'd cold-bloodedly tried to murder Callard; they'd do the same to make sure she remained quiet.

After a bumpy few minutes, they came out the other side of the field and reached a proper road, at least much better than the two before it. Graham stopped the car, thoughtful for a moment. Finally he turned and met her gaze, returning briefly to the charming persona of their earlier meetings. "You could come with me. I'll be rich, and we did hit it off, I thought. Say this car is found in the Firth in a day or so. Who's to say we didn't have a terrible accident and both die?"

"And live on the run with stolen money?"

"We'd be safe now that Vincent is out of the way. The authorities know nothing about a cache of gold coins."

"But I'm not the only one who knows about the treasure."

"Your gentleman friends? They'll go looking for you in Dumfries, giving me the time I need. All I require is the start you've got on figuring out the clues."

"And if I don't tell you?"

His boyish face turned malicious. "I can make your life difficult."

Graham had allowed innocent people to be tortured and killed when he might have stopped it. He'd made an attempt on Callard's life, leaving the man seriously injured. Determination to have the treasure had made him into almost as great a monster as Vincent had been.

255

"We haven't got it all," she said resignedly. "We were working on it when you arrived."

"Tell me what you've got. Once I hear it, I might be able to contribute."

There was nothing to do but cooperate, at least for the moment. "The first clue pointed to Kirkfort, no surprise there. 'The primrose way' refers to hell, but we don't know which area around here would be associated with that."

Graham laughed aloud, indicating a sign to the left: *Kirkfort 1 km*. They had made a large circle and were approaching from the east. "Heydie's Water, I'd say."

She heard "Hades water" but didn't get it. "What?"

"It's a stream we played in as boys. It's spelled *H-E-Y-D-I-E*, but we always called it Hell's Water because we liked the sound of it."

"That makes sense. John waded upstream along several rivers in his search."

"I remember that. What's next?"

"The *f-o-e-o-l*'s way."

"And that would be?"

"I don't know." She didn't want to give up too much. If she could make herself useful, maybe she'd live long enough to escape. "It might be misspelled. We had trouble due to the age of the script. I think the word is *fool*."

"The fool's way? What is that? It sounds familiar."

"I'd need to see the play again."

Regarding her closely for a moment, he turned boyish again,

and she marveled at his ability to switch the charming manner on and off. "What if we go and find the treasure ourselves? I know the area, and you seem to have found the right approach to the clues."

She knew she should play him, agree to be his partner and encourage the belief she'd assist in his plans, but she hesitated a second too long, unable to summon the proper demeanor. Graham's gaze took it in, and he nodded as if confirming what he'd suspected.

Mercedes could almost see the possibilities that flowed through his mind. With her clues and a bit of luck, he might find the treasure before his associate arrived, have it all for himself. He was wondering if he could alter the plan, bypass his partner's expertise, and dispose of the goods himself. Graham was driven by greed, and she had to make the most of it. Once there were two of them to elude, she'd be even worse off. Her best chance was to be helpful until a chance to escape arose. She played her next card.

"Of course, it's the 'Tomorrow' speech! They made us memorize it in high school." She recited what she could remember: 'Tomorrow, and tomorrow, and tomorrow,/ Creeps in this—' something—" She fumbled for the adjective and found it—'creeps in this petty pace from day to day,/ To the last syllable of recorded time;/And all our yesterdays have lighted fools/The way to dusty death.'"

"Very pretty. So the fool's way is to the grave."

"A graveyard? On Heydie's Water?"

With a jolt that made her grab again for a handhold, Graham braked and frowned at the road's edge, looking for a place to turn the car around. "I know exactly where to look."

CHAPTER THIRTY-ONE

Colm put down the telephone in the inn's entryway as David came by with a small leather valise. Glancing at his face the older man asked, "What is it?"

"Inspector Callard has been in hospital for several days. He was hit by a car as he crossed a street in Dumfries. The driver didn't stop and has not come forward."

"Who sent that young man then?"

"He was sent to interview Mercedes, not to arrest her."

"What did the station at Dumfries say about it?"

"Not much, but I gather there's no suspicion that Mercedes Maxwell engaged in criminal activity. No officers were sent to bring her in."

"Then Graham is was working with this Vincent?"

"Or working against him." Colm chewed his lip nervously. "I think two forces are operating here. Vincent hunted Paul Prescott down and killed him after Mercedes left the tour group, which means Prescott must have known about Drake's treasure."

"And he told someone else before he died?"

"According to the news, the last anyone saw he was talking on the phone at the pub. It couldn't have been Vincent, so that means there's someone else involved."

At that moment a blue-topped head appeared around the doorway arch, familiar to Colm but causing David to start.

"Oy," it said diffidently.

"What are you doing here?" Colm demanded.

Lonnie chose to take that as an invitation. He entered the room but stayed near the entry in case flight was required. "I've come to help," he declared with a sniff that involved most of the muscles in his face. Colm merely raised an eyebrow. "I felt real bad about scarin' the lady and all, since it wasn't like I thought. And I was leavin' town, like you asked me to," Lonnie emphasized the verb a touch for David's benefit, "but then I saw the lady in a car with a police officer, and I thought she might be in trouble."

"You might say that." Colm was impatient to get to the point of Lonnie's return.

"Since we talked, I done some investigatin' of my own. This police officer, he's the one had me follow her. Said he was her husband, like I told you, but now you and the lady told me different, so I wondered why she's going somewhere with him." Sniff. "Is things all right?"

Cutler picked up his case. "We should take the Rolls. It's got eight cylinders."

"Eight is good," Colm agreed and headed for the door. As he passed, he gave Lonnie an appreciative clap on the shoulder that sent him stumbling forward. He nevertheless grinned at Colm's retreating figure, concluding he'd done the right thing for once.

***

Graham backtracked half a mile, turned up a lane so steep that he had to put the engine into low gear, and proceeded to a spot where he could pull the car off the road and into some trees. Once he judged they couldn't be seen from the narrow lane, he made a phone call. His face showed frustration when there was no answer,

259

he ended up leaving a long message. Once he'd concluded the call, he ordered Mercedes out and waited until she came around to his side before he climbed out himself, never taking his eyes off her.

Around the small copse where he'd stopped was pastureland, too sloping and rocky to be used for much else. On their left the rise was gentle, allowing grass to grow and enough space for the car to pull off the roadway. On the right it sloped more radically away from them into a scraggly thicket that rolled downhill until only the tops of the trees were visible.

Opening the trunk, Graham pulled out a knapsack. "Always be prepared, that's my motto. We might need some things before we're done."

The path he indicated was narrow and curvy, made by cows meandering through day after day with occasional droppings along the way to confirm the fact. They walked single file in the waning daylight, Mercedes wishing she had better shoes. If she was going to escape, she'd have to seize the first chance that arose, and her lace-up shoes would have served her better.

They made their way down the steep but passable path about half a mile before she heard the stream gabbling its way across in front of them. Soon the trees opened up and there was Heydie's Water, cut through the path of least resistance by years, probably centuries, of patient, constant dissolving of whatever lay beneath it. Here too were the cows, grazing listlessly. One black and white occupant of the riverbank raised her head as they passed, watching them askance, as if not wanting to be caught looking.

"Upstream," Graham ordered, and she obediently turned right, picking her way along the bank. Their way rose now, climbing in the opposite direction of the water's flow at least as steeply as the way they'd come down earlier. Here there was less of a path, for the cows had no reason to travel upstream. There were brambles everywhere, and she soon burned with scratches on both arms and even on her legs as the sharp spines sliced through her clothing. Once they clambered over a low stone wall that served as a land boundary and probably had since medieval times.

Twenty minutes later the bank widened again as the river crossed a flatter, though not flat, plot of land. Dim shapes rose across the stream and to their left. Standing stones came to mind first, but closer observation revealed tombstones, all ancient and most aslant, lining the bank for perhaps a hundred yards and stretching about the same distance away from the water.

"It's an old Maxwell clan cemetery Paul and I found once when we were fishing. Who'd have thought it held the secret to Drake's treasure?"

"We don't know that yet."

"I do. I feel it." He was exultant. "I've found what no one could for centuries, and it's only a matter of time until it's mine. Ours," he amended, continuing the fiction he might include her in his plans.

"If we can unravel the clues."

"I am confident we can do it together. Now what's next?" He stepped ahead of her in anxious haste.

"What's left is 'a—or an—painted devil the man of blood.' I think it's two clues."

"Yes, a short phrase beginning with *a, an,* or *the* fits with the others."

"We copied 'an painted devil', but the *n* was questionable. Probably a painted devil."

Graham waved a hand to indicate she should wade the tiny

stream. "Unlikely to find devils depicted in a graveyard. Angels are much more likely."

The water wasn't deep and the bed was rocky, so they barely wet their feet. The graveyard lay on an incline, the oldest graves along the stream and later ones farther up. Not much of the original lettering was visible on the tombstones after centuries in the elements. The dignified skeleton of an ancient chapel occupied the uphill end of the spot, facing away from them and toward what must have been the original path to the place. All that remained of the structure was a stone facade. The rest, probably wooden, had long ago disintegrated.

The quiet, antique atmosphere of a cemetery would normally have pleased Mercedes, who had always found such places restful rather than eerie or depressing. The thought of the dead buried here was not frightening. It was the living man behind her who was a threat.

Stashing the gun in its holster, Graham began examining tombstones, moving eagerly from one to another of the larger ones as he examined their ornamentation. Mercedes waited until he was a few steps away. Her mind worked feverishly. The stones would provide cover, and if she could make it into the woods, she could hide there until it was dark. By the time Graham realized she'd run, got the gun out, and fired, she'd be too far away for him to get a clear shot. She hoped. As he moved away, intent on finding his painted devil, she bent to a crouch and headed for the trees, heart pounding.

A shout behind her spurred her legs—and her heart—even faster. Trying to remember what she knew of flight under fire, she kept low and zig-zagged, making a harder target to hit. Still, at any moment she expected to feel a bullet burn into her back.

She made the trees and kept running, amazed at her luck.

Graham would follow, but she meant to get as far away as possible. She ran clumsily, however, her feet slipping in the flimsy shoes. Dodging branches and sucking air in great gulps, she expected to hear Graham's steps closing on her at any moment.

Instead she heard a scream of pure terror, all the more frightening because it was a man's scream. It ended abruptly, and there was silence.

It wasn't silent around her, for Mercedes crashed through the brush like a startled deer. She knew she should be quiet, but it was also critical to put distance between herself and pursuit. Branches that had scratched before gouged at her now, but she ran on, unheeding. She lost one shoe and then the other but kept on. Suddenly the woods opened, and she hurtled into the clearing. The water! Should she cross it or return to the anonymity of the trees? If Graham had seen her, it was suicide to go back. She waded the cold, shallow stream a hundred yards down from her original crossing, wincing at sharp rocks that jabbed into her bare feet.

Her panicked mind formed a hasty plan: Graham would assume she'd run downstream, but she forced herself to slow and circle back, quietly now, and hide just along the wood-line surrounding the graveyard. She angled her way up the hillside, approaching the edge of the wood and paralleling the path by which they'd come. Shaking and desperately trying to still her ragged panting, she finally chose a place to hide, a spot where a tree had fallen over a small gully, making a tent of its dying branches. Crawling under them and down into the base of the pit, she pulled loose, dead leaves around her until only her face was exposed. Satisfied she was almost invisible, she lay alert for any sound for a long time. There was nothing but the thump of her heart as it pounded away the adrenaline rush in her blood, quieting somewhat but still ready for flight.

Mercedes waited, terrified, curious, and confused. As her breathing slowed, quiet returned, unbroken except for normal forest sounds: the chirp of birds, the lowing of cows grazing nearby, and even the rustle of a squirrel returning to its normal scurrying up and down nearby trees. After an hour with no disturbance of these prosaic noises, the events of the day caught up with her, and despite the hard ground and her fear of discovery, she dozed.

It was full night when she awoke, and she started in panic before remembering where she was and why. The forest was still peaceful, with only soft, unthreatening sounds. She had no way of knowing if Graham was still looking for her or had given up and returned to his car. He might be lying in wait. That was a problem only if she returned by the path, which she had no intention of doing. Stealthily she rose and exited her hiding place, shaking the musty-smelling leaves from her hair and clothes.

She kept to the trees, cutting toward the path as best she could in the weak light of the skinny slice of moon. The way was steep, and at times she had to use tree roots for handholds. Cringing each time she made a noise or shook a branch, she continued cautiously up the bank until it leveled somewhat. There was the path, so close she could make out the line of it, lighter than the darker forest floor. She stood for a moment, her exhausted brain unable to make a decision. Though dangerous, the path would bring her more quickly to possible help, and it would be easier on her bare, chilly feet. Making her choice, she stepped out of the trees.

It was easier going, but her strength was almost gone. She stumbled blindly, trying to keep quiet but too tired to think straight. She was almost expecting it when strong hands went round her, one covering her mouth and the other encircling her waist. She struggled fiercely until a voice in her ear said, "Mercedes, it's me!" The grip relaxed and she turned to face Colm, his fair hair silvery in the gloom.

"Colm! Jared Graham—he—" she whispered.

"Aye," he answered in what passed for a whisper to Colm but was more like the drone of a bee. "I was stupid to believe him, but I'm not totally daft. Once he'd gone I did some checking. Then your pal Blue Hair showed up and told us Graham hired him in the first place."

"How did you find me?"

"He had to be taking you to the treasure site. David and I were frantic. We tore all over Kirkfort asking who could associate a spot in the area with Hell." He chuckled in spite of himself. "We insulted a few of the locals just by asking. Finally Mr. MacPhearson, the clever old gnome, made the connection from Hell to Hades to Heydie's, and Bob's your uncle."

"What?" She frowned at the unfamiliar idiom.

"Never mind. Did Graham find the treasure?"

"I don't know. I ran off, and he shouted once, and then he—he screamed."

Colm digested that. "Let's take a look, but quietly, okay? I don't think this can be good."

It wasn't. Colm led her back down the path, then pulled her into the trees where they could observe the dark area below them. After a long time of waiting watching for movement or sound, he told her to wait and went on alone. It was an agonizing ten minutes before he returned. She couldn't see his face, but she heard shock in his voice. "Graham's dead. And Vincent's here."

"Vincent?"

265

Colm gripped her arm, his strength supporting her. "I didn't want to worry you, but while you slept this morning I went back to the spot where he went over the cliff. There's a ledge a few feet down. With a bit of luck he might have survived, waited there till daylight, then climbed up to the surface and gotten away."

Remembering the oddity of the silence following Vincent's fall, Mercedes' earlier sense of dread returned. She pictured him crouched on a rocky outcrop, listening to their conversation, perhaps even smiling at the thought they'd be less careful now that they thought him dead. Graham certainly had been, had not once considered he might be followed, maybe even preceded, to Heydie's Water. And he'd died because of it. "We have to get away from here," she said, shivering despite his warmth.

"David's waiting at the car." He led the way up the hillside, keeping to the trees and making as little noise as possible. She followed, her bare feet suffering constant injury as she stumbled in the darkness. She was too afraid to cry out, too determined to slow her pace.

The sliver of moon reflected off David's Rolls, parked on the roadside. Colm was even more careful now, watching for a very long time to assure there was no movement around it. Finally he signaled with his flashlight. In response, the dome light of the car came on. David sat stiffly behind the wheel. "He was going to use my cell and call for help. I hoped someone would be here by now." Colm's tone changed slightly. "I had a devil of a time convincing him he wouldn't be much help crawling over the Scottish landscape in the dark at his age."

Mercedes couldn't help but smile, picturing the argument David would have put up. He still didn't look happy, if the glimpse she'd gotten of his face was any indication of his mood.

As Colm started toward the car, the driver's door suddenly flew open and David shouted, "Run! Get away, Kennedy!" The last syllable was drowned out by a gunshot.

Quickly Colm turned and pulled Mercedes to a crouch, switching the flash off at the same time. As they huddled in the darkness a familiar voice called across the distance, "I didn't kill the old fellow, Kennedy, but I will if you don't do as I say. And I'll make it a slow death."

"Lie flat, Mercedes." His voice was commanding but very, very soft.

"What?"

"Lie flat where you are, in the grass." She did as ordered. "I'm coming!" He shouted toward the car. "Don't hurt him!"

Mercedes hissed, "Colm, what are you doing?"

Barely moving his lips, he answered, "He doesn't know I've found you, but he must know by now I can help him find the treasure. He'll keep me alive. I'll stall as long as I can. You'll have to get help for David, who may be seriously hurt—and for me."

"No!"

"There's no other way. Now stay quiet." At that moment the car's headlights came on, pinning him in their beams. Mercedes ducked her head down and prayed Vincent wouldn't shoot Colm then and there.

"Where is Miss Maxwell?"

"She must have made her way downstream."

"A pity," Vincent said. "I planned to make her Ophelia. A pleasant stream, Heydie's Water." The voice changed. "Come on, then. I'm assuming you know what she knows."

"Yes."

"Then you will live a while longer, and we'll visit the graveyard together." The car door opened, and Vincent was framed momentarily in the dome light. Then the door slammed and there were only the headlights, highlighting Colm and making escape impossible. The beams passed over Mercedes as she kept her head low and lay perfectly still.

In a few seconds a flashlight came on toward the back of the car, and Vincent ordered, "Walk toward me, but stay in the light. If you run I'll kill the old man."

Wordlessly Colm started toward the car. Mercedes lay trembling in the tall grass, terrified for him. There hadn't even been time for a kiss, a caress, a word of goodbye. What if she never saw him again? Contact with Vincent meant death, sooner or later. She had to do what she could for David, but she also had to help Colm. After that she'd worry about the consequences if she had to face Vincent again.

CHAPTER THIRTY-TWO

Mercedes waited until the two men disappeared into the woods, the damp ground cool under her feverish cheek. When she was sure they were gone, she crept to the car and eased the door open, wincing as the dome light came on lest Vincent look back and see it. Inside, David lay sprawled across the front, blood staining his jacket. He was breathing, but shallowly. She touched his face and his eyes opened. "Mercedes? You're all right?"

"You're the one who's bleeding."

"It hurts like the devil too. There's a first aid kit in the back, but I don't suppose it has anything for bullet wounds."

Again moving as quietly as possible, she opened the car's trunk and retrieved the first aid kit neatly strapped against one wall. She returned to David, who had pulled himself to a sitting position and was examining the wound using the rear view mirror. "Where's the phone? We have to call for help."

"Blighter stomped on it," he replied. "Took my car keys, too. He must have been nearby when we pulled up, because as soon as Colm was gone, he jumped me." He added weakly, "I did what I could to help."

"Your warning saved me, and it was very brave. But Vincent has Colm." Mercedes worked on David's injured shoulder as she spoke. The bullet had gone directly through from back to front, and in her decidedly amateur opinion, done no organ damage. The sound of his breathing was fairly normal. Taking bandages and gauze from the kit, she wrapped the shoulder tightly to stop the bleeding.

Once that was done, she helped him into the back seat where he could lie more comfortably and covered him with a blanket from his well-provisioned trunk. "I have to help Colm. If we haven't returned by daylight, try to walk somewhere and get help. In the meantime, lock the doors and say a prayer."

"Mercedes?" His voice was faint. She hated leaving him like this, possibly to die alone.

"Yes, David?"

"Would it help if I told you there's a Glock in the boot?"

Translation took a moment. "You have a gun?"

David looked slightly offended. "I have a permit."

She knew little about guns, but it was no time to turn down a weapon. "Is it loaded?"

He looked even more miffed. "Of course it is. I have no small children to fret over."

***

Vincent and Colm made slow progress. The actor seemed petrified with fear. He stumbled and fell several times, turned off onto wrong headings and had to be ordered back, and generally made a pest of himself with whining. Having enjoyed his performance onstage, Vincent was disappointed to find the actor so pathetic in person.

After a few minutes the light dawned. The man had jumped in with no hesitation to save Mercedes in the alley and again on the cliff. He was not terrified. He was plying his trade. "Kennedy, any more delay and I will shoot you in the right elbow. Test me again and it will cost you the other arm. It takes a long time to die that way."

Colm's manner changed, and even his voice grew stronger. "No Shakespearean death for me? A baker's dozen of bullet wounds?"

Vincent explained patiently, for no one truly understood. "It isn't how they die that matters, it's the tableau created afterward. To paraphrase, the world is my stage, and all the men and women merely players. You might die of a bullet, but I could make you— oh, say Hector, dragged behind a beast. We have no horses nearby, but a cow would do. I will be your Achilles."

Kennedy didn't seem to appreciate the gesture, and Vincent shrugged. No matter.

They crested the last knoll and made their way to the graveyard, crossing Heydie's Water yet again. Approaching the ruined chapel, Vincent used the flashlight to illuminate the facade. Massive columns held a lintel aloft on which the name *Maxwell* had been carved deeply into the stone. Lichen had faded the word into ambiguity. Each column had once been topped with a gargoyle, but only one remained, grinning down at them.

Vincent turned the light past the columns, scanning the hillside that had once braced the back of the structure. Two more columns stood against it, chipped and scarred from the collapse of the walls and roof at some point in the distant past. They stood separate from each other, their crosspiece broken and lying in chunks on the ground around between them.

"Interesting how history moves in spirals," Vincent observed. "The Maxwells built this place, and a Maxwell brought us back to it. I will find her, you know. She won't elude me for long."

Kennedy stopped briefly to stare up at the gargoyles as they appeared in the beam of light. He was apparently thinking harder than ever before, trying to solve the puzzle and prolong his own

271

life. "Another spiral," Vincent commented. "A player was once offered his life if he told the location of the treasure. Now I offer you the same thing."

"I'd guess that like John Romeo, I'm not fated to live long after the telling."

Vincent didn't disagree. "I can offer a brief respite and a quick and painless death at the end. Where do we begin?"

"I don't know." He turned away from musing on the façade and surveyed the graves.

"Don't play with me, Player."

"We were still working on the clues. The treasure is here, but I don't know exactly where."

"It should have been mine years ago." Vincent's outrage began to boil over. "I read the book. I could have solved the riddles back then but for circumstances."

"What circumstances?" He was trying to draw him out, but Vincent only smiled.

"Family problems, which I took care of at a later date. Now you must tell me what you know. I lost the clues in our struggle on the cliffs. I must say, the moments after were quite touching, you and Mercedes."

"You'd have killed her."

"That's true. But you'll pay for the night I spent clinging to a rock" He waggled the gun threateningly. "The clues?"

"Once we knew which letters matter we found words, but they're run together. The first few, 'the least of Duncan's lords,' we guessed must refer to Menteith, the town, not the character. Kirkfort is the spot on the coast directly south of Lake Menteith."

"One gets as much from reading the vicar's notebook."

"Yes. The direction to proceed from Kirkfort came from the second clue: the third witch says the battle will be won 'ere set of sun'. The sun sets in the west."

"Again, very clever."

"Next was the stream. The clue was 'the primrose path', a line spoken by the drunken porter. The primrose path is the way to Hell—hence, Heydie's Water."

"Fortuitous to have an actor of Shakespearean drama along to point these things out."

Colm ignored the jibe. "That led to 'the fool's way' which is 'the way to dusty death,' so we looked for a graveyard. That's as far as we got before you showed up."

"What follows?"

"Seven words: 'an painted devil the secrets man of blood.' I don't know what it means."

"I would say the man of blood is John's clue to who his captor was."

"Willie was certainly a bloody sort."

"No, Reid, don't you see? Reid is 'red,' which implies blood."

"So he identified the man responsible for his death."

"Yes." Vincent had little interest in John's attempt to name his executioner. "That leaves finding the painted devil, which won't be easy in the dark."

Colm tried for a light touch. "I don't mind waiting until first light."

"But there is no first light for you. I have everything I need." Vincent raised the gun.

Grimacing, Colm put up a hand as if to stop the impending bullet. "I know where the painted devil is."

Vincent lowered the gun hand and raised the flashlight to Colm's face. "If you're lying to extend your life a few more minutes—"

"There." He pointed back the way they'd come. "But you'll need help getting to it."

"Enlighten me."

Colm returned to the ruined chapel façade and indicated Vincent should shine his light upward. The gargoyle grinned down at them, its open mouth sprouting a pipe that had once funneled water off the building's roof.

"You might have something, Kennedy. I wonder how one might get up there."

"Climb the ruins and shin the column, I suppose."

"I'm dying to see you do it."

He'd guessed that was coming. "Could I have the light so I can look it over?"

"Certainly. I have another. Poor Jared dropped it when he fell."

"Graham?"

"Yes. An old school chum. Imagine my surprise when I learned it was he who'd interfered in this matter."

"You cut out his heart," Kennedy said, disgust apparent his expression.

274

"*Julius Caesar*," Vincent explained. "The soothsayers told the tyrant to stay home the day he was assassinated. They 'could find no heart in the beast,' remember?" He chuckled in genuine enjoyment of the joke. "It was a bad omen for Bubble as well."

CHAPTER THIRTY-THREE

The cell phone in Jared Graham's pocket pulsed several times, but he was unable to answer any call in this world. At the other end, the caller swore, slammed the phone down, and pushed the *Accelerate* button on his cruise control, nudging his speed even higher. After a moment, he took up the phone again and pushed a speed-dial number.

"It's me. Have you by any chance heard from your cousin tonight?"

"Jared? No, why do you ask?"

"Nothing important, really. He left a message for me, said he'd call back, but he hasn't."

"Is this about that silly scheme of his? Are the two of you hunting treasure?"

The caller paused. "Yes, my dear Aletha, you've guessed it. But don't sound so smug until you hear what Jared found."

***

Vincent watched as Kennedy took the flashlight and examined the façade carefully. The upright columns rose ten feet into the air. The lintel with *Maxwell* carved into it laid across them, and above on the left sat the gargoyle, hunched and humorous for eternity. Behind it were rocks, once part of the hill above, a few rotted timbers, and chunks of stone that might have been decorative pieces, might have been the other gargoyle. It was hard to tell.

Kennedy moved a few large rocks into place at the base of the column to form a climbing platform. Once he was a few feet up, he sought a hand-hold on the ribbed column and began to climb. It wasn't easy. The pillar was too big to reach around, so he had to squeeze with his arms and legs to keep from sliding back down. His fingertips scraped as they fought for purchase on the rough stone. Knowing he was dead if he hit the ground, the actor somehow found places to dig his heels into the surface and slowly inched his way upward. Vincent offered no encouragement, only a few more minutes of life.

***

Mercedes found a flashlight in the trunk of the car along with the Glock. Even more helpful was a pair of ancient rubber galoshes (that was the only word for them), evidently kept there in case David had a breakdown on a wet day. They were too big, but she stuffed the soles with grass, providing squishy but effective protection for her bruised feet.

She crept back down the path they had recently followed, planning on the way. Neither the gun nor the light would be much use when she got to the graveyard. The light would give away her position and, considering the darkness and her inexperience, she might as easily hit Colm as Vincent if she fired the gun.

Creeping along in the dark was difficult. She shone the light briefly every few steps, keeping it low to the ground, and memorized what she saw before going on. Finally she came to the crest of the last rise, where she could no longer chance the flash. It didn't matter. Down the bank she saw two lights, one moving while the other remained still. Hopeful that two lights meant Colm was still alive, she felt her way cautiously down the slope until she could see what the two men saw.

It was Colm's light that moved, and the beam of the other flash followed him. He was examining the columns she'd noticed earlier, what was left of the old chapel. Colm concentrated on the column to the left, which was pretty much intact. At the top of it sat a gargoyle. She immediately recognized it: what was a gargoyle but a painted devil?

The treasure would be there, in columns made hollow to make them less weighty. Was there room inside to hide Drake's gold and leave it undiscovered for four centuries? She hoped so, simply because it would provide a distraction she might use to save Colm's life.

As she watched, she heard Vincent's voice, the tone commanding, but she couldn't make out the words. With a deep breath she edged closer, taking a painfully long time since her grassy boots kept slipping off. Once she reached the softer ground of the riverbank she abandoned them, creeping on hands and knees from tombstone to tombstone.

Colm slowly climbed the column. Vincent's light was trained on him, and she saw his face contort with the effort of holding himself aloft. When he reached the top, he felt tentatively along the lintel, trying its steadiness. Satisfied it would hold him, he pulled himself up and onto it, straddling the lintel and inspecting its surface with his light.

"Nothing." His voice carried through the calm air.

"Try the other side," Vincent called, and he obeyed, sliding carefully along the crosspiece. He inspected the area over the second column with his light.

"I don't see anything that allows access to the column. The lintel is smooth and flat except for a rough spot where the other gargoyle must have been attached."

"I ought to kill you now, Player. What use are you?"

Mercedes took the chance she'd been waiting for. Colm was looking down at Vincent, and she moved directly behind him. Briefly she turned her flashlight on, beam pointed at her face so he saw her there but Vincent did not. She dared only a second of light, but at least Colm would know he was no longer alone against the madman. From his high perch, Colm froze for a second but made no other indication. Lowering himself onto the column again, he slid to the ground.

"So you were wrong," Vincent sneered.

"Wait!" He leaned over and examined the far side of the pillar's base. "There may be something here. The column's been repaired."

Vincent moved toward the spot, and Mercedes ducked behind a tombstone, fearful his light would reveal her crouching there. She needn't have worried. He was intent on the task at hand.

"Where is it? Can you break it out?"

"I haven't anything to hit it with. I'll need something."

"What would you like," Vincent said sarcastically, "a jackhammer?"

Colm kicked at the base of the column and looked behind them, at the pile of debris. "A rock will do."

"Plenty to choose from." Colm kicked again at the pillar, and Vincent began searching the ruins for a suitable specimen. Mercedes again crept nearer. If she had to fire the gun, she knew it had to be from as close as possible.

Locating an egg-shaped rock a little larger than his fist, Vincent tucked it into the crook of his arm. With the light in one hand and the gun in the other, the rock made a clumsy addition, and Mercedes judged it was her moment. He was some distance away from Colm, and the pillar was between them. The weight of the rock changed the angle of the gun enough that aiming it would be difficult. Standing behind the tombstone, she turned her flashlight on, pinning him in its beam.

"Stop, Vincent," she called authoritatively, though both her hand and her voice had a tendency to tremble.

He froze, dropping the rock. He switched his flashlight off. "The Maxwell bitch, is it? Come to frolic with your dead ancestors?"

"Come to stop you making more dead."

"You tried that before. Did you feel bad, little Mercedes? You're not the type who can kill easily."

"Not like you. Colm, can you come here without getting near Mr. Slime-ball?"

"I can." His flashlight went out. Mercedes didn't look, didn't dare let her eyes leave Vincent, but she followed his progress by sound. Vincent gazed at her calmly. He couldn't see her face in the darkness, but he seemed able to. He seemed to be enjoying her discomfort.

"I'm here." Colm's voice came from behind her, and she handed the gun over carefully but with relief. He took it with the confidence of one who's held such things before, but at that moment the flashlight Mercedes held trained on Vincent flickered and died.

"Colm, your light!"

He fumbled to turn it on, but it was too late. When the chapel was again bathed in light Vincent was gone, and it was impossible to guess where. Fear gripped Mercedes as Colm switched off his light and pulled her to a crouch.

Tense seconds followed as they retreated to the shelter of a different tombstone, expecting to be fired upon at any moment. They said nothing for fear Vincent would locate them. Knowing nothing of fear, Vincent didn't mind speaking to them.

"Ah, a graveyard," his voice floated eerily around them, coming, it seemed, from the darkness itself. "Romeo calls it 'the charnel house,' the bed of 'worms that are thy chambermaids.' How often characters come to epiphany in such places!"

Colm pulled her close, making them the smallest targets possible. Now the voice came from slightly above, as if Vincent had moved up the slope. "As he contemplates Yorick's skull, Hamlet recognizes that each of us returns to the earth." His voice took on a theatrical tone: "'Imperious Caesar, dead and turned to clay,/ Might stop a hole to keep the wind away.'" The voice turned softer, almost gentle. "So might we all."

"You first," Colm whispered through clenched teeth.

Though he couldn't have heard, Vincent's voice hardened perceptibly. "I am not afraid to die for what I want, and because I accept the choice, I am stronger than either of you. Will you join your ancestors here tonight, Mercedes Maxwell?" The voice moved constantly, ringing them with mocking sound as it echoed off the stones. Mercedes found herself turning this way and that, her fear intensifying, as Vincent intended.

She felt a tensing that meant Colm had made a decision. "Have you ever fired a gun before?"

"A long time ago, but—"

"Good. Use two hands." He took her hand firmly and thrust the gun into it. A squeeze signified reassurance, and he was gone. She opened her mouth to cry against it but stopped herself, realizing his life depended on her silence. What did he intend to do without the gun?

When she figured out what his plan must be, Mercedes' heart sank. Colm intended to locate Vincent and focus his light on him, allowing her a shot. Colm was the bait, and it was up to her to see he didn't become the next of Vincent's victims.

Several long minutes passed before she heard anything. The sound came from her right, and she turned toward it, straining in the darkness to make out something, anything.

Suddenly the light flashed briefly, and she saw Vincent trapped in its beam. Colm had almost missed him, but she saw enough. He crouched beside the column Colm had climbed, his eager face as horrible to Mercedes as the gargoyle that grinned above. He fired quickly in the direction from which the flashlight beam came, ducking behind the column as he did.

She heard Colm call out, "It's over, Vincent. We'll get you the next time. I'm close, and you're in a corner. You can't climb over the ruins in the dark, and you'll have no cover once I circle that way." Colm's voice revealed he was making an arc around the column. It was a terrible chance he was taking. There was no protection for him at the front of the chapel. The space he traversed was open, and he could be pinpointed in Vincent's light at any moment, making him easy prey. However, Vincent's use of his light would make him a target for Mercedes. Could she take the chance when it came, and would her aim be true enough to save Colm?

Steadying her nerves as best she could, Mercedes set the gun atop the headstone that concealed her. If Colm could target Vincent, she had to do her part. He would create the distraction and provide a view of the target, and she must finish it. Here was the closure she'd sought, but she'd had no inkling it would involve ending the life of another human being.

The light flashed a second time. She saw nothing of Vincent, but the gargoyle appeared to be enjoying the scene. Had he moved? Was he still behind the column? Nervously she adjusted the gun again, resting the butt against the rough stone so her aim would be straight. It occurred to her that the bullet might ricochet, hitting Colm. If that happened, he might be killed, and she'd still have Vincent to contend with.

The light came on again. Still no sign of Vincent, but it gave her a chance to zero in, to make a decision about what to do when next she saw him. He had to be almost directly under the gargoyle, and if Colm moved around the column to the right, Vincent would have to move left in answer. With sudden decision she raised the gun's muzzle to an angle of about forty-five degrees and waited.

Suddenly a gunshot rang out. The flashlight's beam rose crazily in the air then fell, the light rolling and bumping until it came to rest at a downhill angle, lighting the grass on the edge of the pathway. There was no sound from Colm.

Mercedes fired three times, hoping the last burst of light had guided her effectively. There was a sort of rumble as stone hit stone, and a heavy weight dislodged from above and crashed to the ground. A yelp of pain from Vincent testified she'd managed to hit the gargoyle at least once, bringing all or part of it down on him. She prayed it was enough.

CHAPTER THIRTY-FOUR

In the silence that followed her shots, Mercedes was up and after the light, which she grabbed at a run and switched off, giving herself the protection of darkness once more. Then she began a frantic search for Colm on the dark landscape, feeling along the ground uphill from where the light had come to rest. She found him about ten feet away and, setting the gun on the ground beside them, touched his face with relief. He was warm and he was breathing, though there was blood on his face and in his hair. He moved at her touch and groaned. Mercedes touched his lips and said in a low voice, "Quiet! I don't know where he is!"

"I'm right beside you!" came a voice at her back. A hand grabbed her hair, pulling her roughly to her feet. The physical pain was compounded by the realization she had failed. Vincent wasn't dead, not even incapacitated, and now she and Colm would both die. She kicked backward violently, trying to free herself from the cruel grip that kept her tilted backward and slightly off balance. Vincent snarled as her bare foot connected with his shin, but he jerked even more viciously, snapping her head backward and pulling her off her feet. She reached over her shoulder, clawing at his face. As she fell against him, her hand felt something warm and liquid. Blood. Her shot had scored a small victory. It wouldn't be enough.

Vincent babbled in snatches that made little sense: "—mine, and you took it." After a few panting breaths he jerked her head backward again, at the same time avoiding her flailing hands, "—think I'm nothing!"

She ignored his ranting as she struggled against the arm that had closed around her throat, shutting off the air and making it hard to keep fighting. Bursts of colored light exploded before her eyes, and she knew she would die, Colm would die, and perhaps David too, wounded and alone. They'd failed, and Vincent had won.

Suddenly a different sort of light flooded the area, bright and white, causing Mercedes to squint and Vincent to twitch in surprise. "This is the police," an amplified voice said calmly. "Put your hands up and follow directions exactly."

Vincent loosened his grip on her throat, and Mercedes found she could breathe again. Dear, dear David! He'd somehow gotten help.

He did not release her or raise his hands. Pulling her against him like a shield, he shouted, "I'll kill her if you come closer!"

"Mr. Parks, there's no sense in continuing with this. You'll only make things worse."

"Sense? Where's the sense in the world? The gods tease us with glimpses of what might have been, might have had and then snatch it away. We are truly poor players, who strut our pitiful hour on the stage and then are heard no more."

"Mr. Parks." The calm voice obviously belonged to one schooled in dealing with hysteria. "I'd like to talk with you about that. May I approach?"

"If you take a single step closer, I'll kill them both." This precipitated a pause above, and Vincent purred in her ear, "I will anyway, but where's the fun in telling them that?" She remembered of David's gun, somewhere on the ground at her feet. If only she could reach it! "I'll shoot Kennedy first, so you can watch. Then I'll kill you."

"The hell you will," Colm mumbled from below them, and at the same moment his foot came up, hooking Vincent's leg and unbalancing him. Unprepared for an attack from that direction, Vincent fell to the ground, dragging Mercedes with him. She landed on top, leaving her adversary stunned for a second. Frantically she felt for the gun, but it was gone. She sobbed aloud, hands seeking in what she hoped was the right direction.

Recovering, Vincent snarled a curse and raised his gun, taking dead aim at her. Colm was quicker. He fired David's Glock, and Vincent dropped without any attempt to catch himself. He rolled haphazardly down the incline until a tombstone stopped his movement. Other shots echoed from above, and the prone form twitched convulsively several times. Finally silence opposed the uproar of the moments before, and everything was suspended for a few seconds. Vincent lay still, bathed in the police lights. A small, neat hole in his forehead made it clear the other wounds were superfluous.

Hurried steps approached, and voices shouted to them and to each other. Mercedes was up and enveloped in a blanket before she realized she was shivering uncontrollably. Colm was examined by an expressionless policewoman who called for a med kit and began first aid.

The police approached Vincent's body with caution, despite its utter stillness. Examination confirmed he was dead, finally and for certain. The same constable who'd taken her statement the night before assured them that things would be sorted out soon. At a minor commotion above, she looked up to see David striding down the slope on shaky legs, arguing all the way with an officer who vainly tried to keep him from the crime scene. She met him halfway, hugging him clumsily due to his wounded arm and his obvious embarrassment.

"Thank you, David. You were wonderful."

"Didn't do much," he muttered. "There was a cottage not half a mile down the road, and I simply called for reinforcements."

"Half a mile with a bullet hole through your shoulder is still pretty good."

Colm joined them a few minutes later, the area above his left ear swathed in bandage. "They wanted to get me a stretcher, said it's too far for a wounded man to walk." He looked at David with a grin. "I simply pointed you out to them. We'll lean on Mercedes if we need to, right?" Leaving the area crawling with officers, the three began to make their way back to the road.

***

It was daylight when the questions were completely answered and the details explained. Inspector Callard, the constable reported, had awakened from his coma the day before. When informed the string of murders had continued, he'd revealed what Mercedes had told him about the notebook. With that revelation, the second call David made to the Kirkfort police in twenty-four hours concerning abduction had not been taken lightly.

Jared Graham's body was found in the woods, not far from the graveyard. "A bad business," the constable said with a shake of his head. "It's not like us here in Scotland, Ma'am, to have such things happen." She remembered Jared saying something much like that the first time she'd met him. He'd seemed so helpful, when all along he was spying on her, lying, and plotting against her.

Another line from Shakespeare came to mind. Upon hearing that one of his thanes has conspired with the enemy, the old king Duncan, says, "There's no art/ to find the mind's construction in the face:/ He was a gentleman on whom I built/ an absolute trust." She had trusted Jared Graham and his boyish face, and look where it led.

287

Thinking of Graham reminded her of his associate, and she told the others what she knew of their plan. "Interesting," the constable muttered. "The old Maxwell property has been for sale for years with no takers, but only yesterday an offer was made on it."

"I'd be interested in knowing the potential buyer's name."

"I heard it," the man replied, "but I don't recall. He's English, claims he plans to build a cabin here for summer holidays."

"More likely he's Jared's partner," she said indignantly. "Let's see if he still wants the land once the treasure is turned over to the government."

"We haven't found it yet," Colm reminded her.

"But you said there was a patched place in the right column."

He grinned. "I'd have said anything to keep Vincent from shooting me like a partridge in a pear tree."

"We must have a proper search," David declared. "Not poking around at night, but with due procedure. I'm going to see that it's begun as soon as possible."

***

The clamor of a crime scene investigation allowed little privacy, but Colm managed to pull Mercedes aside for a moment as they waited for a ride back to Kirkfort. "Are you all right, love?" The term was common to Brits, she told herself, but it stirred her emotions all the same.

"I'm skinned and I'm scared, but overall I'm feeling very, very lucky. And safe. How about you? Are you really all right?"

"I'll have to curtail some of Nick Bottom's antics for a week or two," he said with a grimace, "but I mend quickly." He brushed her cheek lightly, maybe dirt, maybe affection. "You were very brave out there."

"I was so afraid I'd lost you." She paused, fearing she'd phrased it too strongly. "I mean—"

"I know what you mean. I almost couldn't bear it when Vincent said he'd kill you."

They were silent for a moment, each thinking of what might have happened, facing it so they could put it away in some far corner of the mind. "Mercedes," Colm said presently, "are we headed where I think we are?"

She couldn't resist teasing him just a little. "Where is that?"

"When I first saw you, I was drawn to you by something I can't explain, and nothing that's happened since has lessened that feeling." He pursed his lips, but the words seemed determined to come out, as if he had no choice. "In fact, I never want to leave your side again."

She touched his face, as grimy as hers probably was. "That's good, because I don't think I want you to."

"I tried to hold myself in check, taking your situation into account. You've been under some stress since we met. I didn't want to take advantage of a..."

"Crazy woman?" She laughed aloud, feeling real joy for the first time since that day at Castle Canready. "Oh, Colm, I don't know where this will go. Maybe in a week we'll find there's nothing between us but the story of the time we hunted treasure together."

Colm pushed a stray strand of hair away from her face. "Does that mean we have a week to try things out?"

***

With David's insistent demand that it be done right away, official presences were arranged, and a small army of people returned to the site that afternoon with all sorts of equipment and a corps of accompanying press. In charge of the whole was Nathan Diamond, an architect specializing in historic buildings, commissioned by the authorities to minimize damage and oversee the enterprise.

The columns were examined, but there was no access to the inside without removing the lintel. "Those who hid the treasure couldn't have opened the column and replaced the crosspiece," Diamond said with a shake of his precisely groomed head.

"What if it hadn't been completed yet?" They all turned to stare at Mercedes. "The Maxwells were prominent at the time of Elizabeth. Suppose a family chapel was under construction when the mutineers came looking for a place to hide their gold?"

"You mean they put it in the columns and let the building be finished over it?"

"How would they get it back when they returned?" Diamond asked.

"Smash the columns," David declared firmly. "They'd stolen a whole ship and thrown their officer overboard. They'd hardly have paused at vandalizing a chapel out in the middle of nowhere."

The idea brought renewed excitement, and the two front pillars were x-rayed. The insides were hollow, as Mercedes had surmised, but the space held nothing but air.

It was Colm's turn. Because they'd had more time to think about the treasure's hiding place, their minds ran ahead of the others. "What about the back supports?"

"I thought there had to be gargoyles," said Diamond.

"Perhaps there once were. The back has taken more wear than

the front as the hillside rolled down on it over the years. Gargoyles would logically have been placed at the four corners, both for practical and aesthetic reasons."

"Of course!" David exclaimed. "The extra *n* in the clue might indicate north."

"And that would be the north corner." Colm pointed to the back left pillar.

Diamond indicated his men should move to the back of the structure. The columns here had partially collapsed, and it could be seen that only the bases were solid. The upper sections were cylinders of baked clay, about eighteen inches in diameter and three feet high. The bottom edge of each flared slightly so it fit over the one below it. Once they were in place, they'd been plastered and decorated. Now that the lintel was gone, the upper ends reached upward to nothing.

The crewmen turned their attention to the north column. Its lintel lay smashed beneath it, and the column should have been open to the air. Instead a flat stone had been set over it, as if to protect the interior from rain.

Mercedes' heart beat faster as the workmen put a ladder up to the column and one of them climbed to the top. He removed the stone carefully and handed it to a co-worker below. Then with perverse slowness he took a large flashlight from his belt and directed the beam into the cavity of the column. The assembled group below went very quiet as they waited.

"Here's something," the man called, reaching his hand into the column. He pulled from it a small wooden box, about six by eight inches and three inches high. "It was resting on a slat wedged crossways in the opening."

"Stop right there," a voice called, and those present looked up the slope to see a man descending with purposeful stride. His waxed mustache was no less affected than when Mercedes had last seen him in Aletha's kitchen. Frederick was flanked by two men in suits who could only be lawyers.

"I'll be damned," said Colm.

"What? What am I seeing?" David barked.

"That man is Frederick Gowan," Mercedes told him, "whom we recently met at the home of a friend."

"I guess you were right to run away from me, love. I took you right into the lion's den!" Colm appeared angry at Frederick, at Aletha, and at himself.

"Jared spoke of a cousin who heard the story along with the others."

"But we didn't know she was female."

"He also mentioned his partner Freddy, but I didn't make the connection." It was ironic she'd suspected Aletha of going after Colm but never thought twice about her lover, the self-described "entrepreneur," of going after the treasure.

Gowan waited until he was close enough to speak normally and then addressed Diamond. "This is my property, and I insist you leave at once."

"It isn't your property yet," David growled. Frederick regarded at him as if he were an earwig.

"My lawyers will see about that. I have a court order that puts the entire process on hold until the matter of ownership is decided."

From the ladder, the workman, who'd been forgotten in the

last few moments, gave a shout of laughter. He'd opened the box and now held a sheet of paper from inside. "I don't think there's anything to decide," he shouted, a grin lighting his begrimed face. "The treasure was taken away long ago. This here is by way of an apology."

CHAPTER THIRTY-FIVE

To Whom It May Concern:

My name is Malcolm Seylor, and I am the vicar at Kirkfort. Three years ago, I was set to the task of assessing what should be done with a ruined structure that sat in the center of the village. As things unfolded, I came into possession of a journal that led me to a vast treasure concealed in the column of this chapel by several sailors who had stolen it from its rightful owners. It took me two years and seven months to unravel the treasure's hiding place, and four months more to decide what to do once I found it. At first it seemed obvious it should be turned over to the authorities. But as I looked at my poor community, which was dying by inches, its young people leaving in droves for America, I had another idea. Surely the treasure, after three hundred years, belonged to the land on which it lay. What if the treasure were sold and the funds used to benefit Kirkfort?

It was a difficult decision, because I knew the law would not take my side were my activities discovered. In the end, I took the chance. I had communication with a missionary in the Orient, and I arranged through him to be put in touch with a dealer of antiquities. This man, marginally honest, was willing to overlook certain irregularities in exchange for the profits he would receive. I undertook to ship the treasure to him over the course of a year, labeling the boxes "Missionary Supplies."

Next I had to provide for my people without

incriminating them in the process. Inventing a story of a former local lad who'd made good in America, I set up an endowment for Kirkfort's improvement, using the name of the mutineer I believe brought the treasure to Kirkfort, Lanford Maxwell. I funneled the money through the vicar's hands but put a balance on his power, ordering that the village council must agree to all expenditures. Our first agreed-upon project will be a hospital, built on the site of Willie Reid's fortress, where the prisoner who reached out from the grave to provide the location of the gold died.

Finally I devised qualifications for a "special" vicar, indicating that with so much money to oversee, the person should be carefully chosen from local stock in order to understand local needs. There is provision in the endowment for the education of youth who take up the ministry and return to Kirkfort afterward.

I freely confess I knowingly did wrong. My excuse is the need of my flock, and my vindication will be, I hope, a slow and steady growth of my beloved village. Kirkfort began as a place of evil. I hope I have begun its transformation into a place where good is accomplished. If you seek treasure, look at my village and see if it is not here.

Malcolm Seylor

"The old devil!" David marveled when the letter was read. "He deliberately left out of the notebook that he'd figured it out."

"He left us an explanation," Colm said, "And the chance to solve the puzzle ourselves."

"To find nothing!" Gowan was furious. "The money's been used to pretty up the village."

"And nicely done, too," Mercedes said. "I thought when I first saw it what a lovely place it would be to live."

Without another word, Gowan turned on his heel and strode up the hill. Snatches of polemic fluttered behind him: "—we'll see!"

There was a brief silence behind him, and finally Mr. Diamond said, "I can't say this hasn't been worth my time. Seeing a jackass thwarted, an English one at that—begging your pardon, Mr. Cutler—makes my whole day."

"No offense taken," David said gruffly. "I rather enjoyed it myself. Almost worth a trip to Scotland."

"He'll have things to answer for," the constable put in. "From what you've told me, he is at least guilty of criminal conspiracy, possibly more than that."

"But he has money and lots of lawyers," Colm protested. "You'll never get him behind prison bars."

"Like Willie Reid and my not-so-honorable ancestor Lanford Maxwell. Sometimes people like them get away with their crimes. If Freddy does, we can only hope he pays some other way, as Reid did after killing poor John the Player."

***

A well-dressed, sad-faced man visited the offices of Robert Cecil one afternoon in the fall of 1610. Cecil, recognizing the man's oval face though he'd never met him before, saw him privately. As the visitor entered the room, he automatically took in the details of its spare efficiency: rolls of paper stacked on a table in a corner, a few words scribbled on the back of each as a form of cataloging, extra candles piled on the table between them, for Cecil often worked far into the night, and the only warm touch, a carpet under Cecil's work table, for his misshapen bones chilled easily and pained him.

Cecil was a hunchback whom Elizabeth Tudor, when pleased with him, had called "my Elf." Other times she called him "the Pygmy," a less forgiving metaphor. Now the old queen was dead, and Cecil served the Scottish James as he had served her, ferreting out information to ensure England's throne was as secure as he could make it. He was no warmer than he was attractive, but Cecil was aware of the effect clandestine activities had on the families of his agents. He began the conversation.

"I'm afraid I can give you no news, sir. We have heard nothing."

"I was told as much." The visitor studied the legs of the table before him. He blames us, thought Cecil, as well he may. Still, John had been aware of the danger.

"I am leaving London," the man said. "I have retired from the theater and plan to return to my wife and Stratford."

Cecil was surprised. "You have had success here."

The man's hooded eyes lifted to meet Cecil's. "A man may change his definition of success many times in the course of life, I think."

"True." Cecil's mind skimmed over the past years. The arrangement with John and his twin had been advantageous, allowing John anonymity and his brother time with his family. Well, that was over now, for it was fairly certain John was dead. He'd cheated the Grim Reaper many times, but no one lasts forever.

Cecil put out a hand to John's twin. "May things go well for you. I wish we'd had better news to speed you on your way home."

"Thank you." The man pulled a paper from his vest. "I've written a letter which I ask you to keep in the hope that—" He bit his lower lip. "—you hear from my brother."

"I would be pleased to do so." Cecil took the proffered paper, rolled and tied with a piece of ribbon, and wrote on the outside *John the Player*. He added it to the stacks on the table, assigning it a place of its own.

"Mayhap the opposite will occur," Cecil told his guest gently. "Whatever his situation, John would want to send you word. He might yet write to you in Stratford."

"Mayhap he will." With that the playwright was gone.

CHAPTER THIRTY-SIX

A few weeks after returning home to Detroit, Mercedes received a delivery: a large crate, sturdy and well-sealed. Seeing David's return address, she opened it with some curiosity to find a letter.

My Dear Mercedes,

I am sending a gift, something I have had in my collection these many years. Until I met you, I never realized its import. It is now yours, and you must decide what should be done with it. If Colm is with you (and I believe if he isn't, he soon will be), you might share the decision with him. You have earned this gift many times over, so spare me any protestations otherwise.

In closing I will say I am happy to have known you. I don't like people, but occasionally there is a person or two whom I can tolerate.

With affection,
David Cutler

Unwrapping the heavy bundle inside the box, Mercedes revealed an ancient piece of paper sealed between sheets of glass. The handwriting was terrible, and she struggled to read the message. When she had read it once, she read it again.

And again.

To my dearest brother John,

I despair of hearing from you after so long but will leave this with someone who might see you before I do. I leave London to seek a quieter life; the city without you is somehow diminished. How I wish you had never met the red-haired woman, charming as you found her to be!

No one else helped so much to make my work successful, and I miss your presence every day. If men praise me, I owe a great deal of that praise to you, who encouraged, advised, and listened as I made my poor attempts to open a larger world to my fellow men. We were ever close as boys, and even as you came and went these last years, I always felt your presence. I do not feel it now, and I fear you have left me.

If by God's grace you should return, you might find I have abandoned you, for I am old. You, though the same age to the day, were always younger at heart than I. I pray my dread for you is due to my impending demise and not yours. If you can, come home. If you do not find me there, my spirit will hover nearby, waiting for my double and my opposite, the other half of my soul.

Will

———————————

OTHER BOOKS BY PEG HERRING

Note to Readers: If you enjoyed this book, please leave a review anywhere you know readers will see it. Writers depend on readers to spread the word!

And read Mercedes' next adventure, CHARLIE DICKENS' DOCUMENTS.

Peg's website: http://pegherring.com

Kidnap.org (fun suspense)

Kidnap.org

Standalone Mysteries

Somebody Doesn't Like Sarah Leigh (contemporary cozy mystery)

Not Dead Yet... ('60s-era mystery)

Her Ex-GI P.I. ('60s-era paranormal mystery)

Writing as Maggie Pill

If you like lighter mysteries, and if you have sisters, had sisters, or know a little about sisters, you'll love Maggie's series.

Website: http://maggiepill.maggiepillmysteries.com

The Sleuth Sisters Mysteries (cozy Michigan)

The Sleuth Sisters

3 Sleuths, 2 Dogs, 1 Murder

Murder in the Boonies

Sleuthing at Sweet Springs

Eat, Drink, & Be Wary

Peril, Plots, and Puppies

www.ingramcontent.com/pod-product-compliance
Lightning Source LLC
Chambersburg PA
CBHW070919260626
47162CB00007B/2731